PRAISE FOR LIZ FICHERA'S YA DEBUT

HOOKED

"Fred is a likable heroine, both loyal to her community and determined to create a different life for herself....The high level of emotional drama will appeal to fans of contemporary teen romances, and readers with a special interest in books with Native American characters will be interested in the raw clash of cultures depicted in an Arizona community."
—*Booklist*

"This is Fichera's debut teen novel, and she immerses the reader in the culture of the Southwestern Native American way of life."
—*VOYA* magazine

"I love Fred—she's sporty, smart, stands up for herself and goes after what she wants."
—Miranda Kenneally, author of *Catching Jordan* and *Stealing Parker*

"From the very first pages, this powerful story about the fight for tolerance, equality, understanding and love will have you 'hooked.'"
—Megan Bostic, author of *Never Eighteen*

"I love this book so much!...Now that I've read it, I can say it's one of my favourites I've read this year...It's like *Perfect Chemistry* (one of my fave books ever!) and *Catching Jordan* and golf!"
—Jana, *The Book Goddess*

"Honestly, I did not understand what I was getting myself into when I picked up this book. It was *crazy amazing!* I was intrigued by the story because it was a new idea to me. It was great and I would recommend it to anyone who wants something cute that is a little bit different."
—Gabie, *Owl Eyes Reviews*

"*Hooked* is exactly the right title for this one, because hooked is what I was from page one on. Liz Fichera has written a masterpiece about the troubles of high school, acceptance and how to be yourself."
—Erica, *The Book Cellar*

"*Hooked* is one of the best contemporary YA novels that I've read since *Pushing the Limits*. It is a stunning story about what happens when two people from opposite ends of life fall for each other....Fichera's words are compelling and gorgeous, creating a truly fantastic novel."
—Bailey, *I B Book Blogging*

Books by Liz Fichera

available from Harlequin TEEN

HOOKED
PLAYED

Liz Fichera

played

HARLEQUIN®TEEN

Recycling programs
for this product may
not exist in your area.

ISBN-13: 978-0-373-21094-7

PLAYED

Printed in U.S.A.

For Craig

We know what we are,
but know not what we may be.

—William Shakespeare

1

RILEY

Being the good daughter wasn't easy.

First there was the guilt that gnawed at my self-esteem like a leech whenever I didn't live up to my parents' expectations. That guilt could be triggered by the smallest of things. Like when I snapped at Mom before school because I was late and she didn't appreciate my lipstick shade, and she looked back at me with wide eyes as if wondering whether I was her real daughter or an imposter from outer space. Or when I pulled a B on a chemistry test (my least favorite subject) instead of the A Mom and Dad wanted. For the rest of the day, my anxiety was on overdrive.

Second, because I've had to overcompensate for my loser older brother for, like, ever, old habits were hard to break. The worse he behaved, the better I behaved, because I was the Designated Good Daughter, remember? So when Ryan would come home reeking of cigarettes and beer, or sometimes not at all, and Dad would corner me about him in the family room, I'd make excuses for him. "He had to go upstairs" or "He's getting a cold" were my standbys as I feigned interest in whatever was playing on television. Being the perfect daughter, I got away with my little white lies, and my parents overlooked my brother's shortcomings. It was easier that way. And even though Ryan had recently achieved Good Son status thanks to his new girlfriend, I couldn't shake the feeling that I had to continue to be the glue that kept my family together.

Which was why it made no sense that I'd been going out of my way the past few months to be the Undesignated Bad Daughter. It was like there was another person inside of me with her hands on the controls, pushing my arms and legs, my mouth. My brain. She was definitely stronger than the normal, good me. But this strong part of me kept my confused and frustrated parts together, the ones that I tried to keep hidden from everybody.

You see, being the good daughter wasn't something I wanted. It was just the way the universe arranged things. No rhyme or reason. I'd give anything for a do-over, a chance at some normalcy. A chance to make mistakes and not always feel like bad behavior meant I deserved banishment to a black vortex.

"Just one teeny prick, Riley. Maybe two, at most. Between your eyebrows. You'll never feel a thing," Drew said. "It'll make you look hot." Drew Zuniga had been in dance club with me at Lone Butte High School since freshman year. She was pretty much my only friend, but I was a quality-over-quantity kind of girl—at least, that's what I told myself. It made my friend situation seem Zen instead of serving as reminder that I wasn't very popular, despite having a popular older brother. We had gotten into the habit of chilling at her house after dance practice. It totally beat walking home, especially during the hotter months which, in Phoenix, Arizona, was pretty much every month. And walking was for freshman. The best part was that Drew had gotten a car for her sixteenth birthday and could ferry us around. I had to wait three more months before I'd get to pick out my own car, which was as good as waiting for forever. Today we were standing in her bathroom as I watched her point a clear syringe-like thingy at my face. It was freaky crazy, actually, but Drew was my friend. I trusted her.

The syringe was filled with some type of BOTOX concoction, pilfered from her dad's medicine cabinet. Dr. Zuniga was a plastic surgeon and brought home BOTOX injections for Mrs. Zuniga, who, in her defense, did look like she could fit in with the popular seniors at our school. From a distance, at least.

"But this is creepy." I leaned away from the shiny pointy end as far as the edge of the bathroom counter would allow. "You don't even know what you're doing."

"Sure I do!" Her brown eyes widened with indignation. "I've watched my dad do it a ton. One time I even practiced on an orange. It's just a tiny prick." She paused. "And one time my dad even did it on me. Right here." She pointed to her chin.

"No way."

"Way. See how smooth the skin feels?"

I squinted at her chin. It did look a little different, maybe rounder. Softer. It might have been my imagination but I thought Drew's chin used to look square. Like a boy's. "But this stuff is supposed to be for moms. With wrinkles," I said.

"And you've got a few already, I hate to tell you, *chica*." Drew's eyes swept over my face in full I'm-not-really-a-dermatologist-but-I-play-one-on-TV mode.

"Where?" I turned toward the mirror.

"Right there." She pointed to the skin between my eyebrows, which, okay, had a few stray blond hairs that needed plucking.

"Those are freckles." I frowned at her. Teeny orangey-brown spots dotted my forehead like a dartboard.

Drew ignored me. "It'll tighten that skin right up. This stuff is totally preventative. You'll see."

I swallowed as my knees weakened. I could use a little help, that much was certain, but would it make me look pretty? Jenna Gibbons-pretty? Jenna Gibbons was without a doubt the most gorgeous girl in our sophomore class. To make matters worse for every other girl at school, she had a twin sister, Jeniel, who looked exactly like her but wasn't as outgoing—which was a good thing, because two perfect Jennas on the planet would be more than any girl could handle. With their wavy black hair and killer blue eyes, the twins could seriously be teen models. Why did some girls have all the luck? "But won't it leave a scar?" I said, weakening beneath Drew's unrelenting gaze.

"No scars. It'll just leave a little red mark. Like an ant bite. It'll be gone by tomorrow."

"Tomorrow?" My voice rose. "What about tonight? My mom will freak."

Drew's eyes rolled. "Your mom will be at work, like always." Her hand—the one holding the syringe—lowered.

I swallowed again. Drew had a point. No one would see me. Dad would work late on a case or a trial like always, too. Ryan would be at Fred's house, where he was living practically 24/7. (By the way, Fred was a girl. Fred was short for Fredricka, but Fred hated her name and insisted everyone call her Fred—and who could blame her? She had an old-lady name, even though she was one of the coolest junior girls at school, in my opinion.)

Besides, I'd overheard Shelley McMahon say at lunch that

other girls at school had tried BOTOX, even Jenna Gibbons. That was why I remembered. That was why I was standing in Drew's enormous bathroom, pressed against the double marble sinks, inches from a sadistic-looking syringe, squinting into about one hundred obnoxiously steaming-hot vanity lights. Maybe there was something to this BOTOX frenzy? And maybe feeling pretty was just as important as being pretty. "Okay," I heard myself say. "Do it. Between my eyes. Just once."

Drew flashed a triumphant smile, her thumb ready at the end of the pump. "Trust me, after you see what this will do, you'll be begging for more."

"Won't your dad notice it missing?"

She shrugged. "He hasn't so far."

Then she positioned the syringe inches above my forehead.

I sucked in a breath.

"Lean back," she said, reaching for my neck with her other hand.

Every nerve, muscle and brain cell in my body told me that this was stupid and wrong, but I wasn't in control. It was that other girl inside of me, the fiercer, spunkier one who'd been calling the shots—no pun intended—lately. That voice inside my head kept telling me that I needed to be cooler, more spontaneous. Different. Definitely different. So I leaned back, closed my eyes, tilted my head and begged for *different*.

"Ouch," I said when the needle pierced my skin, freezing my forehead like it'd been doused with dry ice. Then the feeling spread to the rest of my face. "This so better be worth it," I said to Drew through gritted teeth.

Drew took a step back, still holding the syringe in her right hand. She reached inside a jar on the counter that was stuffed with cotton balls.

"It feels like my forehead is on fire."

She dabbed my skin with one of the cotton balls and some other liquid that I couldn't see. "Don't worry. It doesn't last." She took a step back, still studying me, and tossed her ponytail over her shoulder.

"Better not. I've got the leadership conference this weekend."

Drew frowned. "Good gawd! Total dorkdom, Riley. You might as well wave the white flag on your social life right now."

"And what social life would that be?" I didn't bother hiding my sarcasm. Besides, it wasn't as though Drew had a better social life than I did. Otherwise, why would she be hanging out with me? "It's my parents' fault. They're making me go," I added, which was a complete lie. "And it looks good on college applications." Now that was true. It was pretty hard to get into the Art Institute of Chicago—that was my dream— so I figured I'd need all the help I could get, especially since I was kind of mediocre at anything besides art classes, at least as far as my grade point average was concerned.

"Whatever."

I ignored her frown.

But then Drew smiled. She finally said what I longed to hear. What I never heard. "You look different already."

I wanted to believe her. No, scratch that. I *needed* to believe her. It gave me hope. It lifted weight off my shoulders. For a moment, it was as if my life had real possibilities. Potential. Magic.

Welcome to the inside of my crazy head.

2

SAM

My buddy Peter and I hitched a ride in the bed of Martin Ellis's pickup. Martin drove and Vernon Parker called shotgun. There was a party tonight somewhere near the Estrella foothills. When you lived way out on the Rez like we did, sometimes that was as close to real excitement as you got.

Going out beat the alternative, which was stay home, watch my grandmother weave baskets on the front stoop and pretend that my heart hadn't been pulverized into a thousand pieces.

Martin's truck chugged its way along a single-lane dirt road. The sun had already begun to set and by the time we reached the foothills, the sky would be as black as a bruise. Someone would have already started a campfire and (hopefully) someone else would have brought beer—just a can or two apiece, but that was probably all that anybody could sneak from home.

Peter and I clung to the sides of the truck as Martin charged up and out of bumpy washes that snaked across the Sonoran Desert. Peter was another Rez kid and a junior at Lone Butte High like me. Despite being fifty pounds lighter, he was as tall as I was. That's why our legs kept knocking whenever Martin sped like a madman over the washes. Across the truck bed, Peter kept giving me the stink eye from behind his wire-rimmed glasses, even as his glasses kept slipping down his nose.

"Stop it," he yelled over the grind of the engine.

"Stop what?" I yelled back, tasting a thin layer of dust on my lips.

He shook his head. "Stop thinking about it." Peter and Martin were the only ones I'd told, but I was pretty sure everyone on the Rez knew. Even though the Gila River Indian Reservation stretched forever in just about every direction, it was microscopic, if you know what I mean. Sometimes the biggest places could be the tiniest.

I shrugged and looked away from Peter, preferring to stare across miles of brown desert and dried tumbleweeds as if it were the most exciting scenery in the whole world.

As usual, Martin continued to drive like a maniac. Frankly, I was surprised his old man's truck could do more than thirty-five. If the truck were a hospital patient, someone would definitely be reading it its last rites.

I turned away from Peter and focused on the wake of dust that swirled like a minitornado behind us in the darkening sky. If Peter referred to That Which Shouldn't Be Named one more time, I was seriously thinking about ripping off a truck panel. It was bad enough that Peter even thought it. But he surprised me.

"I can't believe you're gonna bail on us this weekend."

I breathed easier and looked at him. "I know. Can't help it. My mom wants me to go." Total lie. My parents, my dad especially, had stopped being interested in what I did at school ever since I'd started going to Lone Butte High. Not sure why, exactly. But it was better for all of us when they stayed out of my business. Besides, they both worked all the time at the casino on the Rez and Mom was studying for her master's degree whenever she wasn't working, so it was probably easier that they didn't have to worry about me. One less hassle.

"Why don't you tell her that you don't want to go? Martin, Vernon and me, we're gonna drive down to Coolidge. Supposed to be a fair in town or something. Maybe even a rodeo." His eyebrows wiggled. "Maybe even hot rodeo queens."

"You wish," I said.

"A dude can dream. What else I got?"

I laughed. But then I dragged my tongue across my lips, tasting more dust. "Too late for me, anyway," I said. "Already paid for it." Another lie.

"Seriously?"

"Seriously." What I didn't share was that Lone Butte High School had paid my registration fee to the Maricopa County High School Leadership Conference. They'd paid the fees for the two sophomores, two juniors and two seniors with the highest GPAs. I happened to be one of the two juniors. Sucks to be the other sixty students who were invited but had to pay out of their own pockets. Now all I had to do was show up to school tomorrow morning and board the bus. It would get me to Monday and put about 250 miles of desert between me and the Rez.

"What do you want with some leadership bullshit?" Peter said. "You need someone to tell you what you already know?"

I swallowed. The truth? I really didn't know. My guidance counselor at school, Mr. Romero, had told me about it. He'd said things like conferences and awards looked good on college applications. He'd said I had to be more of a game player, especially since there was a good chance I was going to graduate early and colleges were already starting to inquire about me. Me. Sam Tracy, the smart kid from the Rez.

Unfortunately I stunk at playing games. Just give me something in black-and-white, minus the sugarcoating. Minus the doublespeak.

A part of me knew I couldn't stay in-state, and I think Mr. Romero would just about blow a gasket if I didn't apply to college, not when my SATs were among the highest in Arizona. Too bad that looking good on paper was more important than simply being smart enough.

I closed my eyes and tried to ignore Peter, even as he teased me for the rest of the ride about being the biggest nerd on the Rez. It was probably true.

Peter was lucky he was one of my best friends. Otherwise I would have tossed him out of the truck, which was pretty easy to do when you were my size.

3

RILEY

Mom dropped me off in the Lone Butte High School parking lot early Saturday morning with my overnight bag. The sun was still rising over the horizon, bright as an orange slice. Small bonus: Mom had just gotten off her hospital shift and her red-rimmed eyes were clouded with fatigue, one of the drawbacks to being a doctor, but a major advantage when you didn't want her to notice stuff. It helped that we had to drive into the sun. That was probably why she hadn't commented about my fave tie-dyed pink baseball cap being tugged superlow over my forehead. I had to hide the results of Doctor Drew's secret BOTOX concoction handiwork. I was lucky it hadn't turned into an infection or a rash or worse. It looked like a couple of ant bites, just as Drew had warned me. She'd conveniently forgotten to tell me, though, that my forehead would feel like plastic. Whenever I wrinkled my nose, my forehead stayed as frozen as stone. Most people wouldn't notice, but most people weren't my mom.

"When should I pick you up?" Mom yawned as I opened the passenger door of her Mercedes. Two yellow school buses waited next to the curb, their engines idling. Students had already begun to board. I recognized a few from Lone Butte, a couple sophomores and juniors, but nobody that I knew well. Most of the ones that I didn't recognize were from other Phoenix schools. One guy was actually wearing a cowboy hat so I figured him for Queen Creek, way out in the boondocks where people still had ranches and dairy farms. Kind of lanky-cute in a Jake Gyllenhaal way.

"Tomorrow night," I said. "We're supposed to be back here by six."

"What time did your brother get home last night?" she asked, her eyes narrowing with newfound sharpness.

I pulled the rim of my cap even lower. "Not late," I lied. "Probably around ten." Another lie. More like midnight.

Mom smiled, just like I'd known she would. "Good. Well, have a good time. Where are you going again?"

"Woods Canyon," I said, but the door had already shut. I had left all the brochures and information about the leadership conference on the kitchen counter, perfectly stapled and organized with pink paperclips and Post-it notes, and, seriously? She'd signed my registration form two weeks ago, so it wasn't like she didn't already know. I didn't want to have this conversation with people staring at us from the bus windows. That was kind of why I didn't wave, either. I mean, it wasn't like she was dropping me off for my first day of kindergarten or anything.

Life would be so much better when I got my own car.

Instead, I pulled out my cell phone from my pocket and fired off a text while I walked to the bus:

The conf is @ Woods Canyon. Info on the kitchen counter. Bye. Love u.

I hoped she got the message. Mom didn't totally get texting and hated that she had to pull out her reading glasses to see the keys. But I wasn't going to call her when I was within spitting distance from the bus. Even though the windows were tinted, I could see the outlines of faces staring down at me and I was a little distressed to see that almost every seat, at least on the parking lot side, was taken.

Two seconds later, Mom surprised me with a reply: Okay. Have a nice time. Love you back. Always. Mom

Mom always signed her texts *Mom* as if I didn't know it was her.

I reached the front of the bus and drew back a steadying breath. Maybe going to this conference was a lame idea, after all. I mean, what normal teenager goes to a leadership conference on a perfectly good Saturday? I should be at the mall with Drew.

I hoisted my bag higher on my shoulder. It wasn't really a backpack but it wasn't luggage, either. It happened to match my pink baseball cap. Pink, in case you hadn't noticed, was my all-time favorite color. Given the choice of pink and anything else, I always went pink. Cheesy, I know, but the color was one of the few things in my life that made me happy. Whenever I saw shades of pink, I smiled inside. I kept waiting to graduate to a more mature color preference, like blue or retro green, but it just wasn't happening. Maybe when I left for college.

Scott Jin stood at the bus door with a clipboard. His eyes dropped to his sheet when he saw me, presumably to find my name. Scott knew me through my brother, like most upperclassman. I think he may have been on the golf team with Ryan before he traded golf for Math Club and Debate, but he always dressed like he was ready to play—brown shorts with perfect creases and golf shirts buttoned right up to his neck. "Riley Berenger," he said, very official-like, without looking at me. "You're in bus number one. This one." He pointed to the door with a blue pen.

"What about when we get to Woods Canyon?" I said. "Where will I be assigned there?"

"Girls will be in one cabin. Guys in the other," he said. He might as well have added "Duh" at the end of his sentence.

"Oh," I said, mildly relieved that this wasn't a sleeping-in-tents-with-an-outhouse affair. The brochure hadn't been completely clear on that point, and camping was not my thing. "I didn't know."

He tapped his clipboard, dismissing me, and I climbed inside.

There was excitement on the bus but it wasn't, say, going-to-a-football-game-at-a-rival-school excitement. This was, after all, a collection of some of the smartest kids in all of Phoenix. Sometimes I had to remind myself that I was considered one of them, especially on the days when I felt like the biggest idiot in the world. Like yesterday, when I let Drew inject my forehead with toxic chemicals. What was I thinking?

The bus driver was reading a newspaper, his baseball cap turned backward on his head. He was chewing on a toothpick that looked as if it had been spinning between his teeth for the past six months.

When I reached the top step, I looked across the bus and saw that all of the seats were taken except for the first two rows behind the bus driver and one empty row near the back of the bus. It might have been my imagination but the excitement on the bus dimmed a smidgen. I pulled my cap lower as I surveyed the real estate. I didn't see any sophomores from Lone Butte, and the juniors and seniors were already sitting with people, talking. There was no way I was walking all the way to the back, so I slipped into the second empty row behind the bus driver. At least I'd have a whole row to myself, so I guessed that arriving late had its advantages.

Behind me, Scott Jin hopped up the stairs, trailed by Mr. Romero, one of the school's guidance counselors. Instead of his usual dark pants, white shirt and either red- or blue-striped tie, Mr. Romero looked almost human dressed in jeans and a white T-shirt that said Someone in Bozeman, Montana, Loves Me on the front. But his brow was furrowed as if he were anxious about something—and who could blame him? No doubt he'd rather be anywhere than camping with two busloads of teenagers. "Time to roll," he finally instructed the bus driver.

Scott and Mr. Romero took the first seat behind the bus driver, thank god. Mr. Romero was okay, but I really didn't want to talk to him for two hours about college applications and test scores, not when I'd downloaded four episodes of *Friends* to my iPod along with five new songs that I was dying to listen to.

The bus driver tucked his newspaper next to his seat, reached for the handle that cranked the door shut and steered the bus away from the curb.

We hadn't even made it to the street when Mr. Romero stood and yelled, "Stop!"

I wasn't the only one to look up in surprise. I hadn't even scrolled down to my first *Friends* episode.

A blue pickup truck sped into the parking lot and headed straight for us.

"What the…" the bus driver muttered as the bus jolted to a stop. It looked like the truck was going to play chicken with our school bus.

I gripped the seat in front of me as a black cloud spewed from behind the truck, which, by the way, looked ready to explode. When it got closer, I could make out two faces behind the cloudy windshield. Boys. The one in the passenger seat was waving his arm out the window.

"Good!" Mr. Romero said, a smile in his voice as Scott returned to his clipboard.

"I thought we had everybody?" Scott said.

"We do now," Mr. Romero said.

Scott's brow furrowed as he continued to study his clipboard. He flipped through a stack of white pages. "Who'd I miss?" he said, as if it were not humanly possible for him to miss anything. Which, for him, was probably true. I'd heard that he'd gotten a perfect score on the math section of the SATs. I mean, who scored perfect on that? That was borderline freakish.

"Sam Tracy," Mr. Romero said as he stared out the front windshield. "But let's cut him some slack, okay? He traveled a long way to get here."

4

SAM

Martin's truck almost stalled three times before we finally chugged into the school parking lot. It was a miracle that his wheels made it at all.

Both my parents had worked late, so if the truck had died, waking them wouldn't have been my favorite option. At the casino on the Rez, Dad worked security and Mom worked in a back office, "counting the money," she always said, but really, she was an accountant for the tribe, and a damn good one. Dad was Gila and Mom was Havasupai and they'd been together since the summer of their senior year when they'd met at some high school summer program in Oklahoma. Figures that two Natives from Arizona would have to travel across state lines to meet. According to Mom, they'd fallen madly in love that summer, which was impossible for me to picture. You had to know my dad to understand—and knowing my dad, even a little bit, was one of the hardest things in the whole world. Harder than AP physics. Dad wasn't exactly the flower-and-chocolates type. "Your dad's just not sensitive like you are, Sam," Mom had whispered to me once when

I was about ten years old and I'd made him a Father's Day card at school. "But he loves you, even if he doesn't say the words. It's what he thinks in his heart that's most important." Dad had looked at the card I'd made and smiled, sort of, but then he'd closed the card and placed it facedown and never looked at it for the rest of the weekend. I knew, because I'd watched him. I'd never made another card for him again. "But you're more alike than you realize," Mom had added, which I absolutely had not believed. Still didn't. Sometimes I wondered if I was adopted.

On a good day, you'd never hear Dad utter five words, least of all to me, but I supposed that came in handy when most of your day consisted of sitting in a smoky haze and watching for people who cheated or misbehaved while playing slot machines or blackjack. I knew that my parents loved me. At least, my mother told me she did all the time. I just wished that I could hear my father say it, even once, before I stopped caring altogether.

Fortunately for my parents, they usually worked the same hours, but that was unfortunate for me from a ride perspective. So Martin really had saved the day by offering to drive me to school at the butt-crack of dawn on a Saturday morning, on the condition that I stayed later at last night's party.

"How are you gonna stay awake long enough to reach Coolidge?" I stifled another yawn.

"I'll sleep when I'm dead," Martin said dully, his eyelids as puffy as mine.

"You sound like a rapper."

"Don't I wish," he said. And then he flashed some sign with his fingers. I had no idea what it meant, but I was sure it was stupid.

I didn't know how I was going to make it to noon on prac-

tically no sleep, much less through the rest of the weekend.
I figured I'd catch some z's on the bus ride.

"There they are." I pointed to two yellow school buses.

"Dude. I'm just tired. Not blind." Martin slammed down
on the accelerator, grinding it to the floor.

I could smell something burning. Motor oil? It was plum-
ing somewhere in the back of the truck. I felt kind of bad leaving Martin, especially since there was a pretty good chance
he'd need a ride home. "Call Fred's brother, Trevor, if you
break down again. He's good with cars. He'll tow you home
if you need it. There's a pay phone by the front of the school,
next to the drinking fountain."

Martin nodded. "I'm not worried," he said, and I smiled
to myself.

Martin was about as good a best friend as a dude could
have. We'd known each other all our lives. We grew up together. Our dads grew up together. It was like we were brothers, not friends. "Thanks, man," I said as he approached the
buses.

"No prob, bro," he said. "Just don't turn dork on me, okay?
I've got a reputation to uphold." He smirked, one arm draped
lazily across the wheel, even though he was practically playing chicken with a school bus full of high school students,
not to mention a couple of teachers.

I chuckled. "Sure. Reputation. Got it."

Thanks to Martin, the bright yellow bus had no choice
but to stop. Its brakes even screeched a little.

Ouch.

I sure hoped that Mr. Romero wouldn't be too mad at me,
but what could I do? It wasn't like we'd be able to catch up
to the bus if we road-raced down the freeway.

"Sure you want to do this?" Martin asked. "I can always
keep driving. Here's your chance."

Chance. I needed one. I needed a hundred. "Yep. Got to." I reached for the door handle. "Besides, I think Romero is ready to dive through the windshield. Can't back out now. He's probably pissed."

"Okay." Martin didn't sound convinced. He paused. Then he said, "You know you can't avoid her forever."

I sucked back a breath, hitching my backpack over my shoulder. I looked at Martin for an instant without saying anything. Then I said, "I know. But I can try."

Martin just shook his head.

"Later, dude," I said.

"Later. See you Monday."

I closed the door—more like slammed it, because the rusted door stuck a little—and then jogged the six steps to the waiting bus.

Even through the windshield, I could see at least thirty faces, including Mr. Romero's, staring back at me like two rows of dominoes. A few mouths hung open.

"Okay, you idiot," I muttered to myself. "You asked for it. Now deal."

When I reached the door, it was already open.

Mr. Romero stood at the top of the stairs. His mouth twitched in one corner below his salt-and-pepper mustache. I couldn't tell whether he was angry or glad to see me.

"Sorry I'm late, Mr. Romero. Had some trouble with the truck." I nodded back at Martin's ride, as if its mechanical limitations weren't obvious. Martin turned and headed back toward the freeway as blue-black smoke billowed out of his tailpipe. He was never going to make it to the Rez.

"I can see that," Mr. Romero said. "Well, glad you made it. Now have a seat. We're already behind schedule."

"Sorry," I said again as I looked over his shoulder at all the faces on the bus. As usual, I was the only Native. I recognized maybe six people on the bus including Matt Hendricks from advanced chemistry. He nodded. I nodded back. Unfortunately the seat next to him was taken.

"You'll have to put your backpack under your seat."

"No problem," I said, removing it from my shoulder. Other than a toothbrush and a change of underwear and socks, it was pretty empty.

There was an open seat up front next to a girl dressed in a pink sweatshirt and pink baseball cap. It was blinding, really. For some reason, she kept pulling her cap lower like she was in disguise. But I recognized her.

"Hi," I said, slipping into the seat. There was barely any room for my legs. The bus driver closed the door and the bus lurched forward.

"Hi," she said. "I'm—"

I interrupted her with my sigh. "Yeah, I know who you are."

The bus lurched again and we all lunged forward, grabbing the seats in front of us. For some stupid reason, I put my left arm out to stop her from crashing her head against the seat.

"Um, thanks?" she said, turning sideways to look at me and then my hand on her shoulder.

My hand snapped back and I nodded, facing forward, wishing I could have found a seat all to myself.

She began to fidget with her hands before fumbling for the iPod in her lap. "Oh. Well..." Her thumb pressed one of the buttons, probably a little harder than she needed to. A notebook with some sketches and doodles sat on her lap.

I leaned my head back, hoping that I could sleep most of the way. Just my luck I had to sit next to Ryan Berenger's sister, who was every bit as annoyingly perfect as her brother.

Maybe worse. The clothes, the pale skin, the graceful way she crossed her legs like a pretzel all the way down to her ankles.

It was going to be a long ride.

5

RILEY

Oh. My. God. What a jerk. Drew was never going to believe this! I pulled out my cell phone and began to text her.

I should have taken that seat way in the back, after all, despite the sea of juniors and seniors. I'd had no idea that Sam Tracy was so in love with himself. *I know who you are?* Seriously? I mean, get some manners.

I had seen him talking with Fred a couple of times in the cafeteria, and he'd seemed nice enough on school territory. Obviously I'd misread him.

My nose wrinkled. *Great!* And he reeked, too. Eau de Charcoal Grill.

Because he was so tall, I supposed he'd want to claim most of the leg space underneath the bench in front of us. Not gonna happen.

Once I got my internal hyperventilation under control, I uncrossed my legs, taking as much space as I could. Then I finished a quick text that Drew wouldn't see until at least noon and pressed the volume button on my *Friends* episode. I'd rather listen to Chandler and Joey and sketch in my notebook any day than attempt conversation with Sam Tracy, especially now.

Mr. Romero turned around. He looked at Sam and me over the tops of his wire-rimmed glasses. "Could you pass these backward?" he said, handing us a stack of papers. "It's the agenda for the weekend."

I removed one earbud, one eye trained on my iPod screen as I grabbed the papers with my right hand. It was my favorite *Friends* episode, the one where Ross gets his teeth whitened so pearly white that they glow in a black light. Hilarious.

Mr. Romero stood. "Can I have your attention?" His chin lifted while his eyes swept over the rows. "Pause the texting for a moment, people. I promise your brains won't self-destruct."

A few people chuckled as the bus grew quiet.

Mr. Romero moved to the center of the aisle, still hanging onto the back of the seat with his free hand as the bus headed down the freeway toward the rising sun. "Since we've got three hours to kill till we reach the campground, we might as well go over a few details. As many of you know, we've reserved two large cabins—one for the girls, the other for the boys."

"Damn," someone behind me said, feigning disappointment. People around him laughed.

Mr. Romero smirked. "Watch the language, Mr. Wolkiewski," he said.

"Sorry, Mr. Romero," Logan said, but he didn't sound the least bit sorry.

Mr. Romero continued. "Anyway, we've got a busy weekend planned and you can read all about it on the agenda that's being distributed as I speak. There will be competitions and contests, and tonight we will have a barbecue. Keeping up so far?"

No one spoke. Most of us were too busy looking over the agenda. It seemed that at any given hour there was an activity—from rope climbing to scavenger hunts to leadership tests that were supposed to reveal our leadership styles. I had a style? It kind of looked like the weekend had the potential for fun, in a weird, dorky way. I did always like variety. I pulled out my pink highlighter.

"As soon as we arrive at the campsite, we'll unpack the buses, get you settled and then get started on the first activity. Everyone has been organized into teams. They're listed on the back of the agenda."

I flipped over the page and scanned for my name. There were twelve groups of five. I was on the Green Team. One name jumped out at me right away: Sam Tracy.

It was impossible not to groan.

Then I stole a sideways glance. At that same moment, Sam and I locked eyes for a millisecond. He had these impossibly dark eyes, the intense kind that looked like they knew what you were thinking, even before you did. We both looked away so fast that I had to wonder if we'd eye-locked at all.

I guessed he was as excited about seeing my name alongside his as I was. His loud sigh and accompanying frown as he stared at the page were dead giveaways. I just wish I knew what I'd done for him to hate me so much.

Maybe I was making something out of nothing. I did that a lot. It was a sickness.

To stop stressing, I began to sketch in my notebook. Before I realized what I was drawing, Sam's angry dark eyes began to take shape on my page.

6

SAM

I folded Mr. Romero's fancy agenda and stuffed it in the back pocket of my jeans. Then I sank lower in the chair until my feet popped out from underneath the bench in front of me. I leaned my head back, closed my eyes and begged for sleep.

The next thing I knew, my head had bounced onto Riley's pink shoulder. It felt as if it had been pounded against a two-by-four.

"You mind?" She glared at me, her blue-green eyes stretched wide below the brim of her baseball cap as she held a thick pencil in midair. Jeez, she looked exactly like her brother with that same know-it-all, confident face that always got on my last nerve.

"Sorry," I mumbled with a headshake, sitting upright, facing forward, hoping that drool hadn't made an appearance.

Just then, the bus exited the freeway. My ears began to pop, and I was pleased to see that we had already reached the top of the Mogollon Rim. A brown sign with white letters welcomed us to the Woods Canyon Lake campsite, and the bus pulled off the highway and proceeded along a narrow two-lane road. The bus shook from side to side as it made its way deeper into the campground on a stretch of road that alternated between pavement and dirt. Exactly as I remembered.

I hadn't been to Woods Canyon since I was a kid. One August weekend, my parents and Martin's parents had lugged all the kids, including his older brother and sister and my older sister, Cecilia, to the campground. Martin and I were probably around twelve years old. We thought it was killer to be camping in tents and fishing for trout. Our parents were thrilled to escape the desert heat and probably a weekend of night shifts at the casino. Who knew then that I'd be back five years later with two busloads of students that I barely knew?

Mr. Romero stood, stretched his arms overhead and then turned to face us. The look on his face demanded our attention. "Look, I know you're all pretty anxious to get off this bus and have some fun. I am, too. So that's why I'm going to ask you to dump your bags quickly once we reach the cabins. Don't worry. Nothing will happen to them." He rubbed his hands together and squinted his eyes. "And I hate to be the bearer of bad news but your cell phones probably won't work way out here." He chuckled.

A few people gasped and I rolled my eyes.

I was probably the only person on the whole bus without a phone—not like I didn't *want* one, but it was the kind of luxury that I couldn't afford. Mom said that if I wanted my own I had to pay for it. Maybe I would when I started college. I'd be able to work full-time during the summer before the first semester. Vernon Parker was the only one of our friends back on the Rez who had one, although I wasn't sure why. Who was he calling, if not us?

As soon as the buses rolled to a stop in front of two large cabins that I didn't remember from my previous visit, Mr. Romero directed all of the guys to the monstrous log cabin on the right and the girls to the equally large cabin on the left. The buildings looked like college dorms, only in the woods. I think I would have preferred to sleep outside.

"Leave your bag on a cot in your respective cabins, use the facilities if you need to and then hustle back outside for the first team-building activity," Mr. Romero said as we began to file off the bus, stretching and groaning from having sat for close to three hours. "Don't forget to grab a water bottle from one of the ice chests and then gather on the picnic tables with your teams." I took a deep breath and forced myself to channel Mr. Romero's enthusiasm.

Fifteen minutes later, I heard Riley's voice outside the guys' cabin. It cut through the wind whistling through the pine trees. "Green Team!" she said. "Green Team, over here!" She was waving a pink scarf over her head, the same one that had been wrapped around her neck like an intestine in the way that girls liked to do. Two boys and another girl gathered around her at one of the ten wooden picnic tables that surrounded a half-dozen grills and ice chests.

"Good," I muttered to myself. Matt Hendricks was on our team. At least I'd know someone besides Riley, who I really didn't want to know at all. I bristled at the way she was waving the damned scarf, an obvious attempt to assume the team leader role. She was already taking charge. Should I be surprised? Like brother, like sister.

I was the last one at the Green Team picnic table. "What's the first activity?" I said.

"We're supposed to give each other nicknames," Riley said, not meeting my gaze. She jumped off the table holding a plastic bag. From the bag, she pulled out pens and those peel-and-stick My Name Is name tags. She proceeded to give each of us a name tag and a pen, although for herself, she grabbed a pink pen out of the front pocket of her sweatshirt.

"What. A regular black pen isn't good enough for you?" I said, admittedly a weak attempt at humor, though Matt chuckled as we fist-bumped before straddling the picnic bench.

Riley rolled her eyes. "Ha. Ha. I think I already know your nickname."

"What's that?" I sat across from Riley.

"Lame Comedian."

"Ha. Ha." I mimicked her tone.

"So," Riley said as the five of us stared at each other around the picnic table. "Nicknames?" Her gaze swept over us, prompting us to begin. Her eyelashes dipped when she reached me.

After a handful of quiet, uncomfortable seconds in which we all had to listen to Riley tap her pink pen against the wooden table, I said, "Um. Suggestion. Shouldn't we introduce ourselves first? You know, try and get to know each other?"

"Would you like to be team leader?" Riley's eyes widened.

"Do we need one?" Before she could reply I said, "My name is Sam Tracy." I turned my attention to the other faces at the table. "I'm a junior at Lone Butte. I live on the Gila River Rez. That's me." I swiveled toward Matt.

"Hey," he said. His leg began to shake against the bench. "I'm Matt." He even gave a little wave. "Used to go to Lone Butte. Now I'm a junior over at Hamilton." He paused to drag a hand through what little blond hair he had. "Live in Phoenix. Born in Chicago. I guess that'll do." Matt turned to the girl beside him.

The girl next to Matt crossed her arms when everybody looked at her. Hazel eyes widened behind her wire-rimmed glasses. She forced a nervous smile and spoke just a hair louder than the whistling pine trees surrounding us. "Cassidy Mc-

Mahon." We all leaned closer. "Basha High sophomore." She
spoke very fast, as if she wanted to get the whole introduction thing over with, and who could blame her. I hated these
kinds of things, too. "I collect comic books," she added, her
pale cheeks blushing as she said it.

Cassidy turned to the boy wearing a baseball cap who was
seated across from her. He sat sideways with his legs pointed
away from Riley so I didn't get a good look at him at first.
But then he spun around to face everybody, a piece of brown
grass spinning between his teeth. "Jay Hawkins." He said his
name like he couldn't wait to tell us. Like it was a piece of
vital information necessary for human survival. I couldn't
help but groan inside. Jay Hawkins was one of my least favorite people at Lone Butte, even one notch lower than Ryan
Berenger, and that was saying something. "And I really hate
these team-building things or whatever they're called. When's
lunch?" Jay added, which got the others to chuckle. Naturally he didn't bother with any further details, because guys
like Jay Hawkins assumed the rest of the world already knew
about him. Humility was not one of his strengths. He turned
to Riley and flashed a set of perfectly white teeth instead.

Riley beamed back at him, tugging on the scarf that had
found its way back around her long neck.

It was hard not to eye roll, watching the silent flirting. Of
course Riley fell for it. Girls always did.

"Well, I guess that just leaves me," Riley said, tapping her
pen again against the table. I noticed she bit her fingernails.
As if she could sense me and everyone else at the table staring at them, her fingers curled around the pen until finally
she hid her hand beneath the table. "I'm Riley Berenger.
Sophomore at Lone Butte High." She smacked her lips, as if
considering what else to add. If I knew her, she had something clever memorized, no doubt recorded in her notebook

in her perfect handwriting with her perfect hot pink pen. "I love to dance and I love to draw."

Then she turned to me, like I was supposed to add something additional to our introductions, which, in her defense, I did suggest.

Before I could respond, Jay leaned forward and looked straight at me. He had on his pretend-serious face. "Dude. I'm curious. What do you like to be called? I mean, Gila, Indian, American Indian, Native American? What?" He paused. "Sorry for asking, but I never know. It's confusing." If it had been anyone else, I would have told him that it was a legitimate question and there were a lot of names, some of which I truly hated, but Jay was hardly sorry for asking. His tone was anything but innocent.

I let a few uncomfortable seconds pass between us. Then I said, "Just Sam. I prefer to be called Sam."

Softly, Riley said, "Fred told me that she prefers to be called Gila first. Then, Native. Then—"

I interrupted her. "Well, that's Fred."

"Well, you have to admit, it does get confusing sometimes. Right, Sam? Knowing what's right. What's proper. What's best."

I finally broke my gaze from Jay and turned to Riley. "You don't have to remind me about that, Berenger." *I deal with it every day*, I wanted to add. Of course guys like Jay Hawkins would never have to deal with it. It wasn't something that they'd have to stress over for one solitary second.

Riley's eyes grew big and she pulled her cap lower on her forehead, like she wanted to cover her whole face. Like she preferred that I look away. So I did.

"Then *Sam* it is," Matt added brightly, trying to inject some lightness into the discussion. "I can live with that."

I nodded at Matt, once, as Jay grinned. "Yeah," Jay chimed

in. "Just Sam it is." Jay had gotten under my skin and that pleased him. I could kick myself for letting him get the best of me.

Our group grew quiet again. After a few more seconds, Riley cleared her throat. "I think we should probably decide on nicknames before we run out of time," she said, tapping her pen all over again.

"How much time we got?" I asked, grateful for the tapping. Grateful to move away from a topic that no one ever understood and one that was almost impossible to explain.

"Mr. Romero said we had until he started to grill the hot dogs for lunch."

Naturally Riley continued with more directions. "I suggest we write our names on the back of the name tag and then pass it around the table so that everyone gets a chance to write a nickname for everybody."

"Okay," I said again. "Anyone else have any other ideas?"

"What do we base the nicknames on?" Matt said. "I don't get it...."

Riley looked down at the agenda, turning it over for the instructions. "Says here that we're supposed to base them on *first impressions*." She air-quoted. "And then see if our impressions still hold by tomorrow."

I turned over my name tag. I wrote *Sam* on the back and tossed it in the middle of the table. "Give me your best shot."

7

RILEY

Grumpy? Needs a Haircut? Condescending? He Who Irritates? Those were the nicknames for Sam Tracy floating in my head.

Poor Jay. Why did Sam have to be so snippy about his question? It wasn't dumb. Sometimes I wondered the same thing, especially when I heard so many names and labels bandied about. It *was* confusing. Somehow I would need to come up with a less caustic nickname for Sam by the time my fingers found his name tag.

And why did he think I was trying to take over the team? I was merely getting us going. No one else had stepped up.

I nibbled at the end of my pen and pushed Sam Tracy out of my mind and focused on the other name tags tossed into the middle of the table.

I reached for Cassidy's first. Hers was easy. We'd taken a watercolor class together at the YMCA a couple of summers ago. She was killer smart and I loved her retro eyeglasses. Very John Lennon. *Batgirl*, I wrote on the front of her name tag, because she loved comic books. I smiled to myself. Cassidy would love that nickname. Then I reached for Matt's name tag.

I'd never really talked to Matt before, even when he went to Lone Butte. The only thing I knew about him after his introduction was that he had one of the deepest voices ever. And cute lips. So I wrote *Barry White Impersonator* and hoped he would get the humor.

Next was Jay's. I peered at him in my periphery and watched him smirk at the name tag in front of him. I hoped it wasn't mine. I couldn't help myself. I wrote *Hunk* and then quickly slipped the name tag upside down to the center of the table and then, reluctantly, reached for Sam's.

I squeezed my eyes shut and then tried, really and truly tried, to come up with a nickname that wouldn't be mean. Or hateful. Because I so desperately wanted to write *Grumpy*. That nickname fit Sam oh, so perfectly. Was there a nicer word for *grumpy?* If only my phone had internet access. I could check a thesaurus....

Finally I opened my eyes, let loose a relieved exhale and wrote *Complicated*. There. That was totally Sam Tracy.

Behind us, Mr. Romero yelled, "Okay, folks. Five more minutes till chow time! Let's wrap it up!"

Everyone on our team stopped writing and pushed the five name tags back into the center of the table. I was dying to read the nicknames on mine.

Since no one else reached for them, I picked up the name tags, clicking them against the table like I was readying a deck of cards. Then I passed each person his tag.

I sank onto the bench. Like an idiot, I'd totally forgotten that I used my pink pen. Everyone else had used their black pens. How could I have missed that? It was all Sam's fault! He'd gotten me so unnerved with the whole icy, just-call-me-Sam discussion that I completely spaced it out.

Dang it.

Across from me, Sam's right black eyebrow shot up as he studied his nicknames.

I looked down at the ones written on my name tag.

Smart. Okay, I liked that one.

Bossypants. Huh? Who wrote that one?

Thorough. Humph. That one was completely lame and boring.

But it was the last one that ignited fire through my veins: *Pink Girl.* I'd bet my new iPad that Sam Tracy wrote that one. He thought it was funny to make fun of my clothes? How nice.

I peered at him through my eyelashes. It was impossible not to glare. The jerk. Naturally, now that I wanted his attention, wanted him to know how much I was beginning to loathe his existence, he turned his back to me the moment I looked at him. He must have realized I'd figured out his clever nickname for me. He didn't even have Matt to chat up anymore. Matt had grabbed his name tag then jumped up to help Mr. Romero with the intricacies of hot dogs and hot-dog buns. There were two stone barbecues on the other side of the picnic tables and Matt began to line the hot dogs into neat little rows on each metal grill. Sam was watching them from his seat at our picnic table as if grilling meat were the most fascinating thing in the whole world.

Pink Girl came from Sam, I was sure of it.

"Don't forget to wear your name tags!" Mr. Romero shouted, turning in a half circle so everyone could hear him. "Then step right up and grab a paper plate and a bag of chips. Scavenger hunt starts in thirty minutes." He glanced up at the sky, at least what little we could see through the tops of the pine trees. He had to yell to be heard over the wind whistling through the branches. "You'll be pairing up with people on your team. Some teams are larger than others but everyone should have a partner!"

I walked closer to the barbecue grills. The hot dogs had already begun to sizzle. "Mr. Romero, do we pick our partner?" I asked, hoping—praying—that I could pick Jay or Cassidy.

Mr. Romero scratched his head. "We'll do this one by birthdates. The person or people closest to your birthday will be your partner."

I turned back to my Green Team and said, "My birthday is March sixth."

Jay said, "Mine is October twentieth."

"Mine's November fifth," Cassidy said, her eyes brightening behind her glasses as she beamed at Jay. My body slumped with that news.

Sam sighed. "Mine's February twenty-third." He looked straight across at me, his jaw stiffening.

I turned to Matt. He was already stuffing his mouth with a hot-dog bun. "When's your birthday?"

"September first," Matt said as bits of bread flew out of his mouth.

Ugh. I mentally counted the extra days for leap year, but not even leap year could save me. Sam and I were officially scavenger-hunt partners.

Kill me now.

8

SAM

I had barely started eating my third dog when I heard her voice. It was impossible not to moan.

"Looks like we have to find stuff around the forest," Riley announced behind me.

I turned midbite and then decided to dump the rest of my hot dog.

Her nose wrinkled as she rattled off the list for the scavenger hunt. *Jeez, did she ever relax?* "Pinecones, bark, berries and…stuff."

"Yeah," I said again, although I hadn't really studied the list. I mean, how hard could it be to find stuff that littered every foot of the forest?

"Even petroglyphs," Riley added.

I squinted at her. Okay. That could pose a challenge.

"How do we take a petroglyph from a rock?" She paused from reading her list, which, I noted, was already highlighted pink in places, along with some intricate curlicue doodling and fancy arrows around the margins.

I shrugged. "I suppose we have to figure that out. You got a camera?"

She nodded. "Don't you?"

I didn't answer her question. "Then we'll use your phone to snap a picture. Problem solved."

From the way that Riley's anxious expression softened, I'd like to think that she was impressed with my solution. But then she had to be a brat and add, "Let's just get this over with, okay?"

"Absolutely. The sooner the better."

Behind us, Mr. Romero started barking out more instructions. "Okay, people! Find your partners and spread out. Be back here in ninety minutes! Remember the days are still short. It'll be dark before you know it, and we've got lots more to do before dinner. No messing around out there."

Like that would be possible.

I started walking toward the entrance to Woods Canyon in silence. Riley didn't budge.

"Do you think that's the right direction?" she called after me. "Cassidy, Jay and Matt are headed to the lake. Maybe we should follow them?"

"You can, if you want," I said with a shoulder shrug. "But I think this way's better." Seriously, I didn't think it mattered where we started but there was no way in hell I would follow Jay Hawkins anywhere, at least not on purpose.

"Wait!"

I kept walking.

A second later I heard her footsteps behind me and I couldn't help but smile a little inside. "Okay, okay!" she said. "If you say so. But you better be right."

9

RILEY

Sam Tracy. I grumbled to myself. *Why'd you have to be a Pisces, too?* I pulled on the brim of my baseball cap and followed him deeper into the forest.

I looked down at the list as I walked. *Juniper bark. Prickly pear cactus needle. Pine nuts. Aspen leaf...* There were about twenty items in total, including a petroglyph that, seriously, I had doubts we'd ever find. And I was embarrassed to admit that I really had no idea where to find most of this stuff. "Are you kidding me?" I complained to no one in particular.

"What's the problem now, Berenger?" Sam said beside me.

I slapped the paper against my thigh and looked up at him.

Sam's eyes blinked wide again as if I were irritating him, a look that I was growing used to.

I fought an eye roll.

"I take it you haven't spent much time in the woods."

"Well, not really." I tried to sound like I could care less. "And I suppose you have?"

He nodded. "A bit."

"It's not like I've never heard of these things." My voice got a little defensive.

"But you've never touched them. I mean, outside of books and stuff. Right?"

I didn't answer. Did the school field trip to the zoo in the second grade count?

Sam looked from side to side. We were completely alone. Against my better judgment, I followed Sam, even when almost everyone else had hiked toward the lake, which would probably be way more fun and scenic than where Sam was going. "Well, we better start finding stuff," I said.

His voice was flat. "We're wasting time by arguing."

Wasting. Nice. "I'm not arguing. I'm following." My chin lifted. "Lead the way, since you're the forest expert."

Without another word, Sam picked up his pace and headed toward the Mogollon Rim, where the pine trees stretched even higher into the sky. No doubt we'd at least find pine nuts or whatever they were called.

I jogged behind him, saying nothing, but I did consider flipping the bird behind his jet-black, irritating, know-it-all head…before I found myself concentrating on the shoulder muscles beneath his stretched T-shirt, which, it pained me to admit, were kind of hot. I blushed as I thought about them, grateful that Sam couldn't see my eyes.

10

SAM

Traipsing through the woods with Miss Spoiled Brat looking for nuts and needles. Somebody put me out of my misery. Not exactly what I'd anticipated for my weekend. Coolidge with my buddies and rodeo queens were suddenly sounding better by the second.

I didn't slow my pace to match Riley's, either. Let her try and keep up.

I'd spotted a few aspen trees and even an alligator juniper near the entrance to the campsite on the bus ride in, which was one of the reasons I'd taken us in this direction. I'd bet Jay Hawkins wouldn't have known that. Couldn't Riley just shut up and trust me?

"Okay. Where are we going, exactly?" Riley called out. The thick trees swallowed her voice. She trailed a good five yards behind me.

I lifted my arms in case it wasn't obvious. "Um. Three guesses?"

"Ha. Ha." Her footsteps quickened across the dirt and dry leaves. "If I knew, I wouldn't keep asking."

I didn't slow my pace.

"Wait!" she said. Her footsteps pattered faster behind me and I figured if I sped up any more it would probably be more than a little cruel. Not that she didn't deserve it, especially after the last remark, spoken in the tone of someone used to getting her way all the time.

"I saw some aspens over here," I said without turning, anxious to be done with this scavenger hunt.

"Where?"

"Just follow me."

She closed more distance between us. "But aspen leaves are sixth on our list."

I stopped and she practically crashed into my back. "So?" I spun around to face her.

"So maybe we should do them in order."

My voice grew higher. "Why?"

She looked up at me, wide-eyed. "So we can make sure we get everything."

"That doesn't make sense."

"It makes perfect sense to me."

"Figures." I turned and started walking again as Riley jogged.

It ended up being farther than I thought, but we finally reached the entrance to the campground. Cars and trucks chugged along the highway in front of us.

"Just one aspen leaf, right?" I asked Riley, reaching up to a branch to pluck a decent-sized one.

She studied the list again. "Doesn't say. Let's take a couple, just in case."

I rolled my eyes but said nothing as I plucked two green aspen leaves. In a few months, the leaves would turn golden-yellow and drop to the forest floor. I decided against sharing that tidbit with Riley, especially since she was practically fainting over finding all the items on the list. This girl had serious chill issues.

"What should we put them in?" she asked.

"Unless you brought a backpack, we only have our pockets. I'll put them in mine—"

Riley raised a palm, stopping me. "What if they get crushed?"

I dropped them inside the front of my jeans pocket. "Take it easy, Berenger. They're leaves, not museum pieces."

She looked back at me as if I'd just slapped her.

I chuckled to hide the last-minute remorse in my tone. "I'm sure Mr. Romero won't mind."

"I noticed that Jay brought his backpack—"

"Jay," I muttered. *Again with Jay Hawkins!* "What's the use in bringing a backpack if you aren't smart enough to find any of the stuff on the list?"

"Are you saying Jay's not smart?"

Ugh. She didn't really want to know my answer.

"'Cause he's in all AP classes. Otherwise he wouldn't be here—"

I interrupted her again. "Good grades doesn't always mean smart." Smart aleck, more like it.

"And he led that school drive last year to collect new sneakers for the homeless."

"Purely for show." And to get another photo caption for himself in the yearbook.

"Well, it doesn't hurt, Sam."

"Save it, Riley." I lifted both my palms at her. "I know all about Jay's compassion and brilliance." I wondered if Riley would change her tune about Jay if she knew how he'd teased Peter during freshman year gym class, taunting him about being so skinny. He'd called Peter a totem pole. He'd tried to tease me, too, until I'd put on six inches and twenty pounds the next semester. That had shut him up real quick. Ever since, Jay had resented everything about me, including my growth spurt. I was pretty certain it bugged him that I had a higher GPA than him. Last year I'd overheard him say to another guy—loud enough for me to hear, too—that I received special treatment from teachers, which I totally did not. I worked as hard as he did, probably harder. It had been my experience off the Rez that there was no reaching guys like Jay Hawkins.

Riley closed her eyes, briefly, as she steadied herself with a loud exhale. "Look, I'll carry the leaves. My pockets are bigger." As if to prove it to me, she lifted the front pockets of her pink sweatshirt with her fists still balled inside. I had to admit, they did look pretty roomy. In one of the pockets, the top of a water bottle peeked out.

"Okay," I said, backing away. "You can carry the prickly pear needles. If you want, you can carry a whole handful of those." I meant it as a joke, but Riley wasn't laughing.

Her hands left their pockets and moved to her hips. "What exactly is your problem?"

"No problem," I said, turning toward the four-lane road. We had to cross it to reach the pine trees. "Just trying to be helpful." My sarcasm was a little excessive, but I hardly cared, especially after she'd continued to defend Jay Hawkins. After this scavenger hunt was over, our partnership would end. I'd see to that.

Riley didn't follow me this time. She just yelled at me as I kept moving. "You know, this is supposed to be a leadership retreat. We're supposed to work together. We're supposed to be leaders."

"So *lead*," I said as I kept walking. "Where to next?"

She didn't answer me. I heard her jeans swish as she jogged across the dirt to catch up. But this time she didn't catch up and jog alongside me. She charged toward the highway like she was some kind of world-class runner. A line of cars sped up the mountain. They weren't going that fast, but fast enough.

"Hey. Wait up," I said. Now it was my turn to catch up to her. *Fast when she needs to be*, I noted. *Convenient.*

Riley caught an opening between the cars and darted across the highway to the other side. She ran toward a ranger station that overlooked the entire Mogollon Rim, which also happened to be where the drop-off to the valley below was the most extreme. The tiny parking lot surrounding the ranger station was empty, probably because everyone was on the other side of the campground, fishing. Or looking for stupid forest stuff, if they were part of our school group. "Hey, wait up!" I yelled again, but my voice was drowned out by the engine noise of cars and trailers racing down the highway.

I had to wait a few minutes. At least twenty cars passed before I got an opening in the traffic. Then I ran to the other side of the road, but Riley was gone.

Gone, where?

"Riley!" I called out. In front of me stretched the Mogollon Rim. All I could see were the tops of pine trees, a million triangles in every direction. They swayed like green waves in the wind. I wouldn't be able to see the little mountain towns below until I reached the edge, and even then the towns were miles below, tiny brown and red roofs dotting spaces between green pine trees like Monopoly pieces. I ran to the Rim, expecting to find her near the edge beneath the trees gathering pinecones.

But no Riley.

I stood frozen on the Rim. The wind whipped through the treetops and against my ears. Cold, dry air filled my mouth, stealing my breath as I called Riley's name. The only thing that came back was the muffled echo of my own voice.

I ran along the edge but it was empty. Nothing but red dirt, pine trees and enough pinecones littering the ground to fill a football stadium. So where was she? There hadn't been enough time for her to run very far. She might be fast but, sorry, I was a lot faster.

Was she crazy enough to climb a tree?

Possibly.

My eyes swept across the trees dotting the edge. Their skinny green leafy branches danced in the wind. I paced along the edge, scanning the trees, and then looked down. The drop was nearly vertical. More pine and scraggly juniper jutted out from the side of the mountain like deformed arms.

I cupped my mouth with my hands and yelled again. "Riley!" My heartbeat kicked up a notch. "Not funny! Where are you?" Of all the girls here this weekend, how had I gotten saddled with her?

And then I heard a muffled squeak, somewhere below me. I tilted my head, trying to focus on the sound, trying to place it. Was it an echo? An animal? But from where? I squinted and scanned the side of the mountain, but it was like staring into the bottom of a murky ocean. I saw only endless greens and browns...and then a sliver of hot pink.

"Riley!" I yelled again, walking as close to the edge as I could without my toes curling over. I cupped my mouth, screaming her name as loud as I could, squinting through the branches and leaves. How had she gotten down there? "Stupid girl," I mumbled as dirt crunched beneath my feet. Rocks rolled beneath my toes and I had to stop myself from slipping over the edge.

Riley's voice was faint, but I made out two words. *"Help me."*

11

RILEY

The moment I opened my eyes, the world spun in slow motion.

I lay on my back, staring up at pine trees as tall as city skyscrapers. Their skinny brown trunks swayed in the wind like they could snap at any second and bury me forever. The sharp pine smell filled my nostrils.

I didn't know how long I had blacked out, but the smell must have coaxed open my eyes. Pine needles, pinecones, pine everything was scattered everywhere. Green-and-brown needles stuck to my hair and sweatshirt sleeves.

I couldn't have been out for longer than a few seconds. I'd been reaching out to a tree branch for the perfect pinecone, number two on the scavenger list. All of the ones scattered on the ground were moldy-looking or broken. I needed to pluck the right one. I'd only needed to stretch forward a few inches to reach it....

Then, *whoosh!* My right foot had skidded across a layer of pebbles, and I'd tumbled over the edge of the Mogollon Rim. Next thing I knew, I was lying flat on a piece of rock that jutted off the side of the mountain like a shelf.

Dumb idea, *obviously*, reaching for that pinecone. If I had only taken one of the many zillion covering the ground, I wouldn't have tumbled down this mountain and found myself staring up into the sky—and into Sam Tracy's most assuredly I-told-you-so face. I couldn't see any of his features, just the black and coppery outline of his head. But how was I supposed to know loose gravel lay hidden beneath a carpet of pine needles?

"Sam!" I yelled the moment I heard him call my name. "Help me!" I could guess what he was thinking about me now. The words *crazy, irrational* and *unstable* came to my mind. No doubt he could add a few more nicknames to my Hello, My Name Is tag, which, miraculously, was still stuck to my chest.

"I'll get some help!" His deep voice floated down to me.

I breathed hard, looking all around me. My arms and legs were stuck in branches at the base of a thick pine tree. Suddenly I was less worried about broken bones than I was about bears and mountain lions. The shiny brochures about Woods Canyon had mentioned the wildlife in the area. Certainly all sorts of animals could scale up and down the side of the mountain as easily as I had somersaulted down it, right? "Wait!" I yelled up to Sam, my voice dry and raspy. Yelling burned my chest. "Don't leave me!"

But Sam's face disappeared from the sky. I started to hyperventilate; my hands turned ice-cold and my whole body began to shiver, a slow rumble at first that quickly morphed into full-on panic. My eyes clouded with tears.

I tried to calm down. Maybe I could get myself out. I began to wiggle my fingers and then my toes. When I sat up and leaned forward, a sharp pain shot up my back. Hot tears dribbled down my cheeks. I wiggled my toes again and then raised each leg. It hurt to lift my right leg. My crying turned to silent sobs, the kind where your whole chest heaves in and out. Why had I ever signed up for this stupid conference or retreat or whatever it was called? I caught tears with my tongue.

Then a branch snapped.

My body froze, including my breathing. I tilted my head, listening for movement. Above me, enormous black birds flew in a circle. I untangled my arm from its branch so my fingers could sweep the ground for a stick, a rock, anything hard or heavy. All I could reach was dirt and more pinecones. It was as if the pinecones multiplied times ten every time I blinked. My only weapons were a pink cell phone with no service, a granola bar and a water bottle.

Snap! Crack! The sounds drew closer.

I reached inside my front pocket for my granola bar. Maybe I could throw it and buy myself some time.

But from what? And, where?

Pine needles and pinecones rained down all around me.

I squinted into the wind, anxious to see what predator was moving toward me. The wind howled louder, messing with my mind. It was like I was being slowly surrounded. I began to picture a hungry pack of coyotes, or wolves. Or bears. Lots and lots of hungry bears...

My heartbeat echoed all the way to my temples. Goose bumps snaked up my back. I reached inside my pocket for the water bottle. It was the heaviest thing I had on me and better than nothing.

Snap, crack, snap!

I lifted the water bottle over my head.

And then a set of gray antlers appeared from behind a trunk, followed by a head.

A deer—or maybe it was an elk—peeked at me with beady black eyes from between two pine trees. It lifted its long snout toward the sky, its nostrils sputtering. If not for its antlers, it would have blended into the tree trunk.

"Oh, god." I exhaled. I wondered whether to throw my water bottle at it. I wondered whether it was alone. Maybe I was about to be trampled by a stampede. Panicked, I inched back a fraction against the tree trunk. If I moved back far enough, the lower branches might hide me. But my whole body hurt when I moved even just a few inches. Instead of screaming at the animal and flailing my arms, I simply froze, watching the animal watch me.

The elk lowered its antlers toward the dirt and moved forward. Straight for me.

It took one step, then another, lumbering toward me like it had all the time in the world.

Was this elk psycho? Shouldn't it be afraid of me? But then, why would it be? It was as wide as a horse, maybe even bigger.

Carefully, I brought my arm back, readying my water bottle.

Snap, crack!

More pine needles floated down from the sky.

My head jerked right just as a flash of blue and black tumbled from above.

A set of feet landed with a loud thump between me and the elk.

Sam.

For a big guy, he moved amazingly fast.

Sam whistled, that loud kind mastered by jocks and gym teachers, his fingers spread in his mouth like a triangle.

The elk's ears sprang to attention like pop-up tents before it fled in the opposite direction, hooves clattering across the rock and then back up the mountain until the sounds disappeared into the wind.

"Did you see that?" I screamed, gasping for breath. "I think it was going to attack me!"

Sam bent over, placing his hands on his knees, breathing hard. Pine needles and brown leaves clung to his hair. He shook them from his head and they rained to the ground. Finally, he stood upright, wiping his hands together. "Elk don't attack. He was just curious."

"You didn't see its eyes!"

Sam came closer, peering at me almost the same way as that elk had. "Are you okay?" His tone held more annoyance than concern.

"Yes!" Tears built behind my eyes again, whether of relief or pain I wasn't sure. "I mean, no." I paused to catch my breath. "Did you bring help?"

His dark eyes stretched wider. "You asked me not to leave you!"

I swallowed, hard. "Yeah. Well. I meant—"

"You mean I climbed down the side of this mountain for nothing?" He looked at his hands. They were red and scratched from branches and rocks. His jeans were dirty and ripped like mine at the knees.

My mouth opened but no words came out. Frankly, I was a little touched that he had climbed down after me. And totally shocked, to be honest.

From his back pocket, he pulled out a baseball cap. It was pink.

My hand flew to my forehead. I wondered if my skin was still red and blotchy. Not a great time for vanity, but that's the crazy thought that flashed through my head.

He walked closer, still holding my hat. "So, are you okay or not?"

"I'm…I'm not sure." I began to wiggle my fingers and toes again. "My right leg stings. And my back hurts."

Sam knelt beside me. His hands, big as plates, pressed against my thighs and then ran up my arms, surprising me with a gentle touch.

I stopped breathing, maybe because I wasn't expecting him to go all Mr. Paramedic on me.

"How did you fall, anyway?" His gaze swept up and down my arms.

I shut my eyes, forcing an exhale. "It was stupid."

"Well, obviously."

My eyes popped open but I didn't say anything. Tough to argue with that.

"Can you walk?"

"I'm not sure." I swallowed.

He began to examine my forehead. "Did you hit your head?"

"No. I don't think so."

His fingertips reached for my forehead, never mind that I couldn't feel them. "What happened here?"

Heat rose up my neck and I was fairly certain that my whole face blushed, probably in pink and red splotches, the way it usually did when I got flustered. "That. Well. Nothing. I don't know." I talked faster. "Probably scraped against a pine branch or something."

"Are you sure—"

"Could I just have my hat, please?"

He handed me my baseball cap and I thrust it over my head, covering Drew's handiwork.

"Wasn't there a ranger station up above?" I was anxious to not discuss my BOTOX experiment because, truthfully, that sounded even dumber than my tumble down the side of the Mogollon Rim for a pinecone.

"Empty. I checked."

"Great," I mumbled. "What's the sense in having a ranger station if there's no ranger?"

Sam shook his head. "Off-season, I guess. Doesn't matter now. Let's see if you can walk."

With his arm around my waist, Sam pulled me to my feet. I wrapped an arm around his shoulder and pressed my lips together to muffle the shooting pain at standing up. I'd had sprains before from dance practice, but nothing like this. It felt as though a thousand needles were pressing into my back and leg. By the time I stood straight, I was gasping and unable to stop clutching Sam as if he were a life preserver.

"This doesn't look good," he said, shaking his head as I balanced on my left foot, still leaning against him.

"I'll be okay," I said, gasping for my next breath. "I'll just need to take it slow. I don't think anything's broken."

Sam looked at me and then at the side of the mountain. The climb back up wasn't completely vertical but it would still be a challenge, especially now with my injured leg. He didn't say anything but I knew what he was thinking: it was going to take forever to get out of here.

"I think it helps to stand," I said, trying to stay positive. "I can do this." I glanced at the top of the rim and nodded confidently. "I know I can." I really didn't want him to leave me. I was going to climb up the mountain, inch by painful inch, even if it took the rest of the weekend.

Then the sky cracked open.

"What the…?" I stared upward, numb. Ice-cold raindrops cooled my cheeks.

Sam sighed. "It's the rim. It rains in the afternoon."

"B-but," I stammered. "The sky was blue a second ago."

Rain started to fall harder, white and blinding, almost like hail. The valley below us disappeared in the storm, as if it weren't even there. The temperature must have dropped twenty degrees, just like that.

Sam's arm stayed wrapped around my waist and my arm still wove around his shoulder. It was awkward but necessary, given the circumstances. The corner of his mouth twitched with obvious panic. We stared at each other, wide-eyed, at a mutual rare loss for words.

Finally Sam said, "Let's wait it out. Got no choice." He had to yell over the rain. "We can't climb out now. Too dangerous." Raindrops clung to the ends of his bangs before spilling onto his cheeks. "Let's sit underneath the branches. At least it'll keep some of the rain off."

"But it might start lightning," I yelled back.

His eyes widened. "You got a better idea?"

I shook my head. "Not at the moment."

We turned back toward the tree, me leaning against Sam and Sam dragging me forward. We limp-walked until we dropped in a heap beneath wispy pine branches already heavy with rain.

"How long?" I asked.

Sam looked up. A second ago, the sky had been a hazy gray. Now clouds raced across it, dark as ink blots. "Could be five minutes. Could be five hours. The storm'll let us know, soon enough."

"That's comforting."

Sam sighed. "Sometimes you can't have everything you want."

"You think I don't know that?" The rain fell harder. It landed on my face like pinpricks.

Sam didn't answer with a clever quip like I expected. Instead, he placed a hand on my shoulder. Despite the chaos swirling around us, his touch slowed my panicked breathing. He leaned closer to my ear and said, "It'll be okay. I promise."

Thunder rumbled. Together we looked up at the unforgiving sky and squinted against the rain. "I hope so," I said. "But what else can we do?"

12

SAM

Crazy freaky spoiled white girl! What had she been thinking?

Even worse, what had *I* been thinking? I should never have climbed down after her like an obedient dog.

We'd crawled beneath the closest pine. It had thick, wide branches like a Christmas tree, but the lowest branches didn't touch the ground. Instead of getting completely drenched, our clothes and hair only got annoyingly soggy. It didn't bother me much but I could tell it was getting to Riley.

She kept wincing. I knew that her leg must have ached but she didn't moan much. That surprised me. I figured her for someone who'd be full-blown hysterical by now.

But when her whole body began to shiver, I got scared. I knew what I needed to do but I was pretty sure she wasn't going to like it.

"You're shivering," I said.

"Telll meee something I donnn't know," Riley replied, her teeth chattering. She wrapped her arms around her chest.

"Wait here," I said.

"Where are you going?"

"Not far. Stay here."

"Where am I gonna go?"

Ignoring her sarcasm, I ran to the tree nearest ours and gathered as many dry pine needles and pinecones as my arms could carry. I ran back and forth several times, making a fairly decent pile of dry needles beside Riley. We'd already had a nice pile under our tree, thanks to all the needles that had already dropped, but I knew we would need a lot more.

"Can I help?" she said, but I continued to ignore her. There wasn't time to explain. The rainstorm made sure of that. Besides, what could she do with a sprained leg?

I remembered the folding knife in my pocket. I squeezed it. It was one of those Swiss Army kinds that did everything from slicing through cardboard to popping open bottle caps. Dad had given it to me for my thirteenth birthday, a gift that had surprised me, since Mom was always the one who bought the birthday and Christmas gifts. I couldn't take it to school but I carried it in the front pocket of my jeans at all other times. Practical Dad. He'd told me it would come in handy when I least expected it. Said a man should always carry one. Also said his dad had given him one when he was my age, shiny silver with turquoise inlay, no longer than my forefinger, just like mine. I used it a lot at work, cutting through duct tape and boxes loaded with paper towels and pasta noodles. But today was what Dad would probably call one of those critical times. *Thanks, Dad*, I said to myself as I removed it from my pocket. With a flick of my thumb and forefinger, the knife opened with an easy *click*.

I cut down four leafy, dry, skinny pine branches as fast as I could. I had no idea how long we'd be stranded on this ledge, but I did know we had to stay as dry as possible.

Racing against the rain, I grabbed the branches and hauled them back to Riley. She sat beside the pine needle piles, running her fingers through them, clearly not understanding my plan. The rain continued to pound all around us.

I dropped the branches and then dropped beside her, motioning for her to scoot to the side so that I could begin.

"What are you doing?" Riley said.

"Making a bed for us."

Riley's eyes grew wider. "Will we be here long enough to need one?"

"I'm guessing we might be. And we've got to work before there's no light left at all."

"What can I do?" She grimaced as she pulled her injured leg out of the way.

"Nothing. For now."

I spread the pine needles in a circle big enough for two. Then I placed the branches over the needles, weaving them top to bottom. It wouldn't exactly be plush but it would be better than sitting on the wet ground.

Rain trickled down my back as I worked. *Drip drip drip.* It was going to be a long hour, a long night, a long weekend— I had no way of knowing. If we were lucky, the storm would blow across the valley before sunset and we could try to hike back to the campsite. I started thinking through several scenarios, one of them including carrying Riley on my back. She was tall but thin. I could probably manage it.

Satisfied with our makeshift bed, I leaned back on my heels to give it a final once-over. "Well," I said, turning to Riley.

"It'll have to do," she said, her teeth chattering again.

I sighed and then moved closer to her on one knee and then the other. Without another word, I put my arm around her and pulled her toward me before she could object, which, knowing what I knew about Riley, she would.

But she surprised me. Again.

Instead of complaining, she exhaled against me, curling

into my shoulder. I sat with my back against the tree trunk, Riley's body pressed against my chest. My arms wrapped around her, tighter, as she shivered. Her warm breath heated my neck, the closeness of our bodies heating us both. I tried to ignore that she smelled all *girl,* her hair like flowers mixed with fresh pine. It kind of became hard for me to speak, but after an excruciatingly long silence, I forced out a word. *"Warmer?"* It came out like a squeak. I rubbed the side of her arm.

She nodded, her hair brushing up against my chin. "Should we start a fire or something?"

"It's kind of raining, in case you hadn't noticed."

She turned her face to mine. "You mean, you don't know how to start a fire?"

My back stiffened.

"I thought you would know...." Her voice trailed off.

"You mean, I should know because I'm Native?"

"No," she said, her whole body rising in place. "Because you're a boy. Weren't you a Boy Scout or anything?"

I pulled back and stared at her, speechless. A second ago, we were sharing a moment. Now I wanted to get far away from her all over again, which was pretty much impossible given our current living quarters.

We both seemed to be counting back our outrage. *One second. Two seconds. Three...*

We glared at each other. It became a staring contest.

And then, when we both absolutely had to blink, we both burst out laughing. In that moment it was as if a balloon had popped between us as we sat tangled together on our mostly dry makeshift bed of pine needles and branches.

"Believe it or not, Boy Scouts wasn't exactly a big thing on the Rez."

"Sorry, I didn't mean—" she began, still laughing.

But I stopped her. "Forget it. No offense taken."

"Sure?"

"Yeah." I'd certainly heard crazier than that. During my freshman year, a guy had actually asked me if I lived in a teepee. And he'd been serious. To which I'd replied, "Dude, you need to get out more." It hadn't exactly made us friends, and he'd looked at me strangely for the rest of the semester.

"In case you were wondering, I wasn't a Girl Scout."

"No?" I said. "I thought all girls north of Pecos Road were Girl Scouts at some point. You know, with the lure of the thin mints and all." So much for stereotypes.

"No." Riley lifted her chin. "I was a Bluebird."

"What the heck is a Bluebird?"

"Someone who didn't want to be a Girl Scout."

"Did they happen to teach survival techniques to Blue-birds?"

"No." She looked up at me, totally serious. A raindrop clung to her eyelash and I thought about reaching down to wipe it away with my finger. "But I did get a cooking patch for making macaroni and cheese from scratch."

"Totally useless right now."

"Agreed," she said, grimacing.

We laughed again and Riley blinked, the lone raindrop trickling down her cheek.

I leaned back against the tree trunk again with Riley pressed against my chest. We looked out past the branches. The world had become a gray wall of water, and I wondered how much longer the tree branches would shield us.

Since it looked like we'd be stranded for a while and Riley was tucked inside my arms, I got brave and said, "So, what's with all the pink?"

She turned her head to peer up at me from beneath the

brim of her cap. "What do you mean?" she said, although I knew she knew what I meant. I mean, come on!

"You. Pink. It's all you ever wear."

Her clear eyes widened. "How would you know?" She turned defensive and I immediately felt like an idiot. Here I was just trying to make small talk, and I succeeded in pissing her off again in less than twenty seconds.

Just as I was about to open my mouth and apologize, she said, "What about you? Ever heard of a washing machine?" Her button nose wrinkled for emphasis. The awkwardness between us had returned.

I closed my eyes and counted to three. "I was at a party last night. Got home too late to change."

"How nice for you." She didn't hide the contempt in her voice.

"Our maid doesn't work on Saturdays," I added, matching hers with more of my own.

"Ha. Ha." She exhaled. "Now you think we have a maid?"

"Well, don't you?" Ryan Berenger had gotten a new Jeep for his sixteenth birthday. He wore expensive sunglasses and his parents were members at the country club. Didn't people like that employ maids?

Riley exhaled again, loud. Loud enough for me to hear the disgust in her voice. Or maybe it was disappointment. She shifted in my arms. "Look, could we just not talk?" She tugged on the rim of her baseball cap again.

Now my shoulders shrugged indifferently. "Sure. Just making conversation." I looked out at black clouds blowing straight for us.

"Well, insults don't exactly make good conversation starters."

"Okay," I challenged. "So you say something. We might be here awhile, you know." I hesitated to tell her that it could be more than a little while, especially when she kept reaching for her leg, the one she said hurt the most.

"I wonder what everyone's doing up at the campsite? You think anyone's noticed we haven't come back yet?"

"Maybe," I said. "Maybe not."

"Hasn't it been hours already?"

"Maybe."

"I wonder what they're thinking," Riley said. She had finally stopped shivering.

"Who?" I really hoped she wasn't referring to Jay Hawkins again.

"The other kids."

"What do you care what they think?"

"I always care what other people think," she said. "Years of practice. Can't help it. Don't you?"

I chuckled. "I couldn't care less."

She sighed, heavy. "I wish I was more like that."

"Then why aren't you?"

She looked at the name tag on my chest. I reached down and ripped the soggy thing off.

"I suppose you're the one who nicknamed me Pink Girl. Real nice, by the way. Very original."

"That really fits you. And I may borrow it from time to time. But it wasn't me."

"Seriously?"

"Seriously."

Her chin lifted. "Which one?"

"Guess."

She sighed like she didn't want to play. But then she said, "Bossypants."

I bit back a laugh because that nickname seriously had crossed my mind for Riley Berenger. "Nope. Not me."

She pulled back. "Smart?"

"Nope."

Her voice grew louder. *"Thorough?"*

I smiled down at her. "Bingo."

"But that is so…lame."

"I thought it was perfect for you. The perfect nickname."

"Thorough is for grandmothers and computer manuals, Sam. A girl doesn't want to be nicknamed Thorough." She rolled her eyes and looked away. "I thought for sure yours was Pink Girl." Then she reached for her name tag and peeled it off her sweatshirt. She crumpled it up and slipped it into her pocket.

"So which one was yours?"

"I'm kind of hungry. Are you?" she said, ignoring my dumb question since her pink ink on my name tag made it pretty obvious which nickname she'd chosen for me. I was Complicated, though? What did she mean by that?

"What do you have?"

She reached into a pocket in her sweatshirt. "One water bottle." She reached into her other front pocket. "A slightly broken granola bar." And then she reached inside her pocket a third time. "And one stupid pinecone." She threw it as hard as she could into the slanting rain.

"Nice throw."

"It's a gift," she said.

I looked down at her as she continued to stare straight ahead. Riley's neck was long and pearly white, almost translucent. For some reason my eyes landed on the skin just below her ear and stayed there. I swear I could see her pulse move, and it stole my breath for a second. I did a mental headshake. But before I could stop myself, I said, "You know, you'd be a lot prettier without that hat."

Silence. She turned to me, unamused.

I swallowed, hard. I had no idea why I'd said that. It just popped out. Suddenly I was a fashion expert?

But it was true.

"I'll shut up now," I said.

Riley nodded and looked away. Instead of making stupid small talk, we listened to the rain.

13

RILEY

Sam was seriously starting to freak me out. Why did he say such things? I knew he was a little odd—well, I really didn't *know* that to be a hard fact, but I had heard that he acted strangely.

Scratch that.

More like it was what I'd observed.

Sam often sat by himself in the cafeteria. I knew this because I sat alone sometimes, too. And when you sit alone, pretending to study the math book beside your sandwich or doodle in the corners of your notebook, your eyes tend to scan the whole room beneath your eyelashes. My attention was usually drawn to other loners like me. There weren't many of us but, if we wanted to, we could have started a club.

The one thing that stood out about Sam was that he didn't mind being alone. He wore his aloneness like a badge, challenging anyone to mock him. No one ever dared to look at him funny or anything. It was sort of a mutual unspoken understanding, which I suppose you could negotiate when you were well over six feet tall and, maybe, two hundred pounds.

Even the biggest senior boys kept their distance from Sam. One time I'd sketched his face in my notebook because I liked the way his expression never seemed to change and yet it said everything.

And now he sat behind me, his arms wrapped around my shoulders like we snuggled all the time. Like we were best friends. And he'd said that I could be pretty. What kind of boy says something like that after insulting you a half-dozen times? None that I knew—not that I knew many.

But Sam Tracy was indeed a strange boy. He wasn't like my brother's friends, and it wasn't just because he was Gila or Native or Native American or whatever he called himself, either. He was just different from all the boys I knew. He didn't say much, and when he did he didn't waste time with too many words.

We sat staring out at the rain for what seemed like an eternity, grateful for our little patch of dryness and the heat radiating from our bodies. Then my stomach grumbled.

Weakening, I peeled back the wrapper to our only food source. I wasn't ready to eat pinecones. "What some?" I pointed my granola bar at him.

He shook his head. "Nah. You eat it."

"We can share." I pulled back the paper and broke the bar in two.

Sam lifted his hand. "Better not eat it all at once."

"Seriously?" My voice got higher. "You seriously think we'll be here that long for it to matter?"

He looked up at the tree, considering my question. "Maybe."

So I halved the half and stuffed the other half back in the wrapper. "For later," I said.

Sam took his piece and chewed it slowly, his lips making a perfect circle, which looked really strange on him.

I did the same, trying to savor each morsel like he did. I closed my eyes and tasted the tiny bit of chocolate, a sliver of almond, a breath of dried cranberry and then crunchy honey and oats. It was probably the first time I had ever truly tasted a granola bar, despite inhaling at least two after every dance practice for the last two years. "Not bad," I said when I allowed myself to swallow the last bite.

"I would rather have had your macaroni and cheese." There was a smile in Sam's voice.

"Beggars can't be choosers."

"True," he said.

"Now for the water. Pretend it's champagne."

"Have you ever tasted champagne?"

"No," I said, popping open the cap. "This is pretend."

"Then I'll pretend it's a chocolate shake."

"Yum. Even better." I passed the bottle to Sam. "You first."

First he raised his hand, motioning for me to take it, but I insisted. "Just a sip," he said, finally tipping the bottle to his lips. And a thimbleful was all he took. Barely enough for a bird. "Now, you."

I took the bottle and it took all my willpower to drink just a sip. I could have swallowed a gallon. "I guess if we get desperate we can suck the water off leaves, right?"

"I hope we don't have to."

Lightning flashed all around us and the mountain lit up like a birthday cake. A few seconds later, the sky cracked open even louder than before and I jumped. "This storm is freaky," I said, my knees curling into Sam. "And it feels like it's getting colder." He pulled me closer.

"We've got to do something to pass the time," Sam said. "Or we're really going to go nuts."

"Damn straight," I said, almost leaping into his lap when the lightning cracked again.

"See? You're not as perfect as you think. You even curse."

"Who said I was perfect?"

"No one needs to."

"You don't really know me."

"I know enough."

"Humph," I said, slightly taken aback. "Well, since you've got me all figured out, tell me something about you." I paused, just as lightning filled the sky again, turning everything all silvery-gray. Like a camera flash. "Tell me something no one else knows."

"No," Sam said quickly.

"Why not?"

"Because I don't want to."

"What's it matter? We're not going anywhere for a while. You said so yourself. And besides that crazy elk, we're the only ones out here." Rain splattered above us, droplets bouncing from one branch to another, one pine needle to another. It was as if we sat below a giant fountain, each raindrop trying desperately to reach our hiding spot. "I'll give you the rest of the granola bar if you do." My eyebrows wiggled.

"Forget it."

"You're no fun."

"Wait. I thought I was *complicated?*"

"Touché." I sighed and looked away.

I counted raindrops when the storm quieted for a few seconds. During one stretch, I almost reached one hundred. But the rain always returned to pound around us like an encore. The sky soon became so dark that we didn't even get a sunset.

Sam's shoulders began to shiver. I hadn't thought he ever got cold, but he was wearing only a T-shirt. At least I had a sweatshirt.

This wasn't good.

"Okay," I said, mostly to keep our minds off the growing

cold and our grumbling stomachs. "If you won't go first. I will." I bit the inside of my lip to keep my teeth from chattering, because if they started again I wasn't certain they'd stop.

"What are you talking about now?"

"I'm going to tell you something personal," I said. "And you have to promise never to tell a soul. Can I trust you?" I looked up at him, just as the sky flashed another bolt of lightning, squiggly white lines stretching in every direction. "Promise?"

Sam surprised me by nodding. Or maybe he was shivering again. Whatever it was, I decided to tell him. What if we never made it off this mountain? What if we froze together tonight in each other's arms? What did I have to lose?

I took a deep breath to steady myself and said, "I let my best friend use BOTOX on my forehead on Friday night. That's why I'm wearing this stupid baseball cap."

Dead silence.

Sam's chest began to shake—but not from shivering. From laughter. It was the dry-heave, raspy kind, like he was having difficulty catching his breath. It started slowly and then built to a splitting crescendo.

"Thanks," I said, between his chest heaves. "Thanks a lot. Glad you find it hilarious."

His laughter turned into a coughing fit when he tried to speak. He raised his hand, begging me to wait. Sam's laughter finally subsided until all we could hear were raindrops again.

"Why would you do that, Riley?" He reached for the brim of my baseball cap but I slapped his hand, which only got him chuckling again.

"I'm gullible. I was bored. I don't know. My best friend, Drew, talked me into it. I blame her."

"Does your forehead hurt?"

"I don't know. I can't feel it."

Sam started another laughing fit and I just shook my head at him, biting back my own smile.

When he finally quieted, I challenged him. "Okay, now it's your turn to play. You've got to tell me something juicy, something really personal. And I swear to god I'll keep bugging you till you do. I could bug you all night. I swear, I will." I looked out beneath the branches into nothing but infinite blackness. "We're not going anywhere, so make it a good one."

14

SAM

"I'm not playing."

I was defiant. I even forgot how chilled I'd become for a few seconds. There was no way I was playing Riley's stupid game.

It was such a girl thing. Why did girls always feel compelled to share personal embarrassing stuff? And *BOTOX?* Are you kidding me? Why would a pretty girl do something like that? Girls confused me.

"Please?" she begged.

"No."

"Chicken!"

"Maybe."

"Maybe you'll play?" She tugged on the collar of my T-shirt, hard.

"Never."

"Then I'll have to guess."

In the growing darkness, I heard her lips smack. It was obvious that she was giving this way too much thought. I could practically hear the wheels spinning in her head. Or maybe that was just her teeth chattering.

"Still cold?" I said to change the subject.

"I'm freezing," she said, just as a gust of wind blew through the tree, knocking icy raindrops off the branches. "This is miserable." We shivered in each other's arms.

"Your sweatshirt is wet."

"So's your T-shirt."

We hugged tighter. We breathed heavily for warmth. We rubbed skin where we could reach. We didn't have a choice. And while it didn't seem so bad in the dark, now that we couldn't see each other's eyes, the situation was clearly going from bad to really, really freaking bad. Ugly words raced through my head—*hypothermia* and *pneumonia,* for starters.

"Riley."

"Yeah?"

"Don't take this the wrong way—" I paused for courage "—but there's something we need to do. *Now.*"

"You've changed your mind about playing?" Her voice turned giddy, even as her teeth resumed chattering. I hoped she wasn't starting to crack. I'd read about such things in life-or-death situations. Some people turned crazy as a survival mechanism.

My eyes rolled. "No. I'm not talking about playing your game. Be serious."

"What, then?"

"We have to take our clothes off."

Her body stiffened against mine.

"We're soaking wet," I added by way of explanation. "We could freeze to death if we don't take them off."

"We could freeze to death with them on."

"True." I nodded, trying to play to her reasonable side. "But we should at least…consider it. For body heat."

"Get naked?" she whispered.

"Get naked."

But then her shoulders softened beneath my hands. "Yeah, I was thinking about how to handle the wet clothes, too."

"This is survival," I stammered a little. "Nothing else."

"Agreed," she said. "Survival." She sounded like she was trying to convince herself more than me. "What about underwear?"

"I guess…I guess we can leave those on."

"Okay," she said. It sounded like she was trying to work up her nerve.

At least it's dark, I wanted to assure her, but that sounded like something a creepy guy would say. "I'll go first—"

Riley caught my arm in the dark, interrupting me. "Let's do it together."

"Okay. On the count of three." I counted slowly. "One…"

"Two," Riley said with me.

"Three."

With only a couple of inches between us, we stripped out of our wet shirts. Blindly, we fumbled and felt for a branch beside us to hang them in the hopes that they might dry, knocking arms at the same time.

"Sorry," we said at the same time when our elbows crashed against each other. I winced when hers caught my funny bone.

I doubted that our shirts would dry even a little in the damp night air. Removing our pants was harder. I had to help Riley pull off hers, one slightly soggy leg at a time. When her jeans pulled over her injured leg, she moaned.

"Sorry," I whispered.

She garbled something back that sounded like "sleigh" but it was probably "it's okay."

After helping her, I unzipped my jeans and then shimmied

them down and stripped them off my bent legs without kicking her in the face.

Beside me, Riley shivered even more and I wondered if stripping was the right idea, especially as rain continued to fall. If there had been a more awful night, weather-wise, I hadn't experienced it. This was like a bad horror movie.

As we sat across from each other in our underwear, shivering in the dark, lightning lit up our hiding space. In the flash, I looked at Riley, and she looked back at me. In that instant I saw everything. She was so white she glowed. Her arms crossed to hide her chest. Most of all, I saw that she was as terrified as I was, and for that reason alone I could not look away.

"There's no reason to be embarrassed, Riley. Or scared. I'm as scared as you are." I had to push off to the side of my brain that I had never been with a girl before, naked. Not like this, so close we were practically sharing the same heartbeat. I wondered if I should tell her that? Would it put her at ease?

Instead, when it turned dark again, I reached for her shoulder. "Come here."

A few seconds later, as if she'd needed time to consider it, she crawled to me on her knees. She sat between my legs, facing me. I wrapped my arms around her and she wrapped her arms around me, at least as much as she could. We were chest-to-chest, skin touching skin. I tried not to think about the softness of her skin or the sweet scent of her hair. Instead, I counted backward from one hundred and forced myself to focus on survival. Staying alive. Global warming. Global cooling, more like.

I rubbed her arms, her back. "Better?" My voice cracked.

Her head nodded beneath my chin, fast. Nervous. I could hear each swallow. "You?"

"Yeah," I said. "Much."

Her body froze again and so did mine.

"It's not like that, Riley. I promise."

"Okay," she said, but her voice was still uneasy.

"Let's lie down."

She stiffened again in my arms but I pushed her backward, gently. I cradled her head by my right shoulder and then curled the rest of my body over hers, doing my best not to crush her. Her warm breath heated my neck as we lay on the ground. "Are you okay?"

"Uh-huh," she squeaked.

"Am I hurting you?"

"Uh-uh." Another soft squeak.

"You're lying."

She didn't answer.

I shifted a few inches, as much as I could in the cocoon that we'd made for ourselves. Pine needles poked every inch of my skin. Despite the branches for our makeshift bed, the ground was still rock-hard. I closed my eyes and did my best to relax. Did my best to picture being warm. I pictured a bright sun and a hot, sizzling desert—anything but the soft body beneath me. After a few silent, agonizing minutes, I said, "I know this sounds gross but it would be better if we burrowed underneath the pine needles."

Her hands squeezed my arms. "What about bugs? And spiders? I really hate spiders."

"It's too cold for them," I lied. We'd probably wake up covered in ant bites, but at least we wouldn't freeze to death.

"Okay," she said with so much trust in her voice that I felt equal parts good and bad—good for keeping us warm but bad for telling lies. Suddenly I felt very responsible for this girl in my arms. Riley trusted me. She believed me. I did not want to disappoint her.

We burrowed like animals, digging beneath the branches,

covering ourselves in a blanket of mostly dry pine needles and moss. Then we lay back again, Riley curled into my chest and one of my legs curled around Riley. After a while, our breathing slowed, and there was warmth.

The warmth turned into heat. Blessed heat. Body heat as thick as a blanket. Our shivering stopped and my breathing matched Riley's, breath for breath. I felt her heartbeat against my chest.

I looked up at the sky, breathing easier, but still trying to keep my mind focused on anything but the fact that I was holding a mostly naked girl in my arms and willing the rest of my body not to react. Rain still pattered against the trees and a few drops reached us, but a couple of stars poked through the clouds with the promise that the storm was breaking. Finally.

"Riley?" My voice sounded loud.

"Yeah?" she whispered.

"I'll play."

She gasped. Her chin rose to touch mine and I couldn't help but smile. "You'll tell me something personal?" She sounded doubtful at first. "Really, really personal?"

"Yeah, why not?" I paused to swallow. "But you've got to swear you won't tell anyone. Not a soul."

"I absolutely promise." Her breath hitched.

"Okay," I said. "I trust you."

"Okay."

"Okay," I said again, hesitating all over again. Why had I opened my big mouth?

"You can tell me, Sam," she said with conviction. "I won't tell anybody."

I sighed. Then I took a deep breath. Then another for some nerve. Another patch of black sky cleared above us. More stars twinkled through the tops of swaying treetops. I looked down at Riley and could see the vague curve of her chin, her nose, even the whites of her eyes twinkling in the starlight. She waited for me to speak, barely breathing.

"Sam?" she prodded, lifting herself over my chest. "You're killing me. What. Is. It?"

My secret dislodged like a boulder from the top of a cliff. There was no taking it back. "I'm in love with your brother's girlfriend," I blurted.

Riley gasped again but for a split second I didn't care.

It felt good to be rid of it.

So I proceeded to tell Riley everything.

15

RILEY

Say. What? I raised myself higher on my elbow, knocking the top of my head against Sam's chin.

Okay, I was expecting Sam to fess up to hot-wiring a car or maybe even cheating on a final exam but lusting after my brother's girlfriend, Fred Oday? No. Way. Was he crazy? Fred and Ryan were inseparable. He'd have a better chance dating Lady Gaga.

"You're in love with Fred Oday." I didn't say it like a question.

"Yep."

"For how long?"

"For forever."

"What's that mean?"

"Since we were in grade school."

"No way."

"Way."

"What do you love about her? I mean, aside from the obvious." Fred was brilliant. She was also beautiful in an unconventional way. She was kind of like the exotic foreign exchange student who intrigued everyone without really try-ing. Throw in the fact that she could beat the butts off most of the guys on the varsity golf team and she became A-list material. I couldn't blame my brother for loving her, too.

"Everything," Sam said with a sigh.

He wasn't making it easy. "You need to be more specific."

"She's pretty."

"Tell me something I don't know."

"And she's smart," he added.

"Well, duh."

Sam laughed. "That's not good enough for you?"

"No," I said. "There must be something else, something you're not telling me…."

I felt him inhale deeply beside me. Then he said, "We want the same things."

"You play golf, too?"

"No," Sam said. "It has nothing to do with golf."

"Then, what?"

Sam paused. "It's where we're from…."

"Because you're both Gila?"

"No. Yes. I mean, no. We both have had to work so hard. We understand each other. It's just that we both want…more. More for ourselves. More for our people."

"More, what?"

"It's kind of hard to explain, Riley." Another heavy sigh. "You wouldn't understand."

"Try me. We've got time."

His hand dropped against my back. "There's not enough time to explain to you what I mean. You don't live it. You wouldn't get it. Trust me."

"I'm smarter than you think, you know."

"I never said you were dumb."

"No, you said I was *thorough*. Remember? This is me, living up to my nickname. I need more detail. Now tell me."

Sam chuckled, but it was the kind of nervous chuckle where I knew he wasn't going to share anything more. His legs began to twitch as if they were covered in ants. Very un-Sam-Tracy-like. And, honestly? I was shocked he'd even told me what he had. In a weird way, I felt kind of privileged. Sam didn't strike me as the kind of boy who went around sharing his secrets.

"Tell me more about her, Sam. Tell me more about what you love about her?"

"I haven't said enough?"

"Not even close."

He snickered. "Okay, then. Well, she laughs at my bad jokes. She's kind to people. She's patient—more patient than I'll ever be. And she's determined." He paused. "I think I love that most of all."

After a silent moment, I said, "You know that getting her is impossible, don't you?" I leaned back down from my elbow.

Sam didn't answer.

"Ryan and Fred are so in love that it's...it's almost sickening."

Sam chuckled. "I know."

"I think they're considering getting surgically sewn together."

Sam's chest shook against mine.

"And then I hear that they're going to share the same brain."

"Stop it, Riley," Sam said, laughing harder.

"I'm just telling you. You're asking for the tragically impossible."

"I didn't say that I wanted to go out with her. I just told

you that I loved her. That's my really, really personal thing that you said you wanted to hear. That's all."

"Yes, well. That's…sad," I said, forgetting for the moment that, except for the parts covered by my underwear, my naked skin was touching Sam Tracy, a boy who was in love with my brother's girlfriend. How twisted was that?

"That's the way it is," Sam said. "You can't have everything."

"At least you understand."

"More than you know." He sighed, and for a few seconds that turned into minutes, we said nothing and just listened to the rain *drip-dropping* through the branches that sheltered us.

My eyelids grew heavy as my body stayed warm against Sam's, even as I kept playing Sam's secret in my mind. I couldn't picture it—Fred and Sam? My brother without Fred? To say that it was impossible would be an understatement. There are some people who go together, like dark chocolate and sea salt. Would Sam really have a chance with Fred?

Despite his love for Fred, right now I was glad that we were together. If I had to get stranded in a forest and Jake Gyllenhaal wasn't available, I was glad I was with Sam Tracy. In fact, forget Jake. I'd definitely choose Sam. He'd scaled down a mountain for me. He hadn't left me alone. He was keeping me warm. He was keeping me alive. And he'd told me his deepest, darkest secret.

"Let's try to get some sleep," Sam said. "We'll need our strength for tomorrow if we plan to hike out of here."

I yawned. "You don't want to talk anymore?" I needed to do something to get my mind off what could be crawling around and over the pine needles and dirt that were doing a decent job of keeping the cold away. Just as Sam had said they would. "No more secrets?"

"That wasn't juicy enough for you?"

"Good point."

"I'm tired." Sam yawned.

I sighed. "Okay, you win. I'll shut up."

So I rested my head on Sam's smooth chest, listening as his breathing slowed. Somewhere in the distance, an owl hooted. That's when I realized it had stopped raining. There was still a tiny rumble of thunder, but it sounded miles away.

"Sam?" I whispered. I wanted to tell him that the rain had finally stopped, the storm had passed, but he didn't answer.

And then I began to dream crazy dreams.

16

SAM

Wrapped around Riley, I didn't sleep a solitary second the entire night, but she did.

Riley talked in her sleep, too. She said nothing that I could understand, but at least it helped the night to pass. It was like trying to figure out Latin or something. One time she even giggled. Martin and Peter were never going to believe this. They were going to give me grief for being Mr. Gentleman. "Why didn't you at least kiss her," Martin would probably say. "Or at least brush her breast while your hand was in the general area?"

Truth was, I was scared out of my mind, not that I would ever tell anybody that, least of all Riley. Not even as part of her silly, girly, tell-me-something-really-really-personal game. And, jeez. Why did I have to crack and tell her about Fred? What was the point, anyway? It wasn't as if I had a chance with Fred Oday. I had a better chance of sprouting wings and flying off the side of this mountain.

Two big raindrops plopped square in each of my eyes. I blinked them off. Was it starting to rain again? I rubbed my eyes with my left hand. My right arm had fallen asleep hours ago beneath Riley's head, still cradled against my right shoulder.

Birds began to chirp.

"What's wrong?" Riley's voice was scratchy with sleep. She raised her head and I relished the few seconds to clench my fist and squeeze blood back into my arm's veins.

"Nothing," I said, my voice equally raspy. My entire body—at least, the parts that weren't numb—ached from stiffness and cold.

Her head lowered just as a trickle of yellow hazy light made its way through the pine branches, some still heavy with rain.

I sat up, knocking Riley awake again in the process. "It's morning," I mumbled. Finally. The sun was rising. I'd thought daylight would never get here.

Riley raised up on one elbow and we locked eyes. We could see each other again, not just the whites of our eyes or the dim outlines of our bodies, but everything. Shock then horror spread through Riley's expression as she stared back at me. It was like we were both too mortified to allow our gazes to drift anywhere below our shoulder blades.

I noticed streaks of dirt on her cheeks where dust had mixed with dried tears. Slowly, her gaze traveled down my face to my chest, her eyes widening as if she were just realizing that she'd spent the night sleeping next to me. I tried to keep my eyes locked on her face but I wanted to look at her. Even in the dim light, I wanted to see everything again.

I swallowed and then looked up to keep my mind from going where it shouldn't. I counted backward from ten in my head. The light filtering through the branches changed from a gray yellow to a burning orange, turning the tips of the pine needles a reddish green. "It's morning," I said again, stupidly, as if it weren't painfully obvious.

"Yes," Riley said. "Finally."

In the distance, we heard a new sound. Our heads tilted, trying to focus on it, our gazes turned upward.

"Is that more thunder?"

I kicked off the dirt and needles and jumped to my feet, smacking my head on the lower branches and knocking off raindrops in the process. "That's not thunder," I said, grabbing Riley's pink sweatshirt from the branch where it had hung all night. "That's a helicopter."

In my boxers and bare feet, I burst from beneath the pine tree, looking for a patch of flat surface, someplace where I had an unobstructed view of the sky. I didn't have time to worry about the cold air that gripped my body.

"Hey," I shouted at the sky, white puffs of my breath floating in front of my face. Like a madman, I waved Riley's still-damp pink sweatshirt over my head. I shook it over my head like a flag, back and forth. Back and forth. "We're here!" I screamed at the top of my lungs. "We're down here!" I ran around the ledge, waving the sweatshirt at the helicopter away from the patch of pine trees.

Beside me, I heard Riley. "We're here! Help us!" Riley was jumping on one foot, waving her pink baseball cap in one hand, her jeans in the other.

I turned to her. Her pale skin was covered with dirt. Pine needles and more dirt clung to her hair. I smiled. She smiled, too, flashing her teeth, the only white left on her entire body.

Together we screamed at the top of our lungs, waving clothing, waving our arms. Dancing in our underwear. We must have made quite a sight.

The helicopter's rumble got closer, so close it was almost on top of us. But we kept waving our arms, our clothes. My throat burned from screaming.

The skyscraper pine trees swayed from the force of the propellers. It was like it was storming all over again, except this time pine needles rained down on us in the early morning sun. We had to shield our eyes from blowing dust and dirt.

"They see us!" Riley shouted. "They see us! I'm sure of it."

"I'm glad pink is your favorite color!" I shouted back at her, still squinting up at the helicopter, afraid that if I blinked it would fly away. But through the blowing dirt and dust, I could see the open door on the side of the helicopter. A man in an orange vest waved down at us. I think he flashed the thumbs-up sign.

At the same time, Riley and I turned to each other. She screamed and so did I. Then, hopping on one foot, she jumped into my arms and I rocked back with surprise and relief. I hugged her tightly, my arms wrapped around her body, skin against skin, laughing and fighting back tears.

"You did it!" Riley yelled. "You saved us, Sam!"

I twirled her in a circle as she laughed, warm breath against my ear, her body pressed against mine. I felt like the strongest guy in the world. "No. *We* did it!"

And then I did something I hadn't planned. Still holding her in my arms, my chest pressed against hers, I kissed Riley Berenger.

And she kissed me back. Not a peck. A long one that got my heart racing as fast as the helicopter propeller. The kind of kiss that might mean something.

For a split second, the world stopped spinning. The trees froze all around us. Colors blended together. The air turned sticky hot. All I could feel, all I could see, all I could taste, was Riley Berenger's warm lips smashed against mine.

It was too late to take it back.

17

RILEY

When Sam put me back on the ground, my lips were warm. Everything was warm. And everything was happening all at once and it was happening at some kind of speed that wasn't discernible to the human eye. It had its own pace.

Above us, from the helicopter, someone in a fluorescent orange jacket lowered a cylinder basket. There was already another person inside the basket with a matching jacket. Holding hands, we stood in our underwear on the biggest boulder on the ledge that we could find.

We released hands so that I could slip on my sweatshirt. It was still damp and smelled of pine. I would have preferred Sam's warm arms to my sweatshirt any day. Slipping on my jeans was impossible because my leg still throbbed. I just pushed down my sweatshirt till the ends reached my thighs.

Sam thrust on his jeans and then his shoes. He stayed bare-chested but wrapped his gray T-shirt around his forehead. From the waist up, he looked fiercely Native. He looked as if he'd just stepped off a Western movie set, except for the low-cut jeans and the waistband from his boxers that peeked above the top. I shivered again from the cold. Yeah, it must have been the cold.

As soon as we were reasonably clothed, we held hands again and waited for the helicopter basket to lower to the ground, shielding our eyes from the blowing dust by hugging into each other. The helicopter's propellers grew more deafening the closer they got. We half walked, half hopped toward the lowered basket until Sam swept me into his arms and carried me the rest of the way, taking my breath along with everything else.

The man in the basket gave the helicopter the thumbs-up sign when the basket was inches from the ground. He wore headphones, and a mouthpiece covered his lips. His lips moved but I couldn't hear his words, not at first.

When we were practically on top of him, he yelled, "You kids all right?"

That was an interesting question. Hard to answer. All right? I looked up at Sam and his gaze locked with mine. He was trying to tell me something with his eyes—I was sure of it. But, what? After a few seconds, we both nodded.

"Good!" he said and flashed a wide smile. He was wearing those reflective silver sunglasses. In his lenses, I could see myself in Sam's coppery arms, my knees folded over his hands. Hair flying in every direction, his black against my blond. The man fluttered his fingers and Sam lifted me higher into the basket and into the man's extended arms.

"Her right leg is pretty banged up," Sam yelled. "Might be broken."

The man nodded as he stood me upright, still leaning against him. Then he wrapped me in some kind of life-preserver thingy that was attached to more ropes. My body started to shiver, not with cold but with fright. Now was not a good time to tell anyone that I disliked heights. I still gripped Sam's hand, squeezing it hard.

"It'll be okay," Sam said next to my ear, as if he already knew what I was thinking.

I nodded, looking down at my chest and waist now covered in ropes with silver clips and hooks. The basket was barely big enough for me and the man with the cool sunglasses. I wondered how Sam would fit. He was taller than the man beside me. That worried me.

The man lowered his face to mine. "You'll have to let go of your friend's hand now."

I cleared my throat. "Yeah, okay," I said, but I didn't let go.

Sam placed his other hand over mine and I leaned closer to his ear. "You're next," I said brilliantly when I really wanted to scream, *Why can't we go together?* We had done everything together in the past twenty-four hours. It seemed cruel to all of a sudden be pulled apart.

Sam's fingers inched away from mine but my fingers gripped his. "Wait!" I yelled.

The man stopped talking into his mouthpiece and Sam stayed beside the basket. The sun glinted off his chest and I could see every muscle, every indentation. His hair flew about his face but I could still see the whites of his eyes through the strands. Sam tilted his head toward me, waiting for me to say something.

"I'm going to help you get Fred!" I shouted.

The relieved smile on his face faded to something else. He started to shake his head.

"Yes!" I said. "It's the least I can do. You saved my life. I want to help you. We can do this, remember?"

Sam stepped farther away from the basket, his palms raised. I watched him until the basket sailed straight up into the sky, in between a thousand pine trees, and then into the helicopter. I forgot all about the nausea building in my stomach as we shot up into the clouds.

Through the open door of the helicopter, I watched as Sam looked up at me, his hair flying about his face, his hand shielding his eyes. I watched him until he was just a speck on the flat mountain rock. Then I wondered if he really saw me at all.

18

SAM

Our parents and Mr. Romero were on hand to greet us when the emergency helicopter landed, but I wasn't sure you could call it a greeting. There was relief and tears and tight hugs from Mom and even a little anger, especially as the Berengers looked from me to Riley and back again. I remembered Dr. Berenger from the hospital, the day that Mr. Oday had had his heart attack. I had never really seen Mr. Berenger before—maybe a couple of times at Fred's golf tournaments, but always from a distance. He looked like Ryan, only older, dressed in khaki pants that appeared to have been ironed. I could guess what they were thinking as Riley and I—filthy, wet and half-naked—sat on stretchers inside the hospital. I knew my parents were wondering the same thing, but they would save their questions for the long car ride home.

"The good news is that the kids are safe," Mr. Romero kept telling everybody who'd listen at the hospital. "Just a few scratches and sprains. No harm done."

Yeah, right. Tell that to Mr. Berenger. He was glaring at me as if I had molested his daughter.

Of course, the Berengers had chartered a private helicopter to whisk Riley back to Phoenix after the rescue helicopter had landed at the White Mountains Hospital. Didn't everybody do that? Insert my extreme sarcasm here.

Mr. Berenger had offered to take me and my parents, too, but Dad had simply said "thank you," and that he and Mom had already driven up in their car, and away we went. How else would we get our truck back to the Rez? I figured that Mr. Berenger already knew that we'd say no, but had asked, anyway, in that crowded hallway with plenty of people to hear it. That was so like a Berenger.

I never got a chance to talk to Riley about what she'd said—about what she'd promised. Not with a dozen paramedics checking our vitals from the moment the helicopter landed. Riley's knee and ankle were sprained, not broken. Her leg had been wrapped in a castlike bandage. They'd given her something for the pain that had made her groggy.

I'd gotten a gash in my leg, probably from when I scaled down the mountain after Riley, that I hadn't noticed. It was covered in red-black mud, the blood absorbed by all the pine needles and dirt from our makeshift bed beneath the tree. The gash required three stitches, but that was really the extent of it. "You're lucky to be alive," Mom said before she burst into tears against Dad's shoulder. Dad's gaze grew darker the harder she cried, and he studied me over her head as if to say, "I expected this to happen." If I didn't know any better, I'd say Dad looked strangely relieved.

"What were you thinking, Samuel?" Mom added between sobs, her eyes red-rimmed and bloodshot. "What were you doing so close to the rim? You should know better!"

I shrugged, embarrassed, feeling guilty that they'd had to miss work because of me. *It was an accident. I didn't plan this,* I wanted to tell them, but I was too numb and exhausted to explain. What did it matter? It wasn't like I could change anything.

"That folding knife you got me came in handy," I said to Dad, trying to lighten the mood in the hospital room, which really wasn't a room at all. It was more like a noisy hallway. But Dad only nodded, as if he'd forgotten that it had been the best and only present he'd ever given me. I was going to take it out of my pocket and show him, but I thought, *Why bother?*

As the tension grew thick between Dad and me, Mom hugged me. Dad just stood behind her, his hands stuffed in his front pockets, his gaze distant, hovering above our heads. When I tried to remember the last time Dad had hugged me, I couldn't. I must have been a baby.

Even in her groggy state, Riley kept telling everybody and anybody who'd listen that I'd saved her life, but, to be honest, I wasn't sure anybody believed her, least of all her parents. They kept looking at me with suspicious eyes, as if I had been responsible for her fall off the Mogollon Rim. I had a feeling that they believed Riley wasn't capable of doing a single solitary thing wrong. Me, on the other hand... I could see the judgment flicker in their eyes, plain as clouds in the sky.

A small part of me thought that maybe they were right. It nagged at me like an itch. I might not have pushed Riley off the edge but maybe I'd driven her to fall. Maybe we should have tagged after Jay Hawkins and all the others. Maybe I shouldn't have taken Riley in a completely different direction for the scavenger hunt. That would have certainly made things easier.

If only I could convince her that I was hardly hero-worthy. I wasn't That Guy. I would never in a million years be That Guy. Let the Ryan Berengers of the world take that role.

I dreaded the long, uncomfortable car ride back to Phoenix. But most of all, I dreaded Monday.

19

RILEY

Monday morning couldn't come fast enough. Mom wanted me to stay home and rest till at least Wednesday, but…well, no way. It was bad enough staying cooped up in my room all day Sunday. Another day of doing nothing and I would freak out.

"I've got an English paper to turn in, and a trig exam. I can't stay home," I said.

Mom finally agreed—she usually did when things like papers and exams were concerned—as I limped my way into Ryan's Jeep, with Ryan carrying my messenger bag. "Well, okay," Mom said. "But call me if you change your mind. The instant your leg starts to bother you, go to the school nurse. And remember, no dance practice."

"I couldn't dance if I wanted to." So that was our compromise. To be honest, a few weeks away from afternoon practice would be a good thing, especially with everything that I had planned.

"At least wear your leg brace."

"Please, Mom. That thing looks hideous. I'd rather limp for the rest of my life."

Major eye roll. "Stop being so dramatic, Riley."

"I'm not. I'm totally being serious."

"It will help your leg heal."

"My leg barely hurts anymore."

Mom and I continued our eyeball war until Ryan revved the engine. Then Mom blinked.

Victory. Freedom. "Gotta go. We're going to be late," I said and blew her a kiss.

Mom waved goodbye once I was belted inside Ryan's Jeep. Worry was etched into every crevice of her face.

"Jeez, Riley. Mom's practically forcing you to stay home and you say no? Are you insane?"

I looked out the passenger window as Ryan backed out. It was hard to look at him straight-on. "I've got a lot on my mind. A lot I have to take care of today."

"You are such a Goody Two-Shoes."

"Shut up, Ryan."

"I think those pain meds Mom gave you messed with your head."

"Thanks for your concern," I replied, deadpan.

Ryan hesitated and then said, "You know I didn't hear about what happened to you until late Saturday night. I was over at Fred's."

My palm lifted. "Naturally."

"What's that supposed to mean?" Ryan signaled left to turn onto Pecos Road and then pressed the accelerator. The Gila River Indian Reservation spanned south as far as I could see.

"Nothing." We drove into the sun and I turned down the visor, and began thinking about Sam.

Ryan chuckled.

My eyes rolled but I didn't turn. "You're irritating me."

"Would you be irritated to know that you and Sam—well,

especially Sam—are all that anyone's been talking about this weekend? It went viral."

I spun around to face him. "Really?" That was a first.

Ryan smirked. "Uh-huh. Thought that would get your attention."

"What else can you tell me?"

"I suppose we're about to find out."

I faced front and smiled. Finally. I would finally be known at school as something other than Ryan Berenger's Little Sister. "I wish you would have said something before we left. I would have done something more creative with my hair. Maybe worn nicer pants." I looked down at my stone-washed jean skirt, smoothing over a wrinkle across my thighs. Then I flipped open the visor mirror.

"You look fine."

I turned. "Really?"

"No." Ryan laughed.

"I hate you."

"I know."

"Jerk."

We didn't say another word until we pulled into the Lone Butte High School parking lot.

20

SAM

I waited with Martin and Peter near the entrance to the freeway for Mr. Oday's van. Martin's truck was in need of a complete overhaul and despite his having worked on it most of
the weekend, the engine wouldn't turn over. Totally dead.
Fortunately Mr. Oday's van was more reliable, though not
by much.

I'd be lying if I said that I hadn't thought about ditching
school at least a hundred times, especially while I'd barely slept
last night, tossing and turning the whole time. It would have
been only the second time I'd done it in my life. I wasn't sure
the time that Peter and I had cut in the seventh grade from
the Rez school to go fishing counted at this point.

"Dude! How was dork camp?" Martin said, his eyes flashing all sorts of crazy. I could tell he knew more than he was
letting on.

"You already know. Why don't you tell me?"

"You were on the news on Saturday—you and Berenger's
sister."

"*On* the news?" Peter jumped in, equally as pumped. "Dude *was* the news."

Martin chuckled. "True, that. My mom said that everyone at the restaurant was huddled around the chef's television in his office, waiting to hear what happened to you. Chef didn't get mad, either. His eyeballs were as glued to the set as everyone else's."

"I thought you were picking up rodeo queens Saturday night."

"We were. My mom loaned us her wheels. Got back here as soon as we saw you headlined on the news, though. And that Berenger chick is pretty hot," Martin said. "Never noticed her." His grin spread. "Till now."

"Shut up," I practically growled.

"So what happened?" Peter said, still with the twenty questions. "What *really* happened?"

I exhaled. It was bad enough that I'd had to explain the whole pathetic tale to Mr. Romero, the paramedics, my sister and, of course, my parents. Now my best friends had to hear all the not-very-interesting details. What was the big deal? "Riley was standing too close to the edge of the Mogollon Rim and she fell. I went after her. It started to storm. We found shelter for the night. Helicopter found us in the morning. The end." I looked down the road, hoping to hear Mr. Oday's van sooner rather than later.

"That's it?" Martin and Peter said together, sounding disappointed.

"That's it."

Martin chortled, bringing his chin close to his neck. "Dude. That's *not* what everybody is saying."

My neck bristled. "Who's everybody?"

"People are saying you and Berenger's sister ran away," Martin said.

"Said you wanted to be alone," Peter added, wiggling his eyebrows.

"Said—you know." Martin's head tilted toward my crotch.

I felt my traitorous cheeks flush. "Who's saying that?"

"It's all over Facebook," Martin said. "Says the cops found you and Riley buck-naked. How come you never told us about her?"

"There were no cops!" Just about a million doctors and paramedics.

Peter ignored me. "Vernon said Twitter was even worse. He got alerts on his phone all night. You even trended, bro!"

"That's just crazy," I said. "Nothing but stupid talk."

"Why didn't you tell us you were hot for her?" Martin pouted. He even looked a little hurt.

I stared back at him, dumbfounded. "Um. Because I'm not?"

Martin paused. Then he said. "Well? Was she?"

"Was she what?"

Martin got louder. "Was Riley Berenger naked?"

My mouth opened and closed. "We were cold," I stammered, looking from side to side as if someone could hear us while we were waiting on a corner in the middle of nowhere. "We had to."

"Had to what?"

"You know. Take off our clothes. Because they were… wet." I cleared my throat. "Because it was cold."

Their eyes grew wide.

"Sweet!" Martin said, grinning, as I glared back at both of them.

"Nothing happened between Riley and me. *Nothing*." I had pushed the memory of our kiss to the back of my mind, as far back as it would go.

They snickered.

"Sure," Martin said, nodding at me in slow motion as if I were a mental patient. "Sure it didn't." But he hardly sounded convinced.

"You always gotta play the comedian, don't you, Martin?" I said, poking a finger at his chest.

Martin turned all serious again. "I'm not playing anything. I'm just telling you what's going round."

"Well, why don't you shut your mouth and stop spreading crazy-ass rumors." Anger began to fill my every pore, my every muscle. I hated losing control, but that was exactly what was happening. So far, the morning was off to an even worse start than I'd anticipated.

I knew they were just joking with me, but I wasn't in the mood for jokes. None of this was funny.

I hadn't been able to study all weekend. I had two exams and a paper due, and all I could think about was what I'd told Riley about Fred Oday. Why had I opened my big mouth? *Then* I had to go and kiss her. Kiss her! What was I thinking? And now I had to run interference with stupid rumors....

"Finally," Peter said, as Mr. Oday's van chugged down the road, dust kicking up behind its rear tires.

We watched the van until it stopped. I lifted my backpack from the ground and threaded it over my shoulder. Then I tugged open the creaky side door.

I squinted inside. Fred sat in the passenger seat next to her father. A Native radio station played through the tinny front speakers, reporting what we already knew: it would be hot and sunny today on the Rez. The Navajos and Hopis were still fighting about water rights. Someone wanted to build a freeway along the Gila River Indian Reservation. There would be a potluck at the community center this weekend. Blah blah blah.

Fred leaned over, her shiny black hair curling around a bare shoulder.

My stomach dropped somewhere around my feet. Whenever I was within spitting distance of Fred, it was like being in an elevator that dropped too fast. All I could do was hang on and hope the sinking feeling would pass quickly.

"Oh, god, Sam," she said. "I heard about what happened. We all did." She nodded toward her dad. Her clear eyes widened with more concern than I deserved.

My chest caved in another notch as I stared at her perfectly soft lips. The sun shone through the window, bathing her bare shoulders in a golden light.

When I didn't answer, she said, "Sam? Are you all right?"

My throat dried up, and I stared mutely back at her.

She didn't want to know.

21

RILEY

After Ryan parked the Jeep, we got out and waited on the front curb, although not close enough to talk. He leaned back on his elbows, ankles crossed, as I pretended to read the first book that I could pull from my messenger bag, despite my best efforts to pretend that the hot throbbing all along my leg didn't exist. I should have worn that dumb brace, despite its hideousness. One thing was certain: Ryan and I were both watching for the arrival of the Oday van.

It was impossible to ignore the stares of people who passed around us, mostly on foot, some pulling alongside us in their cars. "Is that her?" a senior girl whispered. A couple snapped my picture with their cell phones. It was strange. For the first time in my high school career, I was noticeable, all thanks to an ungraceful tumble down the Mogollon Rim.

Normally the Monday–morning buzz was about who'd thrown the best party that weekend, who'd gotten arrested and, sometimes, who had lost their virginity.

I wasn't naive about popularity, though. I'd seen how a person could rise to the higher echelons like a comet—like

Darcy Sherman, a freshman who looked like a senior, following her epic, everyone-was-invited after-hours homecoming party—only to be a footnote by the next weekend. Darcy had been invited to sit at one of the senior lunch tables in the cafeteria, but I'd noticed that she was back with her freshman friends by the time October rolled around. You had to give her points for trying. I wasn't anywhere near that courageous. My brother had gotten most of the brave genes in the family. But that didn't mean I hadn't thought about it.

I'd learned that Sam and I had been on the news about fifteen minutes after Mr. Romero had officially reported us missing, kind of like a televised version of one of those milk-carton things. Fortunately it was my sophomore class picture that had been flashed across all the local television stations. I would have been mortified if they'd used my freshman picture, the one where I still wore braces and was going through an unfortunate stage where I'd always had a too-tight ponytail.

If the attention and whispering from the other students bothered Ryan, he didn't say, although I *had* told him to stop talking to me in the Jeep.

Finally the van sputtered into the parking lot and pulled alongside the curb. As soon as the van stopped, three guys burst out, including Sam. I recognized the other two boys from the reservation. Like Sam, they were quiet and always kept to themselves. The short one—Martin, I think his name was—was pretty funny. I'd had him in a foods class freshman year, and he used to balance olives on his nose when the teacher wasn't looking. I didn't know the other guy very well. In fact, I didn't know his name and, suddenly, that made me a little bit sad. Why didn't I know Sam's friends? If they were as nice as Sam, I would want to get to know them. What was preventing me from walking right up to them and introducing myself? After Saturday, Sam and I were at least friends now. He'd even kissed me—although, when I'd thought more about it, I'd realized it was just a caught-up-in-the-moment kind of kiss that didn't mean anything. Over and done with. Right? He was totally in love with Fred Oday, that much was obvious.

Ryan sprinted to the passenger door and smiled at Fred through the window, saying something to Mr. Oday at the same time. But his eyes stayed locked on Fred. Always on Fred. It was as if the rest of the world didn't exist whenever they were together. I sighed. I certainly had my work cut out for me, but I was up for the challenge. It was the very least I could do, and I wanted to do it. I had to.

I stood up from the curb.

Sam didn't notice me as he bolted around the van and into the stream of students making their way from buses and cars to the front door. Hold on. Was he avoiding me now?

"Sam!" I called, limping in his direction, a good ten paces behind him. It felt like the scavenger hunt all over again, but this time my ankle ached when I walked too fast. "Wait up." He might have been wearing the same jeans and T-shirt from the weekend, something we'd have to work on....

Sam turned. He had a look on his face like he wanted to rip someone's head off. When he saw me, fortunately, his expression softened a fraction. He morphed into the sweet Sam that I'd gotten to know beneath that pine tree.

"We need to talk," I said.

He nodded, albeit reluctantly. "Didn't expect you back at school so soon. How's your leg?"

"Better." I patted my right hip, even though it was an effort not to wince.

"Not much time before homeroom. Can it wait?"

"Nope," I said. "Cafeteria?" I limped toward him.

Students swarming around us stopped to stare, mostly upperclassmen that I didn't know. I pretended to ignore the obvious eavesdropping.

"Yeah," Sam said. He reached out as if he wanted to take my messenger bag, but then pulled his hand back.

"S'okay," I said, adjusting the strap across my chest. "I got it."

"I should study," he said.

"So should I," I said. "But this won't take long."

We moved toward the cafeteria, Sam walking silently beside me, matching me step for step. Whenever we approached groups of twos and threes, the conversations stopped and the gaping started. I wasn't sure Sam even noticed.

I spotted a rare empty corner away from the cafeteria food line and the vending machines. People continued to stare as we walked to an empty table. As we passed, I could hear their whispers, but I couldn't make out much of what they said. I did hear someone say, "So that's Riley Berenger?" Again. Sam kept up his usual stoic, I-don't-care-what-anyone-thinks expression, and I did my best to feign disinterest. It wasn't so hard. For some reason, nothing seemed difficult beside Sam.

Sam sat down and I sat across from him. We plopped our bags beside us. It was a relief to be off my feet.

Leaning forward, I got straight to the point. "I've been doing some thinking."

"So have I," Sam said.

"You have?"

Sam nodded.

"Good. 'Cause I totally think we can do this." I placed my hand over his.

"Wait. Do what?" Sam said, looking down at our hands.

My ribs pressed against the table's edge. "You know."

"No, I don't know what you're saying," he said, but I knew

right away he was lying. I realized that when Sam lied, his eyelids narrowed and for the briefest of moments his irises flickered. I noted that for future reference.

"I said that I would help you with—" my voice lowered another notch "—you know who and I meant it."

"I don't need your—"

I sat back and raised both palms. "Yes, you do, and you shall have it."

"What if I don't want it?"

I leaned closer to him again. My whisper changed to a hiss. "After what you told me Saturday night, I should think you'd be begging me. What have you got to lose?"

Now Sam leaned back, swallowed and then stared at me with a hard gaze. I could tell he was at least considering my proposition.

"Look, I said I could help you have your chance. But winning Fred's heart will be completely up to you."

"This is crazy, Berenger." Sam's head nodded *yes* even though he was all about *no.* "I mean, she's your brother's girlfriend. Remember?"

"I know. And I've thought about that. Ryan could do with a little competition."

"So this is another game?"

"Not at all."

"And you don't think I have a chance." It wasn't a question.

"Now you're the one who's being silly." I paused. "Look, Sam, you're a great guy. Why don't you see that? We've just got to make Fred see it, too."

Sam opened his mouth and then closed it. I wanted to hold his hand again, to reassure him, but I didn't.

Instead I said, "Love is fickle." Then I groaned inside. Suddenly I sounded like an anti-Hallmark card. Not exactly what I was striving for.

The first warning bell for homeroom rang. Saved by the bell. I reached for my bag. "We'll have to meet after school. I'll come to your house—"

Sam nearly leaped out of his chair. "Um. Say what?"

"You heard me. First things first. We'll start with the basics." Another pause. "I need to take a serious look at your closet."

Sam laugh-coughed. "No way."

"Way." I paused. "You've got to trust me, Sam. I trusted you Saturday night. Now it's your turn to trust me."

Sam started to take rapid breaths, the closest to hyperventilation that I'd ever seen him. In a softer voice, he said, "Why are you doing this, Riley?"

I leaned forward and looked from side to side, making certain that no one's prying ears were too close for comfort. "Sam, you're the first boy I've slept with—well, not *slept* slept, but you know what I mean. I told you one of my darkest secrets and you're the first boy to see me in my underwear. I figure the least we can be is friends." I reached for his forearm. Our noses were inches apart. "Besides, I believe in you."

I didn't dare mention the kiss. It would sound so desperate. And, let's face it, for a junior like Sam Tracy, the kiss was probably ancient history. Did guys dwell about kisses like girls did?

And then Sam did it again. He looked at me with his bottomless brown eyes and it was as if his eyes were trying to tell me something that words couldn't.

"Riley!" Drew screeched my name from across the cafeteria, breaking the stare-down between Sam and me. Everyone in the whole room stopped what they were doing. We had no choice but to swivel in our seats and watch her run toward our table.

"Drew. That's my best friend, Drew," I said to Sam as he started to stand and gather his backpack.

"Are you okay?" Drew said when she reached our table, breathless. "Why didn't you answer your texts last night? I've been looking for you all over the place. You weren't by our lockers. Ohmigod, I've been worried sick about you. Are you okay? Are you sure you're okay?" She talked a million miles a minute, her eyes sweeping over me before sweeping between Sam and me.

"I'm fine. No worries. I'm back at school, aren't I?" I tried to laugh off her concern. "Drew? This is Sam. Sam, this is Drew." I really wished she hadn't made such a spectacle and sent Sam running. I wouldn't have minded a few more minutes with him, alone.

"Hey." Sam head nodded toward Drew and hoisted his backpack over his shoulder, clearly eager to leave me to Drew and her inquisition. "See you later?" Sam said to me, surprising me. I was thrilled to know that he was on board with a *later*. There would need to be lots of *laters*.

"Of course." I smiled up at him and he walked away.

Drew tossed her messenger bag on the table and plopped into Sam's seat. "Ohmigod, he is too adorable," she whispered to me, leaning forward. "Tell me everything."

"It'll have to wait till lunch. The bell's gonna ring."

"Are you and Sam, you know, dating now?" She tossed her shiny brown hair behind her back.

I scoffed at this. "Sam and me? No way." Besides, I saw the love-struck way he looked when he talked about Fred— Well, technically, I couldn't really see him in the dark on Saturday night but I'd heard the tug for her in his voice.

"Well, he totally looked into you from what I just saw, *chica*."

"You saw the back of his head, Drew. That's all."

"That's not all I saw. You guys were all over the news this weekend. You looked kinda cute together, too, especially when the news played that clip of you going into the hospital. Sam had his arm around your shoulder like he didn't want to let go."

"We were just exhausted." But I smiled at this in spite of what Drew said. Sam had been so protective and helpful, at least until we saw our parents. It was also fun to think that Drew saw me with anybody, that she saw me as the center of anything. Usually we were always dissecting her latest crush, her issues. "Besides, I have my work cut out for me."

"What do you mean?"

I hesitated. I had to choose my words carefully. I leaned forward another inch and locked onto her eyes. "Can you keep a secret?"

"Always," she whispered.

"Promise? You have to promise, Drew."

Her eyes grew wide. "I swear. I absolutely swear." She grabbed the ends of the table with both hands and stopped breathing.

I hesitated another moment. Then I said, "I'm gonna fix Sam up with Fred Oday." Technically this wasn't part of my promise to Sam. It was okay to share this minor tidbit, right? I wasn't outing his love for Fred.

Drew's eyes looked like they could pop out of her head and bounce onto the table like a pair of gummy bears. "Wait. Your brother's girlfriend? Are you crazy? Why would you do that?"

This was a tougher question. I whispered, "I think Sam and Fred would be perfect together."

"But your brother is totally into Fred." She paused. "Isn't he?" Drew blinked back at me with hopeful eyes, like she hoped I'd say otherwise. I knew for a fact that she'd been crushing on Ryan ever since the day he picked us up from dance practice our freshman year. Drew, along with half the girls at Lone Butte, crushed on my brother. It was sickening, really.

"He is. For now. But you know Ryan. He pretty much has a new girlfriend every time the season changes. Besides, I can't imagine someone as smart as Fred sticking with my brother forever. She's probably growing tired of him already. It'd almost be like I was doing them a favor."

Drew grinned. "You are so bad, Riley."

"Just being a realist."

Drew leaned back in her chair, musing. "Sam and Fred, huh? It's got possibilities...."

Good. I was glad she saw what I saw, but I think what Drew really pictured was herself with my brother by the way her eyes turned all swoony and faraway. I hated to tell her that snagging Ryan was probably a lost cause, but I just couldn't. I could only focus on one project at a time.

"By the way," she said, doing a headshake, "Jay Hawkins was asking about you this morning."

"Jay? Me? When?" The words whooshed out of my mouth.

Drew's eyes twinkled. "Yeah, Jay. In the parking lot. Before school. He parked right next to me."

"Jay knows we're friends?"

"Obviously."

"Well, what'd you tell him?"

"That I was trying to find you, too. He said he'd look for you in homeroom. He asked me how you were doing. He seemed pretty worried about you."

I stood so fast that my chair crashed backward. "Ohmigod, I'm so glad I didn't stay home today. We better go." I reached for my messenger bag.

But the final homeroom bell rang and we were late.

22

SAM

Riley had asked me to wait for her in the parking lot after school. Unless she had her own car, which was doubtful because I'd only ever seen her riding with her brother, our options for getting back to the Rez were limited. That was my ace in the hole. Once she learned that we would need to walk, she'd gladly postpone any crazy ideas about coming all the way out into the middle of the desert to my house. I wasn't going to ask her to hitchhike, either, something I did on occasion.

Go to my house?

Other than Martin, Peter and Vernon, no one came to my house. Ever.

I smiled inside, relieved. With any luck, I'd be able to nip this in the bud pretty quickly.

Then I saw Riley. She walked out the front door by the courtyard, limping, her bag slung across her chest. Students streamed out through the doors alongside her. Everyone walked faster than she did. The top of her blond head bobbed just above the surface of backpacks in every color you could think of. The crowd parted as the sidewalks opened to the parking lot.

When she spotted me, a smile spread across her face and my body froze. This couldn't be good. She looked way too perky for someone with a sore leg who'd just survived an entire day at Lone Butte High School. I was exhausted. Why wasn't she?

"Ready?" she said when she got within a yard.

"Um. Yeah?" I said.

"We're still good to go to your house, right?"

"Sure," I said, unfazed, expecting a short conversation.

"Good." Her lips smacked. "'Cause my brother is giving us a ride."

"What?" It was like a kick to the stomach.

"Oh, good," Riley said, standing beside me on the curb. She looked out across the parking lot just as a silver Jeep—Ryan's Jeep—sped down the center aisle and straight toward us.

"Wait. Your brother?"

"Yeah. Now that golf season is over, he and Fred usually hang. Today they're going to her house to chill instead of ours. Lucky, right?"

"Yeah." I exhaled. "Lucky."

"I know." Her smile widened and I had to wonder if she were really truly listening to me. Every part of me wanted nothing to do with Ryan and Fred, especially not in Ryan's Jeep. Was Riley really that clueless? "I was so glad when Ryan offered," she added.

"He *offered?*" My voice got louder.

"Uh-huh," she said, still utterly and completely clueless.

I moaned. "Riley. I really don't want to—"

"Chill, Sam," she said, interrupting me. "And once we get in the car, let me do the talking."

Like she'd given me a choice.

When I saw Fred through the windshield, seated in the passenger seat of Ryan's shiny ride, my vocal cords twisted into a knot, along with everything else in my body. Not talking would be the least of my problems. Breathing would be harder.

23

RILEY

Fred was the first to speak. "Hey, Ri. Hi, Sam." She sounded so casual. Too casual.

I had hoped that Fred would at least be a little surprised. As an Unofficially Official Observer of students at Lone Butte High School, I was pretty good at picking up on the nuances of people's behavior. And it wasn't as if I hitched a ride to Sam's all the time. I didn't know where he lived—Well, I knew he lived on the reservation but, beyond that, he might as well have lived on Mars. So I was hoping for a little surprise—even a tinge of jealousy would have been nice as I semisnuggled closer to Sam in the backseat, which, I had to admit, felt nice and familiar. It was tempting to reach for his hand. I didn't have to pretend to like sitting close to Sam. After Saturday night, I'd kind of grown fond of it.

Fred's hair cascaded down her right shoulder. As usual, she looked effortlessly beautiful and I was the one who was a little jealous.

Ryan waited till our seat belts were fastened before he pulled away from the curb.

"Hey," I said, breathlessly, nodding at him in the rearview. "*Gracias* for the ride."

"You're going to Sam's?" Ryan replied in the rearview. He said it like he didn't believe me. Like he had to see it with his own eyes. I'd had to tell him three times during lunch in the cafeteria that I needed a ride. I also hated that he'd spoken just now as if Sam wasn't seated right beside me.

Sam stared out the window, saying nothing.

"Sam's gonna tutor me in chem." Chemistry also happened to be my least favorite subject so it wasn't as if it was a total lie. Just a little bitty one. I inched a little closer to Sam and mind-melded, *Look interested!* If I could have somehow inconspicuously lifted his arm and draped it across my shoulders, I would have.

Sam grunted an answer and my lips pressed together.

"Whatever," Ryan said.

"Well, you can't get any better than Sam," Fred chimed in.

"I know," I said. "Stranded together Saturday night, we had a lot to talk about," I added rather vaguely.

Fred turned in her seat. "Really?"

"Really," I said, matching her innocent tone.

"Well, if you had to be stranded, I'm sure glad it was with Sam, Riley," Fred said, turning forward in her seat. "You can't get much better than him," she said. Again. It wasn't my imagination that Fred beamed at Sam.

I squinted at her, trying to divine her obvious double-meaning as Sam exhaled. Clearly Fred had feelings for Sam, probably more than she realized. But Sam continued to glare out the backseat window as if the I-10 Freeway alongside the reservation was the most fascinating piece of real estate in the whole world.

Ryan straightened in his seat. "Gee, thanks."

Fred reached for Ryan's right hand, resting on the console between them. Her lips twisted and then she chuckled. "Come on, you know what I mean."

"No, sorry. I don't." Ryan puffed out his chest a little bit. Ryan and Fred were fighting? Maybe they quibbled like this more than I realized. It suddenly occurred to me that getting Sam and Fred together was probably going to be a snap and I couldn't help but get all warm and glowy inside. By the time I was done, they would all probably be thanking me for getting involved!

Fred turned in her seat toward Sam and then said, "Sam camps out all the time. Don't you, Sam?"

Sam nodded without really acknowledging anything.

"See?" Fred said, turning to Ryan. "Sam's the kind of guy you want around if you get stranded in the wilderness."

"They were two miles from a campsite. I hardly call that wilderness."

Sam stiffened beside me.

"Well, it is if you're stranded on the side of a mountain," Fred retorted, both of them oblivious to Sam and me in the backseat. It was like watching Ping-Pong.

"Well, okay," Ryan said, but I don't think he was convinced. "Hey, Sam," he said, "I guess I should formally thank you for saving my little sister. I haven't done that yet. So, yeah. Thanks."

"Try and be a little more heartfelt," I said.

"I am being heartfelt!"

Sam grunted again, and I made a mental note that we needed to work on the grunting. Sentences with more than one syllable would be required if we wanted any chance of him winning Fred's heart. And, *please*, there was such a thing as too much male brooding. Sam seemed ready to kick his feet through the back window. Didn't Fred see that? Was I the only one picking up on his jealous behavior?

"But could you have at least kept her on the rim more than a day, though?" A tease lifted Ryan's lips, the kind of teasing that I had become used to during the past almost sixteen years. "It was actually quiet around the house on Saturday."

"Ha. Ha," I said, rolling my eyes. "Sam was a real hero. I would have died on that mountain without him. Died! And everybody was talking about how brave he was today, too. Everybody." That shut up my big-mouthed brother.

And that was the truth. People had asked me about Saturday night in every class, during every break, during lunch. Some of the people had never spoken to me before; some I didn't even know. Mostly they'd asked about Sam, especially the girls. And I'd told everybody the same thing: Sam Tracy came back for me. He clawed his way down a treacherous mountain just to reach me. Sam Tracy saved my life. Drew practically swooned over Sam before English class when I'd given her the Cliff's Notes version of Saturday night, announcing that Sam Tracy was officially "hot," although I think she was equally excited to learn that my brother would soon be back on the market.

Even so, it was critical to move quickly. At Lone Butte High School, you could be hot one day and yesterday's news the next—unless, of course, you were lucky enough to be someone like Jenna Gibbons.

I slumped back against my seat and smiled smugly to myself, forgetting my brother's annoying comment as I stared out the window and we drove farther away from the outskirts of Phoenix and into the desert.

This was already starting off better than I had planned. Pushing my brother's hot buttons was easier than I thought. Pushing Fred's would be harder. But that was one thing I'd learned a long time ago as Ryan Berenger's sister: everybody had them.

24

SAM

Get. Me. Out. Of. This. Car.

That mantra looped through my head for the entire ride back to the Rez. On the inside, I was seething so hard that my ribs ached. I was furious at Riley. I hated her brother. I was angry at Fred for bringing the Berengers into our lives. Most of all, I was pissed at myself for being roped into Ryan's car. I would have preferred to walk home in a monsoon, in thunder and lightning, through a raging inferno, than sit in the backseat of Ryan Berenger's Jeep like a lapdog. I had to stop being Riley's science project or charity project or whatever she thought I was, and I planned to get that settled as soon as we reached my house. It was easier to talk to Riley and be real when we were alone.

I opened the car door as soon as Ryan pulled to a stop on the dirt road that ended in front of our house. It was still another twenty steps across patchy grass to our front door. Grandmother was sitting in her favorite metal straight-back chair at the foot of the front stairs, her latest basket-weaving project between her legs. She looked up from her work, but her bony fingers never stopped moving.

"I'll call your cell when I need a ride back," Riley said to Ryan, opening the door and limping toward me as if Ryan dropped her off at my house all the time.

Ryan tooted the horn and then backed up his Jeep until he could turn around and proceed down the road to Fred's house.

"Hi, Grandmother Tracy," Fred yelled from the car window as the car backed up.

Grandmother nodded but said nothing, her fingers barely pausing over the long strips of willow shoots and horsehair that never seemed to leave her hands. Grandmother was half Pima and our house was filled with baskets of all sizes, a craft that she'd learned from her mother and grandmother. Now I supposed I would have to explain Pima artistry to Riley. I moaned to myself again, this time out loud.

Riley shouldn't be here. I shouldn't have to explain. I shouldn't have to explain *anything*.

"Hi, Grandmother," I mumbled as I approached the steps. Her tiny body sat hunched over to the right of the door.

Grandmother nodded. If she was surprised, she didn't show it, but I'd seen Grandmother's expression change exactly three times in my entire life. Nothing fazed her, even a white girl standing at the foot of our front stairs.

Riley caught up surprisingly fast for someone with an injured leg. I didn't slow down for her for a second, not like at school. At the moment, I wanted to explode into a thousand pieces and shake her shadow, but she followed me like a rain cloud.

Grandmother squinted at me behind her thick reading glasses. She waited for introductions. *Great.*

"This is Riley. We're going to study," I added as an afterthought, as if I invited girls over to our house all the time after school—which I did not. This was a first.

"Hello." Riley's voice was bright but cautious. I turned to look down at her, standing at the foot of the stairs, as I reached for the door. Ryan's Jeep was already halfway down the road, brown clouds of dust spiraling into the sky behind his tires. I breathed a little easier, but not much. I had to tell Riley to stay out of my business. Then I had to get rid of her. Since we lived ten miles from anywhere, I was stuck with her for the time being.

"Can I come in?" Riley said in a small voice. She looked from me to Grandmother, who had returned to her weaving.

"Help yourself," I said, opening the screen door and letting it snap behind me.

"Those are really pretty baskets," I heard Riley say as she half walked, half limped her way up the wooden stairs. I tossed my backpack onto the family room couch and stormed into the kitchen. I could still hear her talking to Grandmother. "I don't think I've ever seen one up close. They're so delicate," she added as she opened the squeaky screen door. "Sam?" She stepped into the dark family room as I pretended to look for something to eat in the kitchen cabinet.

"Yeah?" I said in the least friendly tone I could muster.

Riley sighed as she lifted the strap from her bag off her chest. "Don't be mad." She placed it on the couch next to mine.

"Mad? Who's mad?" I wasn't trying to be funny.

Riley stepped closer.

"You could have warned me that your brother was our ride," I said.

"I would have if you had a cell phone. I could have texted you."

I chuckled. "Well, sorry I couldn't be more of assistance."

"Stop it."

"Stop what?"

"Stop being so…angry. Are you this angry at everyone?"

I laughed loud enough to fill all the empty space in the room. It was a mean, maniacal laugh but I couldn't help it. Good thing no one was home except Grandmother. "Just at people who break their promises." And guys like Ryan Berenger, who always got the girl.

"I'm not breaking my promise. I said I wouldn't tell anyone how you feel about Fred, and I won't. I swear I won't."

My nostrils flared.

"We're wasting time and I'm only trying to help you."

"I don't want your help. *You're* wasting time."

"Am not."

"Are, too."

Her arms moved to her hips. "Do you have any idea what everyone was saying about you today?"

"I don't care."

She snorted. "Well, you should."

"Why?"

"'Cause you're officially A-list hot."

"Stop it, Riley."

"I'm totally serious. Every girl at school was asking me about you. They want you. And if they weren't asking, they were thinking."

I scoffed. "Why?"

"You're a hero, Sam! That's why. Every girl loves a hero. Don't you see?" Her eyes bulged.

"Yeah, I see that you're going to be a pain in my ass."

She shook her head. "This is going to be easy. I'll have Fred eating out of the palm of your hand within a week. But we've got to work fast."

"Why?" I said again.

"Because fame is fleeting. Just like love."

"You read too many romance novels."

"Do not. I prefer mysteries."

"This still seems like a huge waste of time. Besides, Fred is your friend, too. Why would you want to hurt her?"

"Hurt her?" Riley's hands moved to her hips. "Did you just see what happened in the car? Were you even listening? Jeez, Sam! Fred and Ryan were *arguing.* I'm sure that wasn't the first time, either. It's only a matter of time. I'm only helping them to see the inevitable. You've got to trust me."

I sputtered, still irritated. Riley was dreaming. Riley was delusional. But she was nothing if not persistent. And what if she were right about Fred and Ryan? Dammit. I was trapped inside my own house.

She took a step closer, her eyes laser-locked on mine. "Now stop acting like a big baby and take me to your bedroom."

I stopped breathing. The only sound came from the *tick-tock* of the kitchen clock. I didn't need a mirror to know that my eyeballs were almost popping out of my head and threatening to drop to the floor.

"And take off your shirt," she added with a sniff. "It's not like I haven't seen you naked."

25

RILEY

Sam stood there, a cereal box clutched in his left hand, completely frozen and silent. And blushing. The blushing part was sweet. You never expect a big tough guy to blush.

When he saw that I was serious, he finally lowered his thick arms and said, "Okay. Follow me. But there's not much to see."

I followed Sam down a narrow hallway covered in brown paneling. It was weird to see Sam in his own house. I mean, it wasn't as though I didn't know that he lived in a house with a family and everything. It was just that seeing him here—in a place so simple and normal with family photos and living room furniture and knickknacks and a grandmother sitting outside—was like I was seeing this new side of him, even different from the gentle Sam I'd gotten to know on Saturday night and definitely different from the mysterious and brooding Sam at school. I was beginning to piece together the real Sam Tracy.

I tried to sneak peeks at the photos hung on the wall but the hallway was too dark and Sam was acting crazy weird as it was. I couldn't get sidetracked until I at least had a good peek at his closet. Then I'd let him freak out—which I fully expected.

We passed a bedroom that I assumed belonged to a girl, given the cute jean skirt and skinny jeans hanging over the open door. "You have a sister?"

"Yeah. Cecilia."

"Older or younger?"

"Older."

"You get along?"

"Usually." I wondered if Sam found his older sister as irritating as I found Ryan.

"What does she do?"

"She works part-time and goes to college part-time."

"What's she studying to be?"

"A librarian."

"Cool." I liked her already.

We entered Sam's bedroom at the end of the hallway. His room had a single bed draped with one of those old-fashioned quilts you see in antique stores, a five-drawer dresser and a nightstand with a brass globed lamp and three hardback books stacked so that all the spines were even. A small window over the bed provided muted afternoon light. It was tidy and looked nothing like my brother's bedroom, where piles of clothes littered the floor like land mines. Sam Tracy continued to surprise me. Instead of clothes, books were stacked in every corner of the room. There was a single shelf lined with small trophies, the inscriptions too small to read. A kachina with a crown of feathers sat on his dresser. I'd never seen a kachina outside of a glass case at a store or museum.

Sam turned on the lamp and a soft golden glow filled the room. He sat on the edge of his tightly made bed, his arms outstretched. "Well. Here we are. Satisfied? Now what?"

I limped to his closet, ignoring the throbbing in my knee. I had done way too much walking today, but it was not the time to complain. I'd wait until tonight when my mother would insist on feeding me another Tylenol, which I would swallow without argument. "Now I look through your closet."

"Why?"

I spun around. "We've got to do something about your look."

"I don't have a look."

"Exactly."

Sam exhaled.

"Stop it with the heavy sighs. You sound like a grouchy old man."

"Stop telling me what to do."

"Once I'm done, you'll be begging me to tell you what to do."

"Doubtful."

I ignored his eyes, which I was certain had begun to drill red-hot holes into the back of my neck.

Metal hangers squeaked as I leafed through his tiny closet. There wasn't much to see. Sam was hardly a clothes-hound, and it was about what I expected. One rod, one wooden shelf. Lots of worn, cotton T-shirts, a couple of button-downs, six pairs of jeans, which, frankly, surprised me, and a black suit that looked six sizes too small. Two leather belts hung on a hook inside the door along with a cowboy hat. I fingered the belt with the round silver belt buckle. The buckle was bigger than my hand. Three pairs of sneakers and one pair of boots neatly lined the floor like soldiers.

"Do you ride?" I asked, fingering the belt buckle.

Sam didn't answer right away, as if he were considering whether to tell me. Then he said, "I did when I was younger, me and my dad. Don't ride too much anymore. Never enough time." He nodded to the shelf. "That's what some of the trophies are for."

"What are the others?"

Sam turned and bowed his head. "A couple of them are from chess tournaments."

I spun around, forgetting the buckle. "You play chess?"

He nodded.

I turned back around. "So do I. I can never find anyone to play with anymore. Ryan used to play with me. Now he spends all his time with Fred." I paused. "Maybe we should play sometime."

Sam hesitated. "Maybe."

"You have horses?"

"Just a pony now in the barn out back. It belongs to Cecilia."

"Does the pony have a name?" I continued to examine each of his shirts before working my way to his jeans.

Another long pause. "Papago."

"As in the freeway?"

He chuckled. "No, as in *O'odham*." He said it with a soft accent.

"Cool. What's that mean?"

"It's a Native thing. You don't want to know."

"Maybe I do?"

Sam shrugged as if he didn't believe me. Or he didn't feel like explaining centuries of Native-American history to me.

"Well, I always wanted a horse. You're lucky. Would you show me Papago?"

Sam didn't answer. He chose to sigh heavily instead.

"Stop it with the heavy sighing, Sam. Girls don't like guys who sigh a lot. It's not fun." I bit back a smile. "How about you show me your pony after I beat you in chess?"

There was a smile in his response. "Don't push your luck, Berenger."

I turned to face him, a little breathless. Sam was so adorable when there was the hint of a smile on his face. "Well, maybe next time. We have a lot to do today."

"Like what, exactly?" The irritation in Sam's voice returned but I ignored it.

"First, I'm going to tell you what to wear tomorrow and for the rest of the week, and you're going to listen to me." I pulled out a T-shirt that wasn't as frayed as the others. It would look totally hot underneath the solid blue button-down in his closet. I brought his shirt to my face. It smelled like campfire. My nose wrinkled dramatically, more for his benefit than mine.

Speechless, Sam turned a shade paler, which was difficult to do when you were as dark as he was.

"Then I'm going to cut your hair."

Sam's jaw dropped.

"Just a trim. Not much."

He appeared to have difficulty speaking.

"Do you have any body spray?"

"I am not wearing perfume!" Sam stood up, finding his voice.

"It's not perfume. It's body spray. For guys."

"Same thing. I am absolutely not wearing any perfume."

"You can and you will, Sam." I turned back to the closet, ignoring his glare. "Girls like guys who smell good." I paused, letting my voice linger. "Fred does."

His mouth snapped shut.

Gotcha, I thought smugly to myself.

"Well, it doesn't matter," he said. "I don't have any."

"Yes, you do. I brought some in my bag. Along with a pair of scissors."

Sam flopped onto his bed, the mattress groaning from his weight.

26

SAM

I realized that the only way that I was going to get rid of Riley Berenger was to do what she wanted. Until her brother came to claim her, I was stuck. In the meantime, I felt like a puppet and Riley was working the strings.

She had completely rearranged my closet—not that there was much to rearrange—even setting out what she wanted me to wear for the rest of the week.

"This shouldn't be tucked in, Sam," she'd said. And "You need to wear a belt with this, not with that." Blah blah blah. "Get rid of that and buy a new pair of stone-washed." More blah blah blah. I had to laugh. Only in Riley's world did people have credit cards with unlimited spending limits. Welcome to my world. I certainly did not.

Riley placed a new bottle of body spray on my dresser. I had to admit, it didn't smell half-bad, although I would never tell her that. She'd sprayed some into the air when I'd refused to let her spray it on my arm. It smelled earthy, like creosote in the desert after it rained. I supposed I could live with that.

She grabbed my hand, pulling me off the bed, and walked

me outside with her hand in mine. Then she found a chair and set it under a paloverde tree. She told me to take off my shirt, again, as Grandmother watched us, never saying a word, her fingers working as feverishly as Riley's.

Riley detangled my hair with the brush she'd grabbed from my dresser. She produced scissors from her bag and began to cut the ends. I watched as at least two inches of my hair fell to the dirt like black smudges.

"Sit still," she said, pulling my hair back. "I'm not cutting that much off. Just the ends. You totally need this."

"I do *not* need this, Berenger."

"Do."

"Don't."

Then Riley combed the hair over my eyes and stood in front of me, her thighs pressed against my knees, my gaze dead-even with her chest. Her skin was as warm as mine.

I closed my eyes, ordering myself to forget the curves and pearly-white skin I had seen beneath her clothes on Saturday night. I'd be lying if I said I hadn't remembered it at least a dozen times since being stranded with her on the side of the mountain. What normal guy wouldn't?

"When I'm done with you, you'll have every girl at Lone Butte begging you to take them to junior prom."

My tongue got lost in my throat. Then I managed to ask, "Who said anything about prom?"

She continued to comb the hair over my eyes. "Well, it's pretty much a given that you'll be nominated for junior court. Jay Hawkins mentioned it to me in study hall today."

"Jay Hawkins?" I blurted. "I told you I can't stand that guy. What do I care what he says?"

"You should care. Jay's popular. He's also on the court committee."

"I couldn't care less. And I have no desire to go to a stupid prom."

"What if Fred wants to go?"

"She's going with Ryan."

"I'm not sure if he's formally asked her yet. A girl likes to be asked, you know."

"Come on, Riley." It was hard not to roll my eyes in frustration. "It's a given that they'll go together at this point. Get real."

"Nothing's a given in high school, Sam."

"Since when are you the expert?"

Her scissors paused in midsnip. "You can learn a lot when you don't say much."

"Are we talking about you?" *Quiet* wasn't exactly the word I'd use to describe Riley Berenger. Did she have an evil twin?

She ignored me.

"But prom is in a month." Never mind that I had no suit, no money and no ride. Not gonna happen.

"And that's why we don't have any time to waste." She combed back my hair so that I could look up at her. Her body blocked the setting sun, which framed her like a photograph, all shimmery around the edges. In this light, her blue eyes darkened like deep water.

I blinked away the thought of Riley's eyes and the way they stared back at me as if I were the most important person in the whole world. "And you think that body spray and a haircut is going to change things between me and Fred." It wasn't even really a question.

She nodded. "Sure. It's a start. And, oh, by the way, you've got plans Saturday night."

I coughed. "I do?"

"You're going to Jay's party."

I sat straighter in the chair, enough so that she had to pull back the scissors.

"I am not going to Jay Hawkins's party, Riley. Never. No way."

Riley's shoulders slumped. Her arms slapped to her sides. "It's probably the biggest party of the year. You've got to go. It's part of the plan." Then she begged. "Please?"

"No. Absolutely not."

Her face crumpled and I had to look away before I'd weaken. Again. I had already let this girl leaf through my closet, cut my hair and douse me with perfume. There was no way I was going to spend a Saturday night at Jay Hawkins's house. "I wasn't invited." Big surprise.

Riley yanked my hair. "Are you kidding? Everybody's invited, even sophomores." She pointed at herself as her eyes widened with delight. Then she proceeded to talk a million miles a minute. "Jay sent out a text to the whole school today. His parents are in Jamaica. I'm going with Drew and I heard Ryan saying something about it to Fred."

I brushed the tiny fallen hairs from my arms. My skin itched as if I had hives, just at the thought of sitting inside Jay's house did, making small talk with people I barely knew— people I didn't want to know. "I'm not going."

"But—"

I stood up. My chair crashed backward. I towered over her, my chest bare and covered by clumps of my own cutoff hair. "Forget it! Now call your brother and have him pick you up. I've got homework."

Riley stood with her arms extended, the scissors still poised in her right hand. Her voice softened. "Come on, Sam. Stop being difficult."

"I mean it, Riley," I said, but there was something about

the way her eyes pleaded with mine that made my knees wobble. I huffed, "We're done here."

Riley looked beyond my shoulder. Grandmother was walking toward us across the lone piece of patchy grass around our house, a light brown basket in her hands.

"For you," Grandmother said, extending both hands. They might have been the only words she'd uttered all day.

Riley placed the scissors on my chair. Then she reached for the basket. "Thank you. It's beautiful." Riley fingered the tight weave. Two rectangles of horsehair dotted each side, the basket no bigger than a fist.

Grandmother nodded at her before turning back to her chair, her hands clasped behind her back as she walked across the yard with her usual deliberate, tiny steps.

Riley looked at me and whispered, "What is it?"

"A basket?" I said in a normal voice, in case it wasn't obvious.

She shot me a glare. "I know that," she said, still whispering. "But, I mean, why would your grandmother give me a present? She doesn't know me."

Grandmother mumbled something, not meant for Riley to hear but I heard it. Loud and clear.

"Sorry, Grandmother," I called after her.

"Sorry for what?" Riley whispered.

"She says I'm being rude. And she's got ears like Superman. Even though she's almost ninety, she hears everything."

Riley cupped the basket in the palm of her hand, cradling it like a fistful of gold.

"It's a dream basket," I said finally. "You're supposed to write down your dreams and place them inside. If you do, they'll come true."

Riley's head tilted, and she beamed at the basket with renewed interest. "Is that a Gila thing, too?"

"No, that's a Grandmother thing. I'm pretty sure she made that up, but it sounds good. And she sells a ton of them."

We laughed, and the laughter lifted some of the tension between us. I did like Riley's laugh. It was the light and girly kind that made you smile just hearing it.

"Wait here," I told Riley. "I'll grab a couple of Cokes and wait with you till your brother gets here."

"Bring out your chess set?" Her lips twisted.

"Okay," I said. "But be prepared to lose."

"Big talker!" She crossed her arms.

I went inside and then returned with two soda cans and a dusty chess set that hadn't been used in forever. The last time I'd played was with Dad during Christmas four years ago. Dad liked chess almost as much as I did, mostly because very little talking was involved. I figured that was why he'd taught me the game in the first place. It was the one thing we could do together. Unfortunately the set now mostly collected dust in my dresser drawer.

For the rest of the afternoon, Riley and I didn't talk about my hair, my clothes, body spray or Ryan and Fred. We just sat beneath the tree, playing chess and talking about weird teachers and classes and nothing in particular until we reached a stalemate. Just us. Just talking. Kind of like Saturday night on the side of the Mogollon Rim all over again except without the torrential rain and lightning and cold. I had to admit that she was better at chess than I'd have thought.

When Ryan pulled up, the sun had almost completely set behind the Estrella Mountains. It didn't seem like another hour had passed, but I guessed it had. I reached down my hand to help her stand and then she hugged me, just like that, like it was the most natural thing. Without a word, we waited for Ryan to stop the car.

As Riley climbed into the Jeep, she said, "Don't forget about tomorrow." Then she winked at me.

Reluctantly, I nodded. I went over Riley's "plan" in my head. It was so not me, and yet she had me cornered as neatly as she had cornered my king in our last chess game.

"Good," she said, lifting her chin with plenty of confidence. "I'll see you in the cafeteria. This'll work, Sam. You'll see."

I looked at Ryan. He was talking on his cell phone as if Riley and I were invisible. He had no clue that Riley's plans involved changing his life forever—well, at least for the rest of the school year, if Riley had her way.

"See you tomorrow," I said, tossing my shirt over my shoulder.

Riley smiled back at me. I was in so deep that I couldn't see the surface anymore.

"Bye, Grandmother Tracy! Thanks again for the basket!" Riley waved.

Grandmother raised her eyes from her weaving and nodded. A small smile lifted her lips.

I watched Ryan's Jeep until it reached the end of our dirt road, bouncing over all the ruts. I remembered that I'd forgotten to show her Cecilia's pony. Oh, well.

Just as Ryan's Jeep was turning onto the main road, Mom and Dad drove up the dirt road from the opposite direction in Dad's truck, dust swirling behind their rear wheels as they chugged toward the trailer. The warm fuzzy feeling from Riley's hug faded. *Great.* They were home early. Just my luck.

Dad parked the truck alongside the house, exactly where he always did.

"Who was that?" Mom called from the passenger window. She pushed her sunglasses onto the top of her head.

Suddenly I felt self-conscious, standing under the tree

without a shirt and with newly trimmed hair. A thousand questions scrolled across their foreheads. I looked over at Grandmother for a little assistance, but she was deep into her next basket.

I turned back to Mom. "Just a friend," I said, picking up the box of chess pieces and crushing a Coke can beneath my foot.

"Wasn't that the girl from Saturday night?" Mom stepped out of the truck. Mom was as sharp as a cactus needle. She never missed a thing.

I nodded.

"What was she doing here?" Mom's eyes narrowed, sweeping over me. Dad joined her from the other side. He dragged a hand through his hair. New lines had sprouted between his eyes. He looked more exhausted than usual.

"Homework," I said, but then I realized how stupid that sounded as I stood surrounded by two inches of my hair, holding my chess game against my hip, Coke cans at my feet, along with an empty bag of potato chips.

Even Dad exhaled, saying nothing. He started walking to the house.

As soon as he was out of earshot, I said, "What the hell is his problem?"

"Watch your language, Sam," Mom snapped.

But I stared at her, waiting for a response, for anything that made sense. "Well?"

"It's been a long day and we're still tired from the week-end. We come home and find you with your shirt off and this girl from Saturday who got you into trouble exiting our driveway. Give us a chance to process, Sam," Mom said. "And give your dad a break today, okay?"

"I've had a long day, too," I said. "Can't I at least get a *hello?*"

"Your father said *hello*. Didn't you hear him?" Mom's brow

furrowed but I think she was rethinking whether she'd heard him say *hello* or simply wished he had.

"I didn't hear one." I rarely saw Dad during daylight hours. The least he could do was acknowledge my existence. Why did I feel like a trespasser in my own home?

"Don't be so sensitive, Sam," Mom scolded, walking toward the house and leaving me under the paloverde tree, confused as usual about how things had gone so terribly wrong. "You know that your father has never been very good with words. It's what he feels inside that's most important." Then Mom stopped and turned. "You could make more of an effort."

I snorted. "An effort to do what?"

"An effort to be more understanding. He's had a lot on his mind lately."

"Like what?"

Mom stopped. "Work. Chasing after idiots all day at the casino. Paying the bills around here. Did you know we need a new air-conditioner and the truck needs new tires?" Her arms folded across her chest. Mom always defended Dad. Always. No matter what I said. "The pressure can wear down a man."

"Well, I've had a lot on my mind, too."

Mom's chin lowered. "You're just a kid. What could be troubling you?"

"You'd be surprised."

Mom chuckled as if I were making a joke.

"I'm serious, Mom. And I am not a kid anymore. I'm seventeen."

Her hands went to her hips. Her voice turned sharp. "You want to be a man? Well, then start acting like one, Samuel."

I spread my arms, frustrated, my breath catching in the back of my throat like a tiny click. "How do I know what to do right if I don't even know what I'm doing wrong?" I turned to the house, looking for Dad, just as the screen door snapped shut. In a softer voice, I said, "I don't even remember how to talk to him anymore." If I'd ever known at all.

"Oh, Sam," Mom said, shaking her head. "You make things more complicated than they need to be."

"What's that supposed to mean?"

"You want to talk to him? Go talk to him." She started walking toward the house again.

"I've tried, Mom. It's impossible." Whenever I tried to talk to Dad about school, about college, even about exams that I'd aced, he looked at me like I'd grown three heads. "Does he even care that I might get a full scholarship to USC, maybe even to Michigan?" I called after her.

Mom stopped again. "Why would you want to go way out to Michigan? All that crime and snow…"

I practically growled. Was she kidding? I'd go to Michigan in a heartbeat on a full scholarship.

"Of course your father cares," Mom said, pursing her lips.

"Does he even know?"

"Well. Yes…" Mom's voice trailed off. She looked toward the house again as if she were considering her answer.

"What am I doing that's so wrong, Mom? Tell me. It's like Dad would rather not even *know* me."

She rolled her eyes. "That's ridiculous."

"Is it?"

She paused. But then she said, "You're a smart kid. You two will have to figure it out."

"Hey, Mr. Michigan," Dad bellowed from the screen door.

I looked over at the house, completely surprised. I hadn't expected to hear Dad's voice for the rest of the day. "Yeah?"

"Feed Papago. Your sister won't be home till late. And

sweep out the stall, too. It needs it." The screen door snapped shut again.

"Well, *hello* to you, too," I muttered.

27

RILEY

Since I'd given Sam his makeover, I figured I could use one, too. Practice what you preach, right?

I'd always wanted a few pink hair highlights and, I had to say, they'd turned out pretty cute. Subtle peekaboos only, not too many. Not enough for Mom to freak but enough to make me feel good, maybe even stand out a little for once in my life. For school, I decided on a black cotton jacket over my favorite pink tee and a pair of my favorite black jeans, the ones that rode low on my hips—lower than all my other pairs. The black jacket helped to hide my self-consciousness while adding some hipness at the same time. My pink-checkered Vans completed the outfit and made me wonder why I always went with my usual six conservative standby clothing options such as pencil skirts and white capris when I had a whole closet full of fun. Drew would be pleased with my choices. That was a given. She'd told me a million times that I had to spice up my wardrobe.

Concentrating in class on Tuesday became impossible, especially when I glanced at the clock in math so many times that Mr. Rainier finally said, "Miss Berenger, do you have a plane to catch?" which, of course, elicited all of the usual stifled giggles from people who were probably as bored as I was.

Little did Mr. Rainier or anyone know that before homeroom I had asked Fred to help me with an English paper. I'd known before she answered that she would say yes and, I hated to admit, her eagerness made me feel a little guilty for even asking, but only for a few seconds. I had my own agenda and I had to act quickly.

Lunch finally arrived.

At a perfectly centered cafeteria table, one with plenty of walk-by traffic, Drew sat to my left while Fred sat to my right. When he'd seen that Fred and I would have our noses buried in *A Farewell to Arms*, Ryan had ditched to have lunch at McDonald's off-campus. Ryan hated any books that didn't include space aliens or private detectives, so it was the perfect ruse to get rid of him for an hour. And, frankly, I was shocked our prime real-estate table was even available and I took it as a sign—another sign that everything I had been planning in my mind for Sam and Fred was meant to be.

At exactly 11:15 a.m., Sam walked into the cafeteria. I knew, because a hush fell over the room. Sam was A-list now and he didn't even know it. I loved that about him. It was a rare quality in high school.

People were still whispering about him, mostly because they didn't really know him. Sam was one of only a handful of Gila River natives attending Lone Butte. Unless you had them in class, you might not know them at all, apart from Fred. Because she was my brother's girlfriend, and the first girl on the Lone Butte High School golf team—the girl who'd led the formerly losing team to win the state championship last fall—everybody knew her. Sam wasn't a jock. He didn't have a big mouth, and he never got into trouble. Of course no one had really noticed him.

Until now.

When Sam strolled through the doors, his black backpack nonchalantly threaded over his right shoulder, it was as if the seas parted. Students—girls, especially—stopped to gape. And I had to admit, he looked good—no, scratch that. Sam Tracy looked *hot*. His hair was perfectly disheveled. His clothes hugged his body a little better, and I noted that he'd layered his shirts exactly as I had instructed.

And there was no escaping those gorgeous dark eyes of his. They didn't change. Now everyone was seeing the Sam that I saw. Sam's gaze swept over the cafeteria as if the room were empty.

"Over here!" I called to him just as soon as everyone had gulped in a long, sweet drink of him.

Sam gave me the backward nod.

"Um. Wow. Is that Sam?" Fred said, staring at him.

"Yeah," I answered with plenty of nonchalance myself. "Didn't you ride in together this morning?" I asked her, even though I knew that my brother had picked her up this morning because I'd ridden with Drew.

"No," Fred mumbled. "That was yesterday."

"Oh," I said, only to fill the silence as Fred faced forward, still looking a little stunned by Sam's entrance.

"Is he helping you, too?" she said.

"No," I said. "I just invited him to eat with us. That's okay, right?"

"Oh," she said again, except this time it came out like a little squeak. Her eyes dropped to the pages in front of her as if she'd just remembered why we were here.

I smiled to myself. But then I squeaked, too. And it had nothing to do with Sam. Jenna Gibbons and three of her friends suddenly stood over our table like a glossy Sephora shadow. "Hey, Riley. Hey, Fred," Jenna said, as if we chatted all the time. "Haven't talked to you in a while."

More like since junior high. "Hey?" I said, but it came out like a question.

"We're dying to hear what happened on Saturday night, with the rescue and all. Are you okay?" Jenna's eyes stayed focused on Sam as he crossed the cafeteria, even as she feigned concern for me. Reluctantly, her gaze dropped to mine. "You should come eat with us sometime," Jenna said.

"Um. Okay?" I said, not sure what she expected me to say first. I hoped she was serious about her cafeteria table. Jay Hawkins usually lunched with Jenna's friends. He'd been seeking me out during homeroom and study hall, ever since the leadership conference. This morning he was waiting for me at my locker. Not sure why, but I wasn't complaining. Little did Jay know that I'd been secretly crushing on him since the first minute of my freshman year. I liked the idea of him, and sometimes that was all you could love about a person.

"And bring your friend," Jenna added, glancing over her shoulder in Sam's direction. She tried for nonchalance, but it wasn't working. "What's his story, anyway?"

"You mean Sam?" I wanted her to beg a little.

"Of course," Jenna said, her glossy smile turning downward. Even frowning, she looked flawless and beautiful. Predictably, her friends giggled. "Who did you think I meant?"

"Sam's pretty busy these days, but I'll see what I can do." I was talking as if I were his publicist or something.

"Yeah. Whatever," Jenna said, hardly deterred. "Do what you can," she added, although from her tone, she fully expected compliance.

I didn't like to admit it, but I admired her confidence. And

I complied. "When we're done here, we'll stop by your table if there's still time before the bell. I'll introduce you to Sam."

Jenna flashed her full-wattage smile. She'd known I'd come through for her. Who didn't? "Thanks, Ri. See ya."

Beside me, Fred stiffened. I wasn't sure whether it was due to the close proximity of Jenna Gibbons and her sidekicks, their overpowering perfume or Sam's suddenly burgeoning social status. Whatever it was, I had a feeling my plan was working.

Anxious to keep it going, I looked past Jenna for Sam, but he was gone.

28

SAM

I stormed into the cafeteria, looking for Riley.

Against my better judgment, I'd done exactly as she told me. I wore my clothes like she showed me. I even wore the damn body spray. Although they were my same old clothes, they itched. They tugged at me in new places. They felt too small, then too big. Everything felt all wrong on my body. Why had I listened to Pink Girl? Why had I let her call the shots? Why had I even let her cut my hair? I should have my head examined and it was time to end this, once and for all. It wasn't right—least of all to Fred.

But the moment I stepped into the cafeteria, instead of Riley, I saw Fred. She was sitting at a table near the windows, the sun streaming behind her. It was as if time froze. All I could hear was my own heartbeat drumming against my temples. When our eyes met, Fred's lips formed the perfect circle. Her smooth skin paled the tiniest of shades. For once, Fred Oday saw me, if only for the briefest of moments. For once, I knew how Ryan Berenger must feel whenever Fred's gaze locked with his. I felt like maybe, just maybe, I had a chance with her. And I liked it.

Then Riley called my name, and the world started spinning out of control again. As I watched, she was ambushed by a flock of girls with glowing faces and shiny lips. I might have nodded at Riley. I might have said *hey*. I couldn't remember.

Instead of walking straight toward Fred and Riley, I dodged for the cafeteria line, my heart beating a million confused miles a minute. Good thing I had an excuse to buy a dry cafeteria sandwich for once.

"Hey, Just Sam!" someone said as I reached across a stainless steel shelf for a turkey sub. I knew who belonged to the voice. I let out a heavy sigh, the same kind that Riley had been chiding me about, but I didn't care. It was impossible for me not to sigh around Jay Hawkins, not to be completely exhausted by his lame jokes, his usual stupidity. It was impossible not to be anything but completely aggravated whenever he opened his mouth and I'd no doubt he preferred it that way.

"Glad you made it out of the rim in one piece." I wished I could believe he cared about anyone but himself. Then he had to add, "How does it feel to be the big hero?" *Great. Yet another thing Jay can resent me for. Add it to the list!* He sidled up to me with his cafeteria tray. We'd barely spoken since freshman year. Suddenly he was talking to me like we rapped all the time. "Riley said it was a pretty scary night." His eyebrows wiggled beneath his baseball cap and I kept sliding my tray along closer to the cashier.

"Riley says lots of things," I said without looking at him

He chuckled darkly. "You're not kidding." I bristled. And I immediately wondered what else she'd been telling him.

"If you'd followed me, you wouldn't have had to freeze your ass off on the edge of nowhere."

"I'll remember that for next time." Just my luck, the lunch

line was moving as slow as sludge and I had Jay Hawkins yap-ping in my left ear. I was tempted to abandon my tray.

"Anyway, I was wondering something...."

I stopped and turned to him. This ought to be good. Jay Hawkins? Wonder? I wasn't sure his brain could handle the pressure. "And what's that, Hawkins?" I hoped he noticed from my tone that I couldn't have cared less what he wondered about.

"You're not in to Riley or anything. Are you?"

I stopped. Then I swallowed, saying nothing. It bugged me that he said it like there was a better chance of an apocalypse right this very second than Riley and I together. I was tempted to rock his world. So I stayed quiet and then took a step closer to the cashier.

He knocked his plastic cafeteria tray against mine. "Well?"

I turned to him when it was obvious he wasn't going to go away. "Why would you want to know?"

"I'm thinking of asking her out this weekend at my party. Maybe take her to prom."

The hairs on the back of my neck prickled. I seriously did not want Riley going anywhere with Jay Hawkins. In fact, I wouldn't wish any girl on Jay Hawkins, especially not Riley. "I don't know" was all I said.

His crazy blue eyes squinted at me like I was an idiot, which I pretty much was with my answer. "You don't know if you're dating her? Or you don't know if I should take her to prom?"

I cleared my throat. "You'll have to ask Riley." I really didn't want him asking Riley anything, but what else could I say?

He gave his usual cocky reply. "I plan to. This weekend." The smarmy tone returned to his voice. "You're coming to my party, right, Just Sam?"

Jeez, he was so sluggable.

Fortunately the lunch lady saved me. "Next!" She waved me forward.

29

RILEY

Convincing Sam to hang with me the next day after school was not as difficult as the first time.

"What's next? Are you giving me a perm?" Sam chided me, but at least he was smirk-smiling when I informed him we'd need to meet again. I even showed him the list I'd prioritized in my notebook.

"Admit it. You're in love with your new hairdo," I said.

"Please don't call it that."

"Guys don't say *hairdo?*"

"This guy doesn't."

I lifted a strand of his black hair and examined it. "Looks ten times better than before. Healthier, too. When was the last time you went to a stylist?"

"No more changes, Berenger. I can't handle any more. I'm serious."

"Never say never," I said. "I never thought you'd wear the body spray."

Instead of catching a ride back to Sam's house with Ryan and Fred, Sam and I took the bus. The ride took forever. It was like crisscrossing the whole state instead of only going ten miles. "Now I remember why I never take public transportation," I told Sam.

Sam turned toward the window. "Lucky you." Then he turned back. "By the way, I saw your new BFF Jay Hawkins in the cafeteria today."

"Jay?" I could barely control myself. He'd gotten into the habit of saving me a seat in homeroom and it had gotten to the point where my heart would race whenever I saw him. I couldn't believe he finally realized I was alive.

"Yeah. You know, Jay Hawkins from the leadership conference. That phony guy with the smart-ass mouth who has mastered the fine art of people manipulation? That guy."

"Stop it, Sam. You're overexaggerating. You need to give him more of a chance. Jay's a nice guy."

"No, he's not. But anyway…"

"But, what?"

"I think he likes you."

I grabbed Sam's forearm. "Really? What did he say?"

"I think you'll find out this weekend at his party."

I heard myself gasp. "Seriously?"

Sam shrugged his shoulders. "I have no idea. But, listen, Riley. The guy's a jerk. Just be careful. Okay?"

I felt my face blush and I had to look away but whether it was from Sam's concern or the fact that Jay had asked about me—again—I wasn't certain. Probably a combination. "Thanks, Sam. That is so sweet." It might also be the nicest thing a boy had ever said to me.

After the bus dropped us off, we had to walk a mile across the desert to reach Sam's house. At least, it seemed like a mile. Better than yesterday or even the day before, but my leg still throbbed the more I walked.

"How are you holding up?" Sam asked me halfway into

the walk. Thankfully he'd offered to carry my messenger bag, otherwise he might have had to leave me for dead next to a saguaro.

"You don't want to know." I pressed a hand against my leg and grimaced.

"You should have gone home after school, Riley. This was stupid."

"No way. Time is ticking. We have much to do. You read my list on the bus. We need to strategize."

"So you've reminded me. But you keep missing the part where I tell you I'm not comfortable with all of this."

I stopped short, my arms slapping against my sides. "Did you happen to notice how Fred looked at you in the cafeteria today?"

Sam stopped, too, but he looked away, pretending to be entranced with a lizard scampering over a rock. I was learning that he employed the look-away trick whenever he knew that I was right. Very convenient.

"I practically had to pick her jaw up off the floor when you walked in! Admit it. My plan is starting to jell."

Sam sighed, one of his long, woe-is-me, tortured ones.

"Enough with the sighing, Sam. I told you it isn't attractive."

He rolled his eyes.

I ignored him. "And when I told her I was going to your house again after school today, I swear I saw her right eyebrow shoot up." I pointed to my eyebrow. "You know, like that." I lifted my brow with my forefinger. "She does that when she's not happy about something."

"Maybe she was just surprised?"

"Pissed, more like it."

"I seriously doubt that, Riley. Anyway, since when do you know Fred so well?"

I brought my hands to my hips. "Are you kidding me? She's over at our house all the time. I have eyes." I paused. "And I'm a pretty good listener, too."

"You?" Sam's eyes widened.

"Darn right."

"Um, Pink Girl, apparently you missed the part when I said I wasn't crazy about your plan. I've said it at least six times. Yet you keep making—" he pointed at my messenger bag "—lists."

My gaze swept over him—the new-and-improved him. His clothes looked better, more styled. His hair looked nicer. Hotter. He was oozing new confidence. No one could convince me that these changes weren't a good thing. It felt good to be part of something big, something that could be special. "Then why did you agree to hang with me today? Something must be working."

He paused as if he had to think really hard about it. "'Cause saying yes to you is a hell of a lot easier than saying no."

Okay, that stung a little. I'd have to analyze that statement later.

Sam started walking again. Looking a little sheepish, his hands stuffed in his front pockets, he said, "So what do they do at your house all the time? You know, Fred and Ryan."

I took a deep breath and then followed after him. "Lots of stuff. Swimming. Watching movies. But most of the time they hang in Ryan's bedroom."

Sam stopped at that little revelation, at least long enough for me to catch up.

"So why am I here today again?" I challenged him. I wanted to hear him tell me that he was going to cooperate. I wanted to see that fight in his eyes. I wanted to know that he would at least try to win Fred's heart. We didn't have much time!

"Yesterday I promised you a ride on Papago. I never break my promises."

Ouch. That hurt. Sam thought he was being clever, playing to my conscience. Trying to make me feel guilty, I'd bet. Well, I never broke my promises, either. I just believed in him. I only wished he'd start to trust me.

30

SAM

Riley had a way of getting me to do things I really didn't want to do, and a part of me admired her for that. No one else had ever succeeded at that, not my buddies, not my parents. Not even Fred, and I'd have crossed the desert barefoot for her, if she'd asked. I was stubborn about change, but when it came to Fred, I was willing to dip my toe in dark waters.

"Do you really need help with chem?" I asked Riley when we reached the road that led to my house. Chemistry tutoring was the reason Riley had given Fred about why she was coming over. Fred had mentioned it to me casually during study hall, but there was nothing casual about it. Riley might be right about Fred's eyebrow. I'd seen it move today, too. Dammit. My life would have been easier if I hadn't.

"I *always* need help with chem, Sam. It's my least favorite subject. In fact, I detest it."

"Why do you take it?"

"My parents make me."

"Why?"

"For some bizarre reason they think I should go into a medical field, even though I hate the sight of blood."

"There's lots of other things you could do with chemistry besides medicine."

She huffed. "Okay, now you sound like my mother."

"But it's true. There's engineering, pharmacy, research—lots of cool things."

"What about art?"

"Art?"

I thought about it but said nothing. She had me there.

"See? My thoughts exactly," she said. "What do you want to do?"

"I'll major in math or science, maybe even both."

"Do you want to go away?"

"Yeah. But I'll come back. I want to come back and help somehow. Teach, maybe. Invent something. Make a discovery that could help someone in our community. I don't know, exactly. Make things better here. Do something that matters."

"Why?"

"If I don't, who will? I mean, those of us that can, should. Not everyone who leaves the Rez comes back. My mom did. She could have gotten a good job in Phoenix or any number of other places, but she didn't. She came back when she didn't have to. I'm pretty proud of her for that. I'm going to come back, too."

"Would you live here?" Riley looked across the barren desert. It was probably the only time she'd heard silence in her entire life.

"Maybe not here. But my heart will always be here." I felt my cheeks darken a little as I shared that morsel. I mean, why the hell was I telling Riley Berenger all this? She wouldn't understand, because she didn't need to. She probably didn't see the beauty that I saw when she looked across the Rez.

She wasn't part of its heartbeat. Her world was different from mine, and I wasn't about to go all cliché and try to explain having one leg on the Rez and the other in the white man's world. She wouldn't understand, and most people who don't usually don't waste time trying to understand those of us that do. I didn't exactly like it, but I'd come to terms with what was long ago. If you didn't, it only drove you bat-shit crazy.

She placed her hand on my forearm, shocking the hell out of me. "Thanks for telling me, Sam. You know, I envy you."

I pulled back. "You envy me?"

"Yeah. You're so sure about everything. The big stuff. The important stuff. I think that's cool."

"You're not?"

"My focus is on you and Fred, and maybe when I'm getting my car. You're focusing on changing the world. I'd say we're different."

That surprised me. I searched her face to see if she was joking, to see if there was the slightest chance she was mocking me. She wasn't. Then she said in a softer voice, "What about Fred?"

"What about her?" Wait. What was the question?

"Does she feel the same way you do about, you know, coming back after college and making a difference?"

"She used to feel the same way," I said.

"Not anymore?"

"I'm not sure. We don't talk like we used to, thanks to your brother."

The crazy glint returned to Riley's eyes. The one that I'd become used to whenever our conversations returned to her misdirected, diabolical plan. Her hand dropped from my arm. "All the more reason to get you two back together—"

I put up a palm, stopping her. "Riley… Fred and I were never officially together. Only in my head."

"Sa-a-am…" She stretched out my name, mimicking my tone. "Just trust me. I know what I'm doing. I mean, come on, it's already working!"

I let loose a long sigh.

"What did I tell you about the heavy sighing?"

I dropped Riley's bag and my backpack onto a chair beneath a paloverde tree next to our house. "When's your brother picking you up?"

She pulled her cell phone from her pocket and looked at it. "We have an hour and a half."

"Ride, first?" I was anxious to change topics.

Riley's face lit up. "Definitely."

I'd be lying if I said I didn't like Riley's smile, maybe even liked to be the one who could make her smile. Her smile was sweet and crazy and maybe even a little sexy all at the same time, kind of like a firecracker. I usually didn't care for perfect white teeth, but on Riley, perfection just worked. Quickly, I looked across the yard at the front door. "I'll grab a couple of Cokes and then saddle up Papago."

"I'll go say hello to your grandmother."

After I got Papago saddled, I led her outside the barn and looked for Riley.

She was leaning back on her knees at Grandmother's feet as Grandmother wove her latest creation in her favorite chair in the afternoon shade alongside the house. Amazingly, Grandmother's mouth was moving. Riley's mouth was moving even faster, which wasn't surprising. What was surprising was Grandmother talking at all. She would never exactly earn any medals as a conversationalist. Sometimes she'd go entire days without saying a single word. Maybe Riley *could* work miracles.

"Hey, let's go!" I called to her. "Papago's getting anxious."

Riley stood, touched Grandmother's hand and trotted across the yard, still limping a little on that right leg.

"What were you two talking about?" I said.

"I was asking her about the materials she was using. Then I asked her if she'd mind if I sketched one of her baskets sometime."

"What'd she say?"

"She said yes."

"Seriously?" Papago let lose a whinny. Some of Grandmother's geometric designs dated back generations. She was usually pretty protective of them.

"Then I told her how awesome you were at school," Riley added.

"What'd she say to that?"

"She said I was welcome back here anytime."

I shook my head. "Riley Berenger. Charming her way across the Rez."

Riley pressed a hand to the base of her neck. "What can I say? It's a gift."

I chuckled. Then I stood by the saddle. I bent over and motioned for Riley to step into my curled fingers. "Come on. Hop on."

For the next hour, Riley didn't stop talking as she rode Papago over the wide-open desert that surrounded our house. I walked alongside, holding the reins, as we wove between sagebrush and up and down dry river washes. Riley rattled off at least a dozen ways she wanted to get Fred and me together, some during school, some right here on the Rez. Then we spent thirty minutes playing chess, and she still kept talking. And she won after only six moves. In my defense, it was impossible to concentrate. By the time Ryan pulled into our yard with his Jeep, my head hurt.

There was no way this could work. Could it?

★ ★ ★

Thursday night after dinner, I walked the two miles from my parents' house to the Odays' trailer. I needed to see Fred's brother, Trevor, and I really hoped—no, I begged and prayed to the Creator, my ancestors and all of the animal spirits and anyone else listening—that Fred was off somewhere with Ryan, as much as that would pain Riley.

Riley had been doing everything she could all week to make sure that Fred's path crossed with mine. On Tuesday, she'd left us both notes on our lockers asking us to meet in the cafeteria, and then made a cheesy excuse about leaving early for a meeting with Mr. Romero. On Wednesday, she'd purposely not given Fred a message from Ryan saying he had to leave school early and couldn't take her home but pressed Ryan's note into my palm instead. When I'd seen Fred waiting in the parking lot for Ryan, I waited with her until it was painfully obvious he wouldn't show and suggested we take the bus home.

It was the first time since Fred had begun dating Ryan that Fred and I had to take the bus home together. It was an hour ride, but it was better than hitchhiking. I'd spent half the ride back to the Rez pretending to read my world history notes for Friday's exam and trying to forget that Fred's arm and leg were within an inch of mine.

The last time I'd been at Fred's house, I'd kissed her on her doorstep. I thought I saw stars when our lips touched. Now, kissing Fred seemed like a lifetime ago. Unfortunately she hadn't kissed me back, not like she meant it, not like the kind of kiss that could lead to more, and that probably explained why my stomach tightened the closer I walked to her trailer. Nothing like reliving rejection, up close and personal.

When I reached the Odays' on Thursday night, two black Labs greeted me at the end of the dirt road that wound its way between the sagebrush to the trailer. Their wet snouts nuzzled both of my palms as they escorted me the rest of the way.

Like all of the homes and trailers on the Rez, the Odays' place was surrounded by acres of sage, saguaros and brown dirt. The closest neighbor was a mile away. A paloverde tree towered over the front of the trailer, brushing its leafy branches against the metal roof every time the wind blew, and blocking what remained of the sun. In the carport next to the trailer, two long skinny legs stuck out from underneath the front of Mr. Oday's van.

I smiled. Trevor. He usually worked nights at the Rez gas station alongside the freeway, but tonight he was home. I figured it to be a sign. I didn't ask about Fred, even if Trevor already guessed the question lurked in the back of my mind like a memory I couldn't erase.

"Hey!" I called out, my voice echoing across the front yard.

Trevor slid out from underneath the van on a piece of dusty cardboard. "Dude!" He stood to greet me. "'Sup?" Before he shook my hand, he wiped his own on the front of his jeans, not that it mattered. Trevor's hands and fingernails were permanently stained from oil and grease. He tinkered with everyone's trucks and cars when he wasn't working on his own.

"Need to talk to you," I said.

"Is our phone disconnected again?" Trevor tossed his braid behind his shoulder. If he noticed my shorter hair, he didn't say.

"Works fine," I said. "Just needed to talk in person."

"You mean, not in front of your parents."

I nodded. Bingo. I wasn't sure my mom would be too pleased with what I wanted to ask him.

"Your old man's still at the casino, right?"

"Where else?" Most of our parents worked at the casino in some capacity.

Trevor motioned to two plastic white chairs underneath the paloverde tree. "Thirsty?"

"Yeah." I reached for my throat like I was one step away from dying. "Just crossed the freaking desert to get here, didn't I?" I ran my fingers through my hair, lifting it off my hot scalp.

Trevor laughed. "Back in a minute," he said as I plopped down in one of the chairs, the two Labs sitting on either side of me.

Alone beneath the tree, I fidgeted in my too-small chair, even though I had been to the Odays' a million times in my life. It was hard not to wonder if Fred was inside. I sighed, loud enough for one of the Labs to raise his snout and look up at me with curious eyes. "Yeah, I know. I need to get a life," I said.

Trevor returned with two Cokes. As he trotted down the stoop that led to the front door, he tossed me a can.

I caught it and cracked open the tab. "Thanks," I said, after a generous sip. "I needed that." The can tingled inside my fingers.

"So what brings you way out here?"

"I need a favor."

Trevor leaned closer. "Lay it on me, brother."

"I need to buy a car." I knew Riley would be pleased, maybe even think I was doing it because of her, but this had nothing to do with her and everything to do with me. I needed my own ride. Bad.

Trevor cleared his throat. "Okay," he said slowly. His eyes began to blink rapidly, considering it. "How much you willing to spend?"

"I got a couple hundred, saved. Maybe three..." I let my voice trail off as I watched Trevor wince.

"That won't buy much."

"Yeah, but I figured if anyone knew who was selling, or if there was anyone on the Rez with a good deal, you'd know."

"A good running car for three Benjamins? That wouldn't last too long."

"Yeah, but you'd tell me, right? You could hook me up?"

"I'll keep an eye out for you."

I slumped back against the chair. That didn't sound promising. I took another long sip from my can. From inside the trailer, I heard the clinking of dishes. The yellow curtain covering the kitchen window fluttered. My foot started to twitch.

Trevor's voice lowered. "Relax, bro. She ain't home."

I swallowed. I wasn't sure if that made me feel better or worse. I knew that Trevor wasn't crazy about Ryan Berenger, either, but it was hard to hate the guy, especially after what he'd done for Mr. Oday when he'd had his heart attack. If it hadn't been for Ryan, Mr. Oday might have died— I shuddered at the thought. Mr. Oday was good people. He was like a second father to me. He talked to me more than my own dad did.

Trevor took another long pull from his can, studying me. "Tell you what. I may have something you'd be interested in…."

I leaned forward, almost dropping my can, as the condensation dripped through my fingers. "What? Tell me. I'm game for anything."

Trevor's head tilted. "Anything?"

"Yeah. Anything."

Trevor stood, wriggled his eyebrows at me and then jogged toward the carport.

I followed after him, along with the two dogs.

He walked to the rear of the carport, past the Odays' mostly rusted van, back where the rays from the setting sun didn't reach. Trevor pulled the cord on a lightbulb above us. It swung like a pendulum, casting a muted glow over a blue sheet covering a bulky object in front of the van.

Trevor yanked off the sheet. "How about this?"

My eyes about popped out of my head. I almost began to hyperventilate. Speaking became difficult. "Your motorcycle?" I finally croaked out the words. I loved this bike. Trevor had even let me ride it a few times around the Rez in the past. "But...uh..." I stammered. "I don't have my motorcycle license. Yet. And what'll you drive?"

"I got another bike. Don't fret. This is my backup." Trevor was always tinkering with something—the old red Cadillac next to the carport, motorcycles, even bicycles.

I approached the motorcycle, my hands extended but touching nothing. It was like approaching something priceless and unattainable. Sure it was dusty and the wheels were caked with dirt. But the black leather seat stretched the length of the bike and it could haul ass.

"A 1995 Honda Shadow. The leather side-bags are original." He patted the seat. "You've ridden her before. But are you interested in buying her?"

Words continued to elude me. "Yeah..." I blurted finally. How could I refuse? "But how much?"

"You can have her for one-fifty."

"No way." Trevor had to be joking. "But it's worth ten times that!"

Trevor nodded, still grinning. Then he folded his arms, watching my eyes sweep over the motorcycle like it was beyond my reach. "Hey, I know what it's like to want wheels. And my dad driving you to school every day?" He grimaced. "Dude, that's lame."

I exhaled in continued disbelief. Staring back at the bike, I felt as if my whole body was about to float into the air. "You have no idea."

He chortled. "Oh, but I do. I remember all too well. A dude's gotta have his own wheels. Period."

"Funny, that's what a friend of mine keeps telling me."

"Dude gotta name?"

I wasn't about to tell Trevor that the dude was Riley Berenger, although I wasn't sure she'd had a motorcycle in mind when she suggested it. "No one you know," I said. "Just a friend."

Trevor smirked. "Uh-huh. You got a girlfriend now, don't you?" His eyebrow arched.

"No!" I said. "Well, yes. I mean, no. Well, kind of."

Trevor chuckled, his arms across his chest. "Which it is?"

I looked straight back at him and sighed. "To tell you the truth, I have no idea. All I can tell you is this girl confuses the hell out of me."

Trevor patted me on the shoulder, still laughing. "S'okay, Sam. Take it easy. Girls have a way of doing that to us."

I looked back at the bike and my stomach sank again. "But I don't have the money on me." I couldn't peel my gaze away from the bike. I thought that if I didn't keep staring at it, my future would disappear into thin air.

Trevor raised his palm. "Don't worry about the money tonight. Give it to me whenever."

"For real?"

"It's yours. Take it!"

"I really don't know what to say." I shook my head, breathing hard. It was the most beautiful moment in my whole life. Finally, my own wheels. I felt ten feet tall.

"Don't say anything. Just jump on her and ride. Just like I've showed you." He reached around to a metal shelf in the corner, grabbed a black helmet and tossed it at me.

I caught it in one hand, cradling it.

He grinned. "At least now I don't have to give you a ride home."

A smile stretched across my face that could wrap clear around my head and back again.

The key was already in the ignition, a white rabbit's foot dangling from the ring. Trevor turned it. He grabbed the bike by the clutch lever and shifted it into Neutral as he kicked the stand sideways. Then he pushed the bike from beneath the carport. He'd let me ride his bike lots of times in the past. The first time was when I was fourteen. I'd made circles in the desert and driven down dirt roads, but I had never taken it off the Rez.

"Jump on." He moved to the side, and I reached for the levers. "Feels familiar, right?" His grin widened.

Familiar? I grinned back. The bike fit me like a glove. I put the helmet on the ground and then swung my leg over the seat, sinking into the leather. I twisted the throttle and let the engine growl a little louder. It was the most beautiful sound in the world. The sound of freedom.

"Pretty sweet ride, ain't she?" Trevor said over the engine.

Sweet didn't exactly describe it. Heaven? Winning the lottery? Nothing was better than this bike, my hands getting reacquainted with the levers like they were old friends. I didn't know what to say. I'd walked over to the Odays' simply to talk to Trevor. I hadn't expected to leave with a rockin' motorcycle! I knew my mother would be all sorts of crazy when she saw it, but I was too stunned, too elated, to care. Dad? He'd hardly notice.

Trevor looked down at the gas gauge. "She's gonna need some gas soon. Only got a quarter of a tank. Come by the station tomorrow. I'll even give her a bath for you."

"I'll bring your money, too."

"No rush. Just take good care of her, okay?"

I nodded. I wanted to hug the guy, but of course, I didn't.

"Chicks always dig guys who ride," Trevor said, his arms crossed over his chest again. "Remember that, Sam."

I felt heat rush up my neck and I was thankful that the sky was almost black. "I'm just glad I can get myself to school."

Trevor smirked, like he didn't quite believe that was my real reason for wanting the bike.

"Seriously, dude," I said. "I'll take care of her. Promise." I scooped the helmet off the ground.

"Oh, I know you will. Got no doubts on that." He moved to the side so that I could idle the bike to the dirt path that led away from the trailer. But then he reached for the right lever, stopping me. "Hey, you want to wait around for Fred?" His tone was equal parts hopeful and doubtful. "Still early."

"Nah," I said, feeling all fidgety again. "Better get home. I got homework to do."

Trevor's nose wrinkled. He didn't believe me, either. But he lifted his hand and waved me away, anyway.

Homework? *Seriously?* I wanted to ride all the way to Tucson and back on my brand-new bike. I wanted to fly.

Just when you didn't think the universe could be any crueler, it threw you a bone.

Trevor's nose wrinkled again but this time he lifted his chin and sniffed the air. Over the engine he yelled, "Hey, dude. Wait. Are you...wearing perfume?"

I shook my head and exhaled. "Don't ask."

And then I sped away.

31

RILEY

As I waited for Drew to pick me up for Jay Hawkins's party on Friday night, the phone rang throughout the house.

"Hello?"

"Hey, Riley." It was Fred. "Ryan around?"

I pulled my shoulders back, steadying my resolve. Then I swallowed. "No," I lied. Ryan was in the shower. I swear he took longer showers than I did. "Isn't he at your house?" I added. The one thing about lying is that it gets easier the more you do it. And I'd been doing my fair share lately. Nothing major—just a little fib here and there to get Sam and Fred in the same hemisphere and see if nature could take its course. I thought I'd seen Fred weakening a couple of times this week, especially when she'd looked at Sam as if she were seeing him for the first time, now that he dressed like he cared. Now that his face wasn't hidden by waves of uncombed hair. And it wasn't just my imagination that he was looking more confident, too.

"Ryan was supposed to call me," Fred said. "At least, I thought he said he would." Good thing Fred didn't have a cell phone, either, or getting Fred and Sam together would be just about impossible.

"Were you going to Jay's party tonight?" It really wasn't a question, because who in their right mind wasn't going?

"I was planning to. With Ryan," Fred said. "But he was supposed to have called by now."

"Huh," I said. "That's odd. At dinner Ryan mentioned something about going out tonight with a bunch of people to the movies. Something about a new action flick." I paused to run my tongue across my dry lips, ignoring the bitter taste that came with distorting the truth. "But you should totally still come to Jay's party. Everybody will be there. Why don't you catch a ride into Phoenix with Sam?"

"Really?" Fred said, glossing over my suggestion. "Ryan didn't mention the movie to me."

"That's what he said. But you could still come to the party with Sam, right? Maybe you could catch up with Ryan afterward?"

Fred hesitated and I held my breath, waiting for her answer. "Maybe." Then she said, "You're sure Ryan's going to the movies?" It was hard to ignore the hurt in her voice.

"That's what he said at dinner." I maintained my innocent tone. "You want me to have him call you?"

"Yes, please. Thanks, Riley."

"So, I'll see you at the party? Everyone's gonna be there."

"Yes. If I can catch a ride."

Drew texted me: Im outside. "Well, gotta go. Drew's here. See you later."

"Later, Riley."

Click.

I returned the phone to the cradle and started humming. Being someone I wasn't was becoming way too easy. Maybe this new Riley was the person I was meant to be? I grabbed my purse and the overnight bag that I had laid at the foot of the staircase and skipped outside the door and into a Friday night full of possibilities. "'Bye!" I yelled into the house before I slammed the door. Mom yelled something from the kitchen but I was already gone.

"Love the outfit!" Drew called from the driver's window.

"Thanks!" I said, managing a spin near the hood of her car, careful not to reinjure my right leg. It barely throbbed today. The only pink I wore was a thin strip on my belt, which I thought gave my outfit a cool, retro look. The rest was black. Black sleeveless tee, black jeans. I'd even painted my fingernails black.

"New shoes?"

I reached for the door handle? "You like?" They were black-and-white-checkered Converse. Very Gwen Stefani.

"Love," Drew said.

"Good," I said, shutting the door. "But I brought another pair in my bag, just in case you hated these."

"Jeez, Riley. I don't know what's gotten into you, but you should definitely bottle it. You're positively glowing."

We assessed each other's makeup and clothes as we drove to Jay's house with the windows down, radio blaring. My fingers tapped against the armrest and my pulse raced the closer we got to the party. We were going to have an epic time. I could just feel it. I was part of the energy now, the hip part that everyone envied on Monday morning. And the fact that Jay's parents were on a cruise somewhere on the other side of the world was the true pink icing on the cake.

Jay lived in the foothills at the end of Pecos Road, the dividing line between south Phoenix and the Gila River Indian Reservation. His house snaked up the side of South Mountain along with a few dozen others. The neighborhood wasn't as cramped as mine and the homes were even bigger. It was as close to being in the middle of the desert as I'd ever been, other than that time when Ryan and I had raced across the reservation to stop Seth Winter from running over Fred with his pickup last year. That was crazy scary.

When we reached Jay's street, cars and trucks dotted both sides from beginning to end. I thought we'd have to park on another street, maybe even at the end of Pecos Road. But Drew reached inside her purse and pulled out a vodka bottle, surprising me, as she wove her tiny car down the crowded street. She took a sip and said, "Fear not. I know a secret spot." Then she handed the half-empty bottle to me as if we shared alcohol all the time. Tonight was full of firsts.

I tried to pretend I knew what to do with it, but the bottle felt strange in my hands. I didn't want to be left out so I took a sip, just a small one. "Where?" I said. A handprint could measure the space between any of the parked cars. "I didn't know you were so friendly with Jay. Since when?"

Drew chuckled before taking another swig and shrugged her shoulders. "Here and there."

"And you never thought to mention it to me?" My voice grew louder but then she cranked up the radio another notch, blaring a rap song, before she pressed the accelerator as the car climbed up South Mountain. At the end of the street in the middle of a cul-de-sac, a two-story house was set deep into the side of the mountain. Lights brightened every window and at least ten cars covered the driveway like checkers on a board. I could hear music pounding from inside Jay's house over the car stereo.

I stared up at Jay's house. It wasn't the outside that fascinated me but what waited inside. Two weeks ago, I would never have imagined being a part of this. I would only have heard about it with all the other losers on Monday morning who weren't invited. In a way, I should be thanking Sam Tracy and my tumble down the Mogollon Rim.

Drew handed me the vodka bottle and I chugged back a long sip. This time, the burn lasted only a second.

Then, somehow, Drew maneuvered her car along one edge of the driveway, almost taking out the Hawkins's mailbox before parking on a thin strip of asphalt next to the garage meant for garbage cans. She turned off the ignition so that all we could hear was a thumping bass from somewhere inside Jay's house.

Surprise must have still filled my face as I looked back at Drew because she said, "What?" Her eyes were shiny. "What can I say? I've got parking karma." She paused to drink from the now almost-empty vodka bottle. "And I've been here before. Lots of times," she added, almost as an afterthought and almost as if she were letting me in on a big important secret, which she basically was. She capped the bottle, stuffed it inside a brown paper bag and then tossed it behind her seat.

I gaped at her. "How come you never told me?" Especially since she knew I had a crush on Jay. "And since when do you carry alcohol in your car?"

She ignored my second question. "Jay and I had the same babysitter when we were kids. Our parents have been friends forever. It's not like we hang out, though."

"Have you got a thing for him?"

"God, no. He's all yours," Drew said. "Jay's like a brother." She checked her bangs in the rearview. "Speaking of brothers, yours will be here, right?"

"Maybe."

"Just maybe?"

"Maybe, but I really hope not. I'm hoping Sam will come tonight with Fred."

"How's the matchmaking going?"

"Slowly. But surely."

"What if Ryan sees Fred with Sam and gets jealous or something?"

"That could be bad." *Really horribly tragically bad, but, oh, so good for Sam.* My vodka lips sputtered. "Do me a huge favor?"

"Anything."

"If my brother shows up, keep him occupied? Any way you can. This could be your chance, too—you know, with getting my brother." I shouldn't have said that but it was too late to take it back.

Drew looked like she could bust out of the car. "Absolutely."

"He was asking about you today," I blurted. I knew that was a lie, too, even as I said it but I was on a roll.

She grabbed my arm. "Ryan?" Her eyes widened another notch. "What'd he say? Tell me! Don't leave out a single word."

I cleared my throat. "He just asked what you were doing tonight." In truth, he asked what *we* were doing so it wasn't like a complete and total lie. Only a little selective pronoun placement.

She squeezed my arm. "And what'd you say?"

"I may have said we'd be here." That was another white lie. Ryan didn't know I was invited. If I'd told him I was, he would have told Mom, and then Mom would have insisted on picking me up from the party and there was no way I could survive the humiliation of that. Your parents waiting to pick you up outside a cool party? I think not. What I did tell my brother was that I was spending the night at Drew's. That was all.

Drew's expression was hopeful. "Oh, my god. I totally hope he's here already."

I smiled at her. I really needed her to shower Ryan with attention, especially when Sam showed up with Fred. In Drew's defense, my brother did like her. He thought she was really sweet. But he thought kittens and rabbits were sweet, too. That Drew was my best friend did not work in her favor. I didn't have the heart to tell her all that. But, who knew what could happen when you threw people together. People could surprise you.

"Let's go!"

My head was buzzing with excitement and alcohol as we walked across the driveway to the front door. I recognized guys from the varsity football team, a few girls from the junior cheer squad, even a senior girl from dance club, who nodded at me with approval as we passed through the front door. I tried to look disinterested, like I frequented these parties all the time, but my cheeks tightened from holding back a huge smile. Plus I was biting down on the inside of my cheek.

Inside, the house was crawling with kids from school. If I didn't know their names, I most definitely knew their faces. And they weren't the faces I was used to seeing, either.

Music blasted through speakers in every corner of the room. The ear-bleeding levels only added to the excitement. From the looks of the place, I wasn't the only person pumped to be at the party. Drew dropped my arm and wove her way directly to the counter, leaving me at the edge of the room. I bumped someone's shoulder everywhere I turned but no one cared. I smiled to a few of them and head nodded to the music.

I stood on tiptoe, looking toward the kitchen for Drew, when someone dropped a heavy arm across my shoulder.

"Wow!" The voice was clear but faint.

I turned.

"Jay!" I yelled over the music, relieved. My whole body

warmed at the mere sight of his face. He had perfect boy lips. Completely kissable.

He leaned those lips down to my ear. His breath was hot, his words slurred. "Glad you made it, Mountain Girl. You come with Just Sam?"

I pulled back. "Sam? You mean, Sam Tracy?"

"Yeah. Just Sam." His grin turned mischievous.

"No. I came with Drew."

"Awesome." Then his eyes traveled the length of me. "Been waiting for you to get here!" He fingered one of my pink highlights between his fingers.

My skin flushed all the way up to the tips of my ears. Jay was always saying the nicest things. This morning at my locker he told me he liked my tee. "I didn't know you and Drew grew up together," I said but I wasn't sure if he heard me. Someone raised the music volume another thousand decibels.

Jay leaned down, his head bobbing. But his eyes smiled at me, along with the rest of him. Then without even asking me, he placed his wet lips over mine, startling me. I tasted cigarette smoke and beer. It wasn't what I expected.

It wasn't anything like Sam's kiss.

But I wanted Jay to kiss me, didn't I? I'd been thinking about what it would be like to be with Jay Hawkins since freshman year.

When he pulled back, he pressed his hot forehead against mine. "Been wanting to do that for a while. Got carried away. Sorry," he added, although he didn't sound sorry. He looked at my lips for more.

"Really?" I was barely breathing, barely able to speak, my eyes bouncing between his eyes and his lips, wanting to try it again. Maybe we just needed more practice....

"Really. I've been watching you, Berenger. How come we didn't hook up a long time ago?"

Because you never noticed I was alive till now. "I don't know."

"There's something special about you."

Jay Hawkins thinks I'm special? I was too stunned, too happy, too excited—too everything—to do anything except reach up and put my hand on his shoulder.

"I'm not letting you out of my sight tonight. You've been warned." His forehead pressed harder against mine. "You're mine."

My breathing stopped. "I'm not going anywhere." I closed my eyes, leaning into him. I'd waited forever to have this moment.

"You better not." Jay pulled my belt loops till our hip bones pressed together. The next thing I knew, his tongue was teasing my tonsils.

People around us began to clap, loud and steady, like we were about to start a race or something. We were the center of attention. We were the center of everything. It was as if the whole world had landed in my lap. Through my eyelids, as Jay's tongue made itself at home inside my mouth, flashes popped.

Only Drew's tap on Jay's shoulder, motioning with two red cups in her hands, broke us apart. A knowing grin spread across her face as clear liquid spilled from the cups. I was seeing a whole new side of Drew, but then, I supposed she was probably thinking the same about me.

I took one of the cups and chugged it, adrenaline pushing through my veins from the music, the kiss, the drink. The energy in the room. The possibilities.

More flashes and clicks.

My head spun long after the taste from Jay's lips left mine.

After Jay passed me my third drink, I forgot to keep look-ing around the hazy room for Sam and Fred. But mostly for Sam.

32

SAM

I rode my motorcycle out to the Estrella foothills to the usual Friday-night party spot on the Rez.

For once I was glad that it took forever to reach it. The cool night air brushed against my face and through my hair as I flew down the road, listening to the reliable engine roar, making me feel alive. Truth? I could ride all night. I'd already put two hundred miles and three tanks of gas into my new ride since buying it from Trevor. In the dark, racing head-first into the wind, anything was possible.

Martin, Peter and a handful of our friends were already seated around a campfire with flat rocks for chairs in front of a boulder that glowed coppery-orange from the campfire's flames, miles from anywhere. The sagebrush barely curved in the wind as I coasted the bike off the dirt road and parked next to a pickup truck with its passenger door open. Music spilled from inside the truck, but the desert swallowed most of the noise before much of it reached the party around the campfire.

"Dude!" Martin yelled as I approached the group, jovial as

always, a shiny can in his hand and a smile stretched across his face. I wasn't sure I'd ever seen Martin in a bad mood and if anyone had a right to a bad mood, it was him.

People with their backs to me turned and nodded, but their faces were mostly shadowed. They didn't gawk at me like kids did at school. I'd had enough gawking since the Saturday Night Rescue Debacle to last me a lifetime. To my friends, I was just another guy on the Rez.

"Glad you could make it!" Martin added, tossing a silver can at me.

I nodded, catching the cold can in my right hand. Before I sat down on one of the rock seats around the fire, I pulled back the tab and enjoyed a long fizzy sip with my eyes closed. The first sip was always the best. It tasted good going down.

"Have a seat. Stay awhile," Peter chimed in.

My eyes opened and I frowned at him. "Where else am I gonna go?" I looked around the circle at all of the familiar faces, almost twelve in all. I saw them every weekend but there was one face that stopped my breathing, one that I hadn't expected.

Fred? What was she doing here?

Even though my lips didn't say the words, I was certain my eyes said, *Where is Berenger? Why isn't his arm sewn to her shoulders?* Not that they ever partied with us. These days, Fred usually spent her Friday nights on the other side of Pecos Road.

I shot a questioning look at Martin but he only responded with a discreet shoulder shrug.

"Hey. Fred." It was an effort to push out a greeting. I nodded at her as fake casually as I could. Seniors Kelly Oliver and Yolanda Studi sat on either side of her. Yolanda's lips didn't stop moving.

Uh-oh.

Something was up. Kelly and Yolanda always rallied around

Fred when something was wrong. They treated her like a little sister. Seriously, those two girls kind of scared me, Yolanda especially. She was like the short fuse that you never knew when it would blow.

Suddenly my cool, happy vibe shriveled and my heart began to hammer against my chest. And it had nothing to do with Kelly and fireplug Yolanda.

"Sam," Fred said from across the fire in that soft, sweet voice of hers. The one that used to reduce me to a puddle. She smiled at me in the firelight, pulling her knees into her chest. Six months ago and I would have been rendered speechless by that smile. Now? Oddly, I didn't feel that same pull at my heart.

I nodded at her again and chugged another sip from my can.

Fred's eyes sparkled, but there was something hidden behind her smile. I could tell she was uncomfortable by the way her forehead lowered and tilted to the side, her hair falling across her shoulder. Sitting around a fire in the middle of the desert shooting the shit with a bunch of mostly guys drinking beer wasn't exactly her scene. It never had been, even before Ryan Berenger invaded our lives.

Martin broke my trance. "We thought maybe you'd take off for Mexico or someplace on your new wheels," he said, nodding at my bike.

"Huh?" I said numbly.

"I said, why don't you take a road trip?"

I coughed, trying to regain some composure. "Don't tempt me," I said, staring up at an inky black sky that stretched forever in every direction—staring anywhere but into Fred Oday's eyes. They were like truth serum.

"What's stopping you?" Martin said.

"The bike doesn't run on your hot air," I said. "I got a shift tomorrow night. You know how the chef gets when you blow off work." I had to start replenishing my already depleted bank account. After paying Trevor for the bike, I was pretty close to broke and I hated asking my parents for money. Then there were all the demands from Riley about new shoes, new jeans, new everything—most of which I had to ignore. Mom usually gave me cash whenever I needed a little—and never in front of Dad—but I knew things were tight.

Martin's chin pulled back. "Tell me about it. That chef is a real piece of some serious messed-up work." Martin didn't show up once for a weekend shift of bussing tables and the chef had blacklisted him from returning for two months, for which Martin nicknamed him the Chef Nazi. Bussing tables at the Wild Horse Restaurant paid pretty well, and for reasons many of us didn't understand, people came from all over the state, even the world, to eat the chef's Native fare and pay seventy-five dollars for an entrée in the middle of the freaking desert. But, hey. No one complained. It was a good job. It was good for our tribe.

"Dudes," Vernon said, tilting his cell phone high into the air like he was trying to communicate with a satellite. His skinny arm stretched up into the sky.

We all turned to him. Even Fred sat higher. "What up?" I said, noticing that my palms had turned sweaty and it had nothing to do with Vernon's mysterious text message. Even Yolanda's jaw stopped flapping.

"Buddy of mine just forwarded me a text from someone."

"That's fascinating," Martin said and laugher floated around the circle.

Vernon turned to Martin and frowned. "There's a house party in Phoenix tonight. Just south of Pecos Road." Vernon returned to his phone. "Man, there's got to be at least a hundred people on this text. Probably more. This one's gonna be *Project X huge*."

I didn't dare mention that I'd already heard about it from Riley. She'd begged me to meet her there. I still felt guilty for not showing, but she knew how I felt about Hawkins.

Martin sat higher on his rock. "Really? Who's throwing?"

"Doesn't say. Just says to go to the end of Pecos and follow the music." Vernon looked around the group, a smile spreading across his face. "Could be bitchin'. Game?"

Fred sank back, her arms still wrapped around her knees.

Martin pressed his hand to his chest. "What? And leave this lap of luxury?"

"Check it out," Vernon said, passing his phone to Martin. "People look pretty wasted already."

Martin smiled at the phone as his thumb scrolled through some pictures. "Jeez, no kidding." He passed the phone to Peter. Peter passed it to Fred.

Then Fred's jaw dropped. She exhaled, shaking her head. Yolanda and Kelly looked over her shoulder.

"Son of a bitch!" Yolanda said, loud and clear.

Fred just shook her head at Yolanda and then leaned forward and offered me the phone.

"Hey, isn't this your girlfriend?" Peter said.

I leaned forward to take the phone from Fred. "Yeah, that's Riley." But seeing her sucking face with Jay Hawkins made it even worse. I warned her about him but she obviously hadn't listened. My stomach tightened, looking at his hands on her.

"I take it you're not a fan of Jay Hawkins?" I said to Yolanda. At least we could agree on that.

"I'm not a fan of Ryan Berenger," she said with an irritated eye roll. "Especially not tonight."

Puzzled, I scrolled through the photos, expecting more of Riley and Jay Hawkins but my thumb stopped on a photo of

Mr. Perfect Ryan Berenger himself. He was seated between two pretty girls. One of them was Riley's friend, Drew. Slanty wasted eyes. Or maybe it was the camera flash? Ryan's arms were draped across their shoulders.

"Oh," I said to no one in particular. This must be the photo that had Yolanda breathing fire and spitting nails. I could almost feel sorry for Ryan. Almost. If there was one thing that most of the Rez kids knew, it was never to get between Yolanda and whatever pissed her off. You never wanted to get on her bad side. She could let fly expletives better than most guys I knew.

"Okay, Sam. Whatever you say," Martin chimed in. He knew the photo of Riley and Hawkins together was bothering me more than I let on, even more than the photo of Ryan, but Martin also knew I detested Hawkins.

My whole body clenched. "You say another word and I swear I'll toss you into this fire." I didn't know which photo to fixate on—both captured in color and no doubt being loaded onto Instagram and Facebook pages everywhere. I should have been more sympathetic, especially toward Fred, but it was hard not to say "I told you so." With guys like Ryan Berenger, this was bound to happen. He'd obviously grown bored of Fred. Riley was right.

Martin pulled back, laughing. "Chill, bro. Just messing with you."

"Yeah, I know what you're doing." I glared at him as he air-chuckled, obviously spurring more curiosity among the others. "Stop it."

More teasing. "I thought you and Riley were tight."

"Stop. It." My teeth clenched. Anger stormed through my veins. I was exploding inside in a dozen directions.

"I think your new haircut has done something to your brain." More laughter.

"Shut up," I said, but even I couldn't help but chuckle a little at that. Martin had been teasing me all week about the new way I tucked and untucked my shirts, the way I combed my hair. He could still smell Riley's body spray—which I'd decided to keep using, for reasons yet unknown to me—but I just told him Mom bought a new brand of soap.

Martin stood, twirling his keys around his fingers, completely ignoring me. "Who's with me? Let's go crash this bad boy and join the fun."

"Your truck wouldn't make it to the freeway," I said.

Martin spun around, his expression hardening in the glow of the campfire. "Don't knock the ride."

Peter stood. Then Vernon and two others.

Even Fred stood.

Hey, if she wanted to go to some stupid party, let her. Let her see with her own eyes that her precious boyfriend had no problem chilling with other women when she wasn't available.

I drained the rest of my can.

"Sure you don't want to come with us?" Peter said.

"Positive," I said before reaching over to stoke the fire.

"Good," Fred said, the firelight dancing in her eyes. "Because I need to talk to you." The way she said it left nothing open to debate.

My breath froze, but whether it was from the request or the way her gaze gripped mine, I didn't know.

"Now," she said.

I still didn't answer. I was too stunned to say anything.

And then in a softer voice, she begged, "Please."

I didn't stand a chance.

Everyone except Fred and me loaded into one of the three pickups and two dusty cars parked next to my bike. A dozen Rez kids would stand out at a party across Pecos Road like rain on a sunny day, but if enough people from school crashed it, maybe it would be cool.

Fred stood looking at me from across the campfire as if I were the only person on the planet, just like she had on Monday in the cafeteria. Her hands were balled up and stuffed in the front pockets of her shorts. The last of the vehicles chugged to life and caravanned back to the main road. A light breeze lifted the ends of her hair, the fringe on her shorts, and brought a whiff of her shampoo to my nose.

"Why are you here?" I said.

"Same as you." Her shoulders shrugged. "To relax with friends. I know that I don't hang out with you guys often enough…." Her voice trailed off.

"Save it, Fred." I lifted my palm. "Why aren't you with Ryan tonight?"

"Riley said he was out with friends. The movies, or something." Her voice caught a little. "Obviously that wasn't true."

My tongue thickened. *Riley.* "You shouldn't believe everything Riley says."

"Why not?"

"'Cause. You just shouldn't," I said, wondering how much to tell her. What could I tell her that wouldn't make me sound like the World's Biggest Idiot? I was just as guilty as Riley. Guilt flooded my conscience.

"Riley said I should have gone to the party with you."

"Would you have wanted to?"

Fred didn't answer, though not answering didn't give me the kick to the gut that I expected. Instead, in a soft voice, almost a whisper, she said, "Did he happen to say anything to you?"

"Who?"

"Ryan."

Okay, now I was confused. "Why would Ryan say anything to me?"

Another shoulder shrug. "Oh, I don't know. Maybe something in passing. Something during school. Maybe in chem class?"

"Like what, Fred?"

She steadied herself. "Like…why he's acting kind of different lately?"

My skin prickled with more guilt. "Hasn't said anything to me. You better ask him." And, seriously. This wasn't about me. This was about Ryan and Fred. I had to wonder about the strength of their relationship if a little white lie or two from Riley could throw them into so much turmoil. What kind of a relationship was that? If Fred had been my girlfriend, that wouldn't have happened. But she wasn't.

"Oh," her voice quivered. "Yeah. Right. I plan to. I'm sure it's just a misunderstanding. Ryan probably called over at the house after I left tonight. I should have waited a little bit longer for his call. If he called…" Her eyes lowered to a stone in the dirt. She kicked it. "So." She paused, watching the stone shoot across the desert. "Are you dating Riley now?"

A nervous laugh bubbled deep inside my throat. "Um, that would be a no. Besides, didn't you see the photo on Vernon's phone?" Riley had looked wasted in the photo, and I cringed thinking about it. Her eyes had looked heavy and dull, her hair all crazy and spiky around her head, as if someone had raked his hands through it a hundred times. The photo didn't even look like her. What happened to Pink Girl? She was behaving more like Party Girl now, not like the Riley that I had gotten to know on the Mogollon Rim and certainly not like the girl I'd been spending days with after school. But people could surprise you. That much I knew.

"Yeah. Guess not." She bit her lower lip, like she was thinking, so I knew there was more.

"What's really going on, Fred? It's not like you ever partied with us before you started seeing Berenger."

"I just wanted to see how you were doing. That's all. You've been…different lately." Her eyes swept across my face, studying me.

My throat turned dry. "How?"

"Good different." Her hand swept through the air toward me, as if it were obvious.

"Why do you care all of a sudden?"

"I always care about my friends."

My stomach plummeted at that horrible little word. *Friends.* "Yeah, right."

"I mean, not that you aren't a great guy and one of my best friends—"

I raised one palm again and sighed. "Save it, Fred. I get the picture."

But Fred kept walking toward me. Her front toe slipped forward on the same stone she'd kicked in front of her a second ago.

The next thing I knew, she started falling toward me, arms open.

I reached out to catch her.

In that moment, the world went into slow motion.

I looked down at her. She looked up at me. We blinked at the same time. My gaze moved to her lips; her gaze did the same to mine. Then I had to wonder: had Fred planned this? Falling into my arms as if we were in some kind of cheesy movie? Fred wasn't exactly the trip-and-fall type. That was more Riley Berenger's job.

After a thousand years, Fred said, "This isn't going like I planned."

We stopped breathing. The air froze. I swear I could hear my heartbeat.

Finally, we blinked. My eyes traveled down to my hands. They still clutched Fred's forearms, which were soft and warm from the campfire. She didn't pull away. It was as if gravity kept messing with us, pulling us toward each other when it should be doing the opposite. Behind her, embers popped and crackled in the campfire, angry and confused. Just like me.

I blinked again.

The world started spinning.

I cleared my still-dry throat, looking around for my beer can, looking everywhere but down into Fred's dark eyes and the firelight that sparkled inside them. "What's this really about, Fred? Because you're starting to mess with my head."

I dropped her arms and put a few more inches between us. Her hands returned to her pockets and locked at her elbows. I could see each of her knuckles through her pockets. She suddenly looked very uncomfortable, even for Fred. "I'm sorry you think I'm messing with you, Sam. I just thought we could...talk." Her shoulders shrugged. "I've missed you."

"You see me every day." My teeth clenched. What was with women, anyway? I seemed to be surrounding myself with nothing but crazy. First Riley. Now Fred. I wanted to jump on my bike and go.

"I know that I *see* you, but we don't talk anymore." Fred dropped to the flat rock and pulled her knees toward her chest. She began to rock. "Not like we used to. We used to be able to talk about anything. Books, school. College. How we wanted to come back after college and do something good here. Our parents. Everything." Her chin dropped to her knees. "What happened to us? What happened to talking and our long conversations?"

With a heavy exhale, I sat beside her and tossed dried mesquite into the fire, anything to keep my hands busy—hands still red-hot from touching her arms. But the silence between us grew palpable. "So talk," I said finally, my voice sounded irritated. And loud. My gaze lowered to Fred's.

"Tell me about you and Riley. I know something's going on. You can't fool me, Sam. Remember?"

"Why do you care?"

"I told you already. We're friends."

I paused to consider my words. I couldn't deny that Riley could get me excited sometimes, usually when she didn't realize it. "Would it bother you if something was happening between me and Riley?"

Her eyes blinked wide before she turned away. But then she turned back to me again. "Maybe. A little. But I'd be happy for you."

My chin pulled back, surprised. "But what about Ryan?"

"What about him?" Her eyelids lowered, as if she didn't care anymore. But I knew better, despite the photo from the party. Fred Oday was a terrible liar.

"Please, Fred. Now who's being stupid."

"Am not."

"Are, too." I choked out a laugh. "So the guy went to a party and you go all crazy? I'm sure he was just having a little fun. Blowing off steam."

"You think?" Her nose wrinkled with hope. "You think that's all it is?"

My shoulders shrugged. "You'll have to ask him yourself." Why was I defending Ryan Berenger? I seriously needed to get my head examined.

"What are you going to do about Riley?"

Another shoulder shrug. "What can I do? She looks pretty tight with Hawkins."

"But I've seen how she looks at you."

I scoffed at this. Riley looked at me like I was a project. Nothing more, nothing less.

"In her eyes, it's like you hung the moon," Fred continued.

It was difficult to hide my sarcasm. "Yeah. I guess that's why she's making out with Jay Hawkins." Wait. Now what was I saying? Now I sounded jealous.

"I'm serious, Sam. I think Riley would be good for you. You should give her a chance. She's a great girl."

Fred and I didn't speak for a few minutes, listening instead to the crackle of the fire, which was completely fine with me.

Just as I was about to throw another mesquite branch on the fire, Fred said in a soft voice, "Why aren't you at the party with her?"

"Who?" I said stupidly.

She punched my arm. "With Riley, you dummy." She paused. "You know, if you like someone, if you *really* care about someone, you need to go after her."

"I tried that once." I turned to face her, straight on. "It didn't work." My eyes lowered to Fred's lips. Then I said, "And who said I wasn't planning to go later?"

"So you do have feelings for her?" Fred paused again. "That'd be cool, you know."

I leaned back, palms up. "Why would you care?"

Fred placed a warm hand over mine. She tilted her head to my shoulder.

"'Cause I'm always gonna care about you, Sam. Whether you want me to or not." She paused. Then in a softer voice, she said, "When did we stop being us, Sam? You were like a brother to me."

I couldn't answer her. Not because being referred to as a brother hurt me. It wasn't a punch to my gut anymore. But what I realized, sitting with Fred by the fire, was that she'd begun to feel like a sister to me again, like back before we thought about being anyone's girlfriend or boyfriend. Back when everything was uncomplicated and we were just us. Just friends.

We sat together on the rock for a while, listening to the wood snap in the fire as a couple of coyotes howled somewhere in the distance. I inhaled the night, begging for calmness. Inside, my chest was exploding, then quieting, and then exploding all over again with this new revelation. I focused on the darkness, the nothingness that surrounded us, until finally it felt like my world could be okay again, if I just let everything go. If I just let Fred go, once and for all.

I don't know how much time passed—a few minutes or an hour—but when our last log burned itself to a gray ash hulk, my mind had stilled. Despite the darkness, I began to see clearly again.

"Come on," I said. "I'll take you home."

"Don't you want to get to the party and find Riley?"

"There'll be other parties."

Fred sighed but her eyes sparkled. That's when I realized that tears had welled in her eyes but the next time she blinked, they'd vanished.

I smiled down at her, and a sense of relief built between us. Things almost seemed normal again. *I* was finally acting normal again—well, normal for me. "That is, unless you're expecting your boyfriend to drive way out here, searching for you."

She chuckled. "Never say never, Sam."

Dramatically, I pressed my hand to my chest.

Then Fred threaded her fingers through mine, just like old times, and we walked back to my bike. This time it didn't feel weird. Much.

33

RILEY

When my eyes cracked open, I was lying on a bed. Correction: I was lying on silky pillows scattered on top of a bed. Someone was yelling.

The only light in the room came from the outline of a closed door. Behind the door, a woman screamed, "Okay, everybody out! *Now!*" She kept demanding that everyone leave, over and over and over. But why would a stranger yell at me to leave my own house?

Hold up. Where was I?

I raised my head. A shooting pain slashed across my forehead and the room went fuzzy and sideways at the same time.

Then I heard the shuffle of footsteps and doors slamming all around me. It was like a fire drill but there was no fire, not really. Not that I remembered…

But what did I remember?

I remembered arms and legs and zippers and buttons and lips pressing against mine. And heat. Lots of heat. I even had a vague memory of someone sucking tequila from my belly button.

I felt my face flush.

Oh, no.

I shot up higher and this time my forehead exploded. I was tempted to fall back against the pillow till the dandelion fuzziness behind my eyes disappeared, but the shrieking woman made that impossible.

The door burst open, a switch was flicked and the chandelier light above me brightened the room like a thousand suns. It was easier to navigate the room in the dark.

"And you, too, sweetheart," she said, though it was hardly a term of endearment.

I squinted back at her, stunned. Who was she? Instinctively, I crossed my arms over my chest and realized the straps from my tee draped over my bare shoulders. The room temperature dropped fifty degrees.

"Out. *Now.*" She pointed at the door. "Is there a room in my sister's home that you kids haven't trashed?"

I mumbled something that I hoped was an apology, even though I didn't know who she was, what she was talking about or where I was. But then it flooded back to me. I was at Jay's house. There'd been a party, a big one. We were having fun, goofing around. Being stupid. I remembered laughing till my sides ached. Trying things I'd never done before. I remembered kissing. Lots of kissing. And more.

"Look. You've got ten seconds to get out of here before I call the cops." She raised her cell phone, in case I doubted her.

Again, I nodded, squinting against the bright light. My legs wobbled as I stumbled off the bed and tried to adjust and button and zip my clothing. It felt as if the bed were six feet off the ground. It hurt to talk but I finally did. "I just need to find Jay," I said, willing my legs to take me to the door and not fall into the arms of this crazed woman who filled the doorway. Jay was the last person I remembered talking to, although we hadn't been doing too much talking. I remembered his hands on my arms, my legs, my chest. I rubbed my shoulders. They felt as raw as the rest of me.

"Jay?" the woman cackled. "By the time I'm done with my nephew, you won't see him for a month." I did not doubt her.

I need to find Drew and go home. "I'm so sorry," I mumbled again, folding my hands beneath my chin. The lady let me squeeze by and I got a closer look at her eyes. She had short black hair like Jay, with the same clear blue eyes, but they blazed with a fierceness that scared me into silence. I wanted to be far away from her, as far away as I could get.

I stumbled into the living room. All the lights had been turned on so that it was hospital-room bright. The room was empty of people but littered with red cups and beer cans. They covered every available table, end table, armchair and window ledge. Shot glasses lined the ice-cold granite countertop table in the kitchen, a place I vaguely remembered using as a bed. Or was it a stage? Someone had even stuck red cups on top of the lamps scattered throughout the room. The air reeked of cigarette smoke not quite masked by a minty air freshener that only made it worse. All of the family photos and pictures hanging on the wall were slanted. I felt ashamed, looking at all of the innocent faces in them. We'd trashed their home.

Everywhere I stepped, the bottoms of my shoes crunched. The tile was covered with pretzel pieces and potato chips. I had more vague recollections of someone throwing potato chips into the air like confetti during a Katy Perry song, and people laughing and clapping. We'd all thought it was so funny at the time. Everything was funny…except that I could only remember tiny bits, like a scratchy movie reel. Pieces of my evening lay discarded on the floor along with everything else. This wasn't how I'd imagined the party would end.

My forehead continued to pound, but I survived what felt like a twenty-mile trek to the front door by grazing my hand against the wall for support. It took every muscle to open the wooden door with both hands, but it was worth it once I did. The brisk night air hit me like a much-needed slap. I sucked in a greedy gulp, grateful for the oxygen that coaxed open my eyes and brain. The night was strangely silent, so different from when Drew and I had first arrived and the driveway had been loaded with cars and voices and high expectations.

Drew? Where was she?

I had no idea about the time but the sky had that wee-hour nighttime feel. The only people out this late would be cops and people delivering newspapers. And me, apparently. I watched as three cars screeched down the street toward Pecos Road, their taillights pinpricks of red.

"Anybody out here?" I stumbled to the side of the driveway to look for Drew's car but the sliver of concrete where she'd parked was empty.

Growing more frantic, I looked up and down the street. Rather than wall-to-wall cars, it was eerily empty. Now what? I fumbled inside my front pocket. At least I still had my cell phone. I pulled it out. But who would I call? I couldn't call my parents—not that they shouldn't get at least one half-way drunk and panicked phone call from me in the middle of the night, but I really didn't care to be grounded for the next one hundred years. Besides, I'd told them I was spending the night at Drew's.

I sucked in another breath and texted Drew, then waited. And waited. No reply. I squeezed my cell phone. I thought about texting Ryan but in the next heartbeat I decided against it. He'd shown up late to Jay's party. When he hadn't found Fred there, he'd asked me if I wanted a ride home, after not bothering to hide his irritation that I was at Jay's party in the first place. I'd quickly informed him that I'd be going home with Drew, thank you very much. Now I sort of regretted not leaving with my brother. Instead of going home with Ryan, I'd slammed back a tequila shot while Drew and some other girls stepped in and kept him occupied. Soon after, Jay and I had snuck into one of these rooms to be alone. I never saw Ryan again.

There was only one thing to do.

When my eyes opened, my stomach tied itself into one big knot. The fuzz returned to my forehead. Before I realized what was happening, I dropped to my knees and puked my guts out, right there on the pretty red pavers that covered Jay Hawkins's manicured driveway.

Then I picked myself up, knees wobbling, and started walking.

I didn't get too far. I puked again at the corner of Jay's street, right beneath a streetlight. Then I stumbled again as I wiped my hand across my mouth and pointed myself toward Pecos Road. At least the lack of streetlights along Pecos would dull the white fuzz swimming in my eyes.

Other than stopping to puke, it took less time than I thought to reach Pecos Road. Thirty minutes? An hour? Half drunk, half numb, I had no real concept of time. I knew that I reached it when the air became even easier to breathe. Over my right shoulder stretched the reservation, coal-black with specks of yellow light far in the distance.

After a while, headlights from a car appeared in front of me. I squinted at the approaching lights. They drove straight toward me, so I hugged the side of the road, sinking a couple inches into the soft dirt and gravel. I stumbled into the sand, but only for an instant. I was back up on my feet as the car passed me. A pale face glowed green from the panel inside the car. The man just stared back at me as I held in a breath and hugged the shoulder of the road. Was he going to stop? Would he offer me a ride? If he did, was I crazy enough to take it? My whole body shuddered.

The car did not stop. It just kept moving.

And so did I. Faster.

At least he wasn't a cop. I had no idea what time it was, but I was pretty sure I was out past curfew. This was the first time in my whole life that I'd been out so late on a Friday night. The notion thrilled and scared me at the same time.

I pushed forward, inhaling the night air, listening to my footsteps across the pavement, ignoring the building queasiness in my stomach. I figured I had to walk at least another thirty minutes before I reached my neighborhood. "There. That's not so bad," I said aloud, and my voice sounded as if it had been projected on a bullhorn.

Another headlight appeared on the road, bright as a full moon. The engine growled as the vehicle got closer. Like before, I kept to the right side of the road, squinting into the light. My heart pounded against my ribs. What if this was a cop? Or a serial killer? It was almost better when my mind was fuzzier. I didn't analyze as much.

The white headlight blanketed the sky until it cast over me like a net

I took another step to the right, farther off the road, and sank lower into the dirt. My temples thundered, competing with the engine.

The vehicle slowed but its headlight was too blinding for me to see anything.

I raised my arm above my eyes against the glare.

Then it stopped, idling right in front of me. The driver revved its engine, and I jumped.

"Riley?" The voice was incredulous.

I jumped again, pressing one hand against my chest as if that could slow my heart.

"What the hell are you doing way out here?" he said. "Alone?"

"Oh, my god, Sam?" I peered into the headlight, my throat bone-dry.

Sam turned off the headlight and the road turned black again.

"You were supposed to be here hours ago," I said. I sounded angry but at the same time I was ecstatic to see him. My whole body started shaking. I may have been happier to see Sam right at this very second than I was the moment he fell between me and that elk on the side of the Mogollon Rim.

"Sorry," he said, but his tone wasn't apologetic. "I got lost." Sam leaned back on his motorcycle as the engine sputtered.

Quickly, I walked up to his bike and stood in front of him. I couldn't see much more than the whites of his eyes. Everything else about Sam Tracy blended into the night like a great big mystery. Without another word, I lunged forward and grabbed him in a tight hug, startling him. "Hold me." My voice cracked. "Please."

A few beats later, I felt his warm arms wrap around me. Sinking into Sam was exactly what I needed. The tighter his hug, the harder I cried. I couldn't hold it in, either, hard as I tried. Sam didn't say anything. He just held me against his chest and I breathed in campfire and the desert.

I didn't really know how long we stood alongside Pecos Road but it was long enough for my body to calm. When my breathing returned to normal, Sam pulled me back and lowered his face to mine. I was grateful for the dark. "Riley?"

I raised my eyes to his.

He shook me, just a little. "What happened?"

"You were supposed to be at the party," I said, sniffing. "That was the plan."

"No. That was your plan. You know how I feel about Jay Hawkins. I never promised you that I'd be here."

"It was a fun party."

Sam's hands tightened around my arms.

"At least at first. And you were supposed to bring Fred."

"I saw Fred earlier."

My shoulders lifted. "Really? Where?"

"On the Rez. We had a party of our own."

"Oh." My voice got smaller. "Well, good. I hope you had a nice time."

"I did."

"Good," I said again, but for some reason I didn't sound like I meant it. I was just surprised, that's all. Surprised to see Sam. Surprised that he'd spent an evening with Fred, all on his own, without any help from me.

"You didn't by any chance see Martin Ellis, Peter Begay and a bunch of other crazy Native guys, did you?"

"I don't remember seeing them." I didn't remember much of anything. I wasn't sure whether I wanted to remember. Feeling dizzy, I reached for my forehead.

"You okay?" He still held both of my arms and I liked that. I needed that.

"Yeah," I lied.

"You don't look so good."

"Thanks."

"Need a ride?" he said, although he already knew the answer.

"Yeah," I said, anyway. "Definitely." My legs felt heavy, now that I knew I didn't need to walk the rest of the way home. Suddenly the throbbing ache returned to my right ankle. How much farther would I have had to walk? Another mile? Five miles? I really didn't know. It was impossible to tell when you were standing alongside the reservation in the middle of the night. Black and endless, it was like standing on the edge of the world.

"Here," Sam said, letting me go to reach around for the helmet attached to the back of his seat. "Put this on."

The helmet was cold and heavy in my hands. I'd never worn one. I'd never ridden on a motorcycle, either. More firsts.

"I'm glad you finally got a vehicle, but I was kind of hoping you'd buy a car."

Sam chuckled. "Well, maybe next time."

He was in a pretty good mood for it being the middle of the night. "I take it you had a nice time with Fred?" I said.

"Yeah. Real nice."

"Good," I said, but the news stung me a little. Once again, I didn't sound happy for him. I sounded…frustrated? Angry? Confused?

"I take it you had a nice time with Jay?" There was something odd in Sam's voice. An edge?

I blinked, wide. "Yes," I said, although I was still uneasy about the parts that I couldn't remember. The not knowing rooted like a big pit in the bottom of my stomach. "How'd you know?" *And, wait. Is Sam Tracy jealous?*

"I don't think there's a single person at school who doesn't know at this point, Riley."

"What's that supposed to mean?"

"Don't you know?" His tone turned from edgy and maybe-jealous to concerned in the span of two seconds.

"Know what?"

Sam cleared his throat, avoiding my question.

In the darkness, my fingers fiddled with the helmet straps. "Stupid straps," I muttered.

"Here. Let me." Sam reached for the straps and I reached for the sides of the helmet, just in case there was something I could do. His warm fingers kept brushing against my chin until finally, I heard a *click*. "There," he said with some satisfaction. "Now hop on."

I approached the bike. The rear seat was slightly higher, kind of like a perch for the passenger. The bike was also higher than I'd thought. In a very ungraceful way, my leg swept over the seat. You'd never know I'd had eight years of dance lessons, including three years of ballet. I fidgeted and squirmed until the seat felt comfortable. Then the bike rumbled beneath me.

Sam turned. "You gotta hang on, Riley. To me."

"Cool." I reached my arms around his waist. Then I said, "Okay. I changed my mind about the car. I'm glad you got a bike. This will be a good thing. You know, girls really like guys with motorcycles—"

"Just shut up, Riley. And hang on. Tight."

"Tight. Got it." I leaned forward, collapsing against him with fatigue and gratitude. I hung on tight all over again.

"Where do you live?"

My eyes popped open. "Oh, you can't take me there. I need to get to Drew's house. It's not far from mine—"

"Riley…" Sam turned so that his chin grazed the top of the helmet.

My face turned up. "I know. Long story. But I can't go home tonight. My parents think I'm spending the night at Drew's and my stuff is at her place. Even my house keys." Tiny lie. There was a spare key that Mom kept in a planter in the backyard, but there was no way I was going home, not at this hour. Mom would freak. Dad would never let me out of the house again.

Sam knew that I was lying.

"That's not smart. You can get your stuff tomorrow."

"Just go, Sam." I paused to swallow before I leaned my chin back against his shoulder. "Please."

Sam twisted the throttle, a little harder than seemed necessary, jolting the bike. My arms squeezed tighter around his waist.

We raced the rest of the way down Pecos Road, the engine from the bike drowning out everything else, even my conscience and all my lies. I felt warm and safe against Sam again, and I wanted to feel this way for as long as I could.

34

SAM

I was stunned to find Riley half walking, half stumbling alongside Pecos Road. Now I was glad I'd gone looking for my friends at Jay's party. Or had a part of me come to find Riley?

And damn that Jay Hawkins, letting her walk home in the middle of the night. I squeezed the handlebars, tighter. What a douche. I'd no doubt that he'd pushed her to do things she shouldn't have, too.

Riley pointed to a street lined with stucco houses arranged like dominoes, each one looking exactly like the next. They glowed in pinks and yellows beneath streetlights that stretched up a curvy road with perfectly spaced saguaros and paloverde trees. A few front porch lights brightened expansive doorways.

I coasted into the neighborhood, bringing the engine to a purr. Riley pointed to a two-story house in the middle of a street that I assumed was Drew's. I cut the engine as I pulled into the driveway, trying to size up the house. There was no light anywhere inside, not even over top of the front door. One of those obnoxiously cute Volkswagens that always reminded me more of a toy than something you drove on a freeway was parked in front of a planter. A spotlight inside the planter brightened red geraniums that spilled out on all four sides.

I turned to Riley. "Do you have a key?"

Riley's fingers fumbled with the strap beneath her chin until she removed the helmet. She shook her head so that her hair bounced on her shoulders and my breath caught in the back of my throat. Against the dim light, I hated to say it, but she glowed like some kind of butterfly. The ends of her hair framed her face like yellow silk, and I was tempted to reach out and touch a strand. Feeling cheesy-stupid for staring— even dumber for thinking it—I turned forward and forced myself to concentrate on Drew's front door. The red geraniums. Toy car. Dim lights. Anything but Riley.

Riley lifted herself off the bike and then walked around to face me, her hand resting on the handlebar. "No," she whispered. "I don't have a key."

"Huh?" I'd forgotten that I'd asked the question.

"I don't have a key," she repeated. "There's a back stairway that leads up to Drew's bedroom." She paused. "Thanks for the ride, Sam. I mean it. You saved me. Again."

My eyes dropped to her lips. "You sure you're okay?" She wasn't slurring her words as much, and it was too dark to see whether her eyes were bloodshot. From the picture that had been texted around earlier, I was betting they were fire-engine-red.

"Yeah. Sure. Fine."

"Well, it looked like you were having fun."

Riley pulled back. "Why do you keeping saying that?"

I paused, wondering whether I should tell her. I felt like I had to. "There's a photo of you and Hawkins floating across cell phones as we speak." My hands squeezed the handle-bars, tighter.

"Really? What kind of photo?" She sounded more delighted than disappointed, and that bothered me. I wished she'd get hopping-mad angry about it. I wished she'd get wise to Jay Hawkins. Why did I have to be the one to educate her about him? Why hadn't her brother already seen to that?

My stomach tightened along with my fists. I slowed my words. "It was just that you looked like you were having a good time. With Hawkins. That's all." Major understatement.

Her teeth flashed, suddenly more alert. "We did. It was such a fun party. Well, until his aunt started screaming at everybody to leave."

"Jay's totally playing you, Riley. You know that, don't you?"

"Jay's not playing anyone, Sam. He's just a friend. A good friend."

"You need better friends."

"Why do you hate him so much?"

I spread my arms. "How can you stand him? Would a good friend let you walk home in the middle of the night? Alongside a deserted road? By yourself?"

She turned away with an irritated headshake, dismissing it, like she didn't care to think about Jay and his bad manners. "Well, you should have come. You missed out."

"I didn't miss a thing."

"Stop being a baby. Of course you did. Fred, too."

"Yeah, well, Fred told me that your brother blew her off."

Her eyes widened. "Oh, good!" she gushed. "That's what I wanted her to think, especially when she didn't show up with you. That's good for you. Right, Sam?"

"No, it's not. It hurt her. And Fred is my friend."

"I know, but—"

"No *buts*, Riley. I want you to stop this. Stop interfering between your brother and Fred. It's not right."

"But you said you loved her."

My voice got louder. "Yeah, and that means I don't want to see her get hurt."

Riley pouted. "Well, she could have come. She could have been with him. He was there, anyway. The whole school was invited—"

I stopped her again, leaning over the handlebars. "Not me. Not any of my friends."

"Then why did you drive all the way out here?" She leaned toward me, her hands on her hips, so that our chins were only a few inches apart.

"I told you. I was looking for my friends."

For a brief second, her face crumpled, like she was hurt. But it only lasted a moment. Then she raised her chin and said, "Okay, now you're really confusing me." She paused. "Your friends were here? But you weren't?"

"We got some texts...."

"Okay. Probably the same one I got about the party."

I laughed. "Highly doubt that."

"Oh, Sam. Why are you talking in riddles? Just be honest with me."

"I am."

"No, you're not."

My hands twisted around the handlebars. "Look who's talking."

"Now what are you talking about?"

"Nice job keeping Ryan and Fred apart. That's all." I didn't mean it as a compliment.

"That wasn't me."

I knew she was lying. "Yes, it was."

She paused. "I may have mentioned to Ryan that Fred

wasn't coming." Her mouth twisted with mischief. "He waited for her all night, you know."

"Well, from the photo that got texted around, he sure looked like he was enjoying himself."

Riley leaned closer.

"I think he had his arm around your girlfriend and some other girl."

"You mean Drew?"

"I don't know their names. But you pushed them together, right?"

Riley shook her head. "I might have." She looked away. "I don't remember, to tell you the truth."

"Well, congratulations, Riley. I saw Fred tonight, and she was pretty upset."

She spun around to face me. "But...I..." she stammered. "I thought that's what you wanted. I gave you your chance tonight, Sam. On a silver platter."

"One more time, Riley. And I'll say this real slow...." I paused for a breath, mostly to steady my growing anger. "Fred is my friend. I don't like to see my friends get hurt." Then I stopped again. "And I sure as hell don't want to be the consolation prize."

Riley's eyes began to blink, fast, as if she were already recalibrating for a new plan.

I lifted my palm, stopping her. "Enough. No more playing. You're going to have to stop interfering in everyone's lives. Just worry about fixing your own."

Her chin pulled back. "Interfering?" She gasped. "I gave you an opening with Fred." Her mouth opened and closed, as if she weren't sure whether to continue. But she did. "And I'm pretty sure I got you a spot on the junior prom court tonight. Courtesy of Jay Hawkins—"

I was yelling now. "Jay Hawkins?" I hated that his name

took space on my tongue. A dog began barking somewhere in the distance. "Riley. Hear me." I jabbed a finger at her. "I don't want *anything* from Jay Hawkins. Ever. You understand?"

"But…but…" More stammering.

I reached down for the ignition, anxious to leave. I fingered the rabbit's foot at the end of the key. "You want me to walk you around back? 'Cause I better get going, if you don't. This conversation is over." It wasn't easy to look at her at this point, especially after she thrust Jay Hawkins back into my life.

Riley placed her hand over mine on the handlebar and my heart slowed a fraction. "I'm sorry, Sam," she whispered. "I'm sorry I made you angry. Don't be mad at me. I hate it when you're mad. Please."

"Well? You need me to walk you around back, or what?" I looked everywhere except into her eyes. I kept my hand beneath hers.

Slowly, she pulled her hand away before stuffing it in the front pocket of her jeans. "No. Thanks. I can make it from here."

"Okay, then," I said as the motorcycle idled back to life.

"Wait." Riley grabbed the handlebar with both hands, lurching forward a few steps as my bike backed up.

I pressed the brake and stared at her in amazement. "Jeez, Riley. You're lucky you didn't face-plant into the pavement."

Her mouth opened, closed and opened again. Her toe dug into the driveway. Finally, she spoke. "You ever want to run away?"

Whoa. Left field. Wasn't expecting that. I chuckled. "Every damn day."

"Really?"

"Yeah, sure." And that was the truth. "Who doesn't?"

Her hand twisted around the handlebar. "You think you'd ever want to run away with me?" I could hear her breathing. "Like, tonight?"

I was almost too stunned to answer. After I'd just told her to stop meddling in my life? But whenever I was around this girl, I was crazy enough to say yes.

Riley was serious, her expression frozen, waiting for my answer.

I finally found my voice. "Just because I want to doesn't mean I will." My hand dragged over my forehead and through my hair, the tangles pulling through my fingers. "Besides, why would you want to leave all this? And all your new popular friends?" There I went being all Jealous Guy again.

"I'm serious, Sam."

I leaned forward. "So am I."

I fiddled with the key again. "Look, you better go in. And my parents are gonna worry. It's late."

"Party killer," Riley said, trying to laugh it off like her idea was all one big joke, but I could tell she was fuming beneath the surface. She'd expected a different answer from me.

"I gotta go."

Riley pulled on the handlebar again. "Wait."

I stared back at her, saying nothing.

"Thanks," she said. "I just wanted to say thanks." She sounded sincere. I hoped she was. "You saved me again, Sam. I just wanted you to know that I appreciate it."

After a handful of seconds, I said, "You're welcome, Riley."

Then out of nowhere, in a softer voice, she said, "I haven't forgotten that kiss the morning we were rescued, Sam. Have you?"

I hadn't, either. But I had to wonder if this was Riley or the alcohol talking. "I shouldn't have done that," I said. "I wasn't thinking."

"I'm glad you did."

In the next heartbeat, she leaned forward and kissed my cheek, soft lips against my skin. Not quite a peck, but not quite a lingering kiss, either.

Before I could reach for her—because in that moment I could have—Riley spun around and disappeared into the darkness alongside Drew's house, her hair the last bit that glistened in the night.

For the longest time, I sat on my bike, just shaking my head at the darkness. "Women," I muttered finally. I'd never understand them.

Before someone could call the police about a strange guy on a motorcycle loitering in a neighborhood where he did not belong, I strapped on my helmet and sped back down the street to Pecos Road. I played back my conversation with Riley over and over as I rode into the night, her kiss still on my cheek, the touch from her hand still sending electrical currents up my arm.

I'd never been more mixed up in my entire life. My life had grown seriously out of control.

I pulled back on the gearshift. The sooner this side of Pecos Road found itself in my rearview mirror, the better.

35

RILEY

Drew could barely stand to look at me the next morning. I had hoped it was because of her hangover but it wasn't. She hadn't even suggested we go out for mochas before she dropped me back at my house. We always did mochas after a sleepover. Our conversation had sounded something like this:

"Your brother was so not into me last night, Riley. You lied to me. You gave me false hope."

"I did not." Then I hesitated and felt all sorts of guilty, especially when I saw the hurt in her face. "Well, I probably should have warned you it wouldn't be easy."

"You should have warned me about a lot of things, especially about listening to you."

"I'm sorry, Drew."

"I kept him occupied, just like I promised. But I felt like a total idiot, especially when he kept asking me and everyone else with eardrums, 'Have you seen Fred?' It was pathetic. I hate to disappoint you but your matchmaking plan is seriously flawed."

"I'm so sorry, Drew. Really, I am." I could apologize one

hundred times but there was no placating her. She was pissed at me, *really* royally pissed at me, for the first time since we'd been friends. I had planted the seed that she had a chance with my brother and from the looks of things I would regret that for the rest of my life.

"You know what I think?" Her bloodshot eyes got all squinty when she had said this, too, almost to the point where it scared me. "I think you came up with this stupid match-making ruse just to get close to Sam Tracy. That's what I think."

I didn't answer her.

After Drew dropped me off, I spent the rest of Saturday in my bedroom, sulking and waiting for the anvil in my head to disappear.

I was listening to country music on my iPod with my eyes closed, sipping a 7-Up, when someone knocked on my bedroom door. I ignored it.

But then the knock turned into a pound.

Bam-bam!

I pulled out my right earbud. "What?" I yelled at the door and then reached for my temple. The inside of my head had been drumming all day due to my first (and preferably last) hangover.

"It's me. Let me in."

I rolled my eyes at the door. "Go away."

He knocked again, louder than before. This time he was close to breaking down the door.

"Go. Away!"

"Riley, open the door. We need to talk. Don't be a baby."

I dragged myself off my bed. Ryan never dropped by my bedroom to chat. Obviously he needed a favor. "Make this quick," I said, unlocking my door.

Ryan stepped around the door as I held tight to the doorknob. His eyes swept over me and then my unmade bed. The clothes I'd worn to Jay's party hung on the back of my desk chair. Even from across the room, I smelled the cigarette smoke as it mixed with the fresh air from the hallway. "You look like hell," he said, moving to the window to open the shade.

Bright light flooded the room, stinging my dry eyes. I looked down at my gray sweatpants and rumpled matching T-shirt. "Gee, thanks."

"Seriously, Ri."

I chuckled. "Okay, I believe you. I look like crap. Thanks for the fashion update. Please leave now."

Ryan plopped on my bed, sending my sketchbook onto the floor and I cringed. I wasn't expecting a sit-down. "I told you," he said. "I wanted to talk."

"Don't you have another sister to irritate?"

"Just close the door," he said. "Relax, would you? I won't bite." Ryan leaned against my pillow and crossed his legs at the ankles. They stretched the length of my queen-sized bed. When I didn't move away from the door, he pleaded in a softer voice, "Come on, Riley. Please."

I shut the door, hard. And then listened a moment for signs of Mom and Dad through the door. I hadn't heard either one in the house the whole day. Dad often went into the office on Saturdays and Mom had probably been called in to the hospital on one of a zillion emergencies. People always seemed to have more accidents and heart attacks on the weekends. So it was just my brother and me. All alone. *Oh, joy.*

I dragged my feet to my desk as if I were wading through chest-high water and plopped into my chair. I drew up my knees and looked at Ryan. "Okay. What?" I said in my best I'm-bored voice.

Ryan leaned forward. "What is going on with you?" he asked.

My eyes widened. Well, this was a first—my big brother caring about someone other than himself? "What do you mean?" I treaded carefully.

His hands spread open. "I mean, you're not *you* lately. You're…someone else."

I exhaled a chuckle. "I hate to disappoint you, but I am very much me. I've never been more me in my whole life. I've just been having a little fun for once. What's the big deal?"

He glared with disapproval but I held his gaze.

When I didn't blink, he said, "So, let me get this straight. Suddenly you're hanging out with the Jay Hawkins clan, you smoke and—" he paused, sniffing "—you obviously like to get hammered all of a sudden. This is the new-and-improved you? This is fun?" His tone was incredulous.

"Don't be a hypocrite, Ryan. You've been doing it for years."

He pushed back on the pillow. "I did try it. I've tried everything. And it's totally not worth it. Remember?"

How could I forget? I was always the one stuck at home listening to Mom and Dad fight about Ryan while he was off at yet another never-ending party. I was the one who'd answered the front door to the police when Ryan had held a party in our backyard and a neighbor had complained about the noise. I was the one who had to watch Mom cry in frustration every time Ryan stumbled home drunk. Let him get a taste of what I had to go through. "That was you," I said. "This is me."

"And I don't like what I'm seeing."

"Ask me if I care." My chin lifted. "Besides, it's not for you to decide."

Ryan sighed. "Riley…this won't end well."

"Quit your worrying, would you?"

"Well, stop acting stupid and the people who care about you will leave you alone."

"I'm not being stupid. I know exactly what I'm doing."

"No, you don't."

"Yes, I do."

"No, the hell you *don't.*"

My voice rose. "At least I'm having some fun for a change. At least people are paying attention to me in the first place!"

Ryan leaned forward on one knee. "Is that what this all about? Attention?"

"No," I said. "Yes. I mean, *no.*" I gripped the sides of my head. "Just leave me alone, will you?"

Then his eyes narrowed. "And another thing. Why did you tell Fred I was going to the movies last night?"

"I didn't." *Oh, no.*

"Yes, you did. She told me this morning when we talked it all out. Why have you been lying to us?"

I looked away. I couldn't look at him.

"Fred and I had planned to hang out last night. When I drove to her house, she was already gone. I thought maybe she'd gone to Jay's party."

"I thought you didn't like Jay Hawkins. Why would you want to go to his party?"

"I said I didn't like my sister with Jay Hawkins. And don't change the subject."

"You've known Jay forever. You used to be in Little League together."

"That was grade school, Riley. Jay changed in high school. He's full of himself. I really can't stand him."

I shook my head, frustrated. Then I bolted upright and stood beside the chair, my arms folded tight across my chest.

"Get out, Ryan. I'm done talking." My forehead throbbed harder.

Ryan leaped off the end of my bed and towered over me, his hands on his hips. "I'm just worried about you, Riley. After last night, now you've got a reputation. Is that what you want?"

I gasped, feeling like I'd been punched in the stomach. "So I kiss Jay Hawkins and I get a reputation? That's original."

"You did more than kiss."

"So what?" I felt heat rush up my neck. "And how would you know?"

"I think it's pretty much a guarantee that everybody knows about you and Jay."

"Well, what's everybody calling Jay?"

Ryan's jaw hardened. "Lucky."

"Huh." I choked out a laugh. "That's rich."

His nostrils flared. "I'm going to talk to him."

I jabbed my finger at him. "Stay out of this, Ryan. Stop treating me like a child. It's none of your business."

"Like hell it isn't."

Ryan walked out the door and turned as my temples tap-danced against my skull. His gaze battled mine. Then he looked behind me, like he was seriously considering walking back inside my room for Round Two. "Consider yourself warned," he said, lowering his voice.

"Consider yourself a moron." I slammed the door in his face and began pacing in my room. I had to get out of here or I was going to explode.

Then I thought of our old Lexus, parked beside the garage. No one ever used it unless one of our other cars was in the shop. Mom hung the extra car keys next to the back door. I wondered if the Lexus had any gas.

36

SAM

I knew something was wrong when Mr. Romero stormed into the cafeteria before homeroom on Monday morning.

"I need to talk to you, Sam. *Privately.*" Mr. Romero towered over my table, tapping two fingers against the edge like they were keeping time.

The hairs rose on the back of my neck. "Okay," I said, stuffing my math and physics books into my backpack, doing my best to ignore the stares from the students around me. Teachers usually stuck to the teachers lounge. Rarely did they cross the invisible dividing line into the cafeteria before school, not unless the building was on fire and there was no other way out.

I followed Mr. Romero as he walked out of the cafeteria and into the hallway. He always walked like he was late for a bus.

As soon as we reached his office, Mr. Romero closed the door, motioned to one of two brown chairs and then took his place behind a desk that took up most of the room. Behind him hung his framed degree from the University of

Arizona and some type of counseling certificate. Three perfect piles of white paper made a line on his desk, along with a coffee cup and a brown sack in the corner that I assumed contained his lunch.

"If this goes late, I'll write you a pass," he said, moving one of the piles so that he could fold his hands in the middle of his desk.

I nodded as I dumped my backpack on the empty chair beside me.

"I'll get right to the point." His fingers reached up to smooth down his mustache. "What can you tell me about Riley Berenger?"

I swallowed. Okay, call me stupid, but I hadn't seen that one coming. "What do you mean?" It sounded lame but it was the first thing I could think of. Was he accusing me of something?

"Well, she's been acting differently since the leadership retreat. It's obvious you two have grown close since the rescue."

My eyes widened. *It is?*

"I've seen you together in the cafeteria and in the parking lot after school."

If he noticed my surprise he didn't say. "I thought maybe she's confided in you…."

"I haven't noticed anything different about her," I said quickly. Perhaps too quickly. "I don't really know her." At least that part was true. Just when I thought I knew Riley Berenger, she did something that totally blew me away. Like tell me she liked when I kissed her.

Mr. Romero's eyes narrowed. "Nothing? You've noticed *nothing?*"

"You mean, like at school?" Wow. That sounded lame even to me, but I was stalling, wondering where this conversation was headed.

"Well, okay. For starters. Her teachers tell me that she's been late on assignments and falling asleep in class, even behaving rudely. That's not like her. Why would she behave that way?"

"To be honest, Mr. Romero, you'd have to ask her." My innocent tone rang false but I wasn't about to tell him that she was meddling in other people's business. "Or maybe her brother."

"I intend to, Mr. Tracy. But you're an upperclassman and a respected member of this school. I value your insight. I was hoping you might be able to shed some light on the recent changes in her behavior, especially since—" he paused to clear his throat "—the night you spent together on the Mogollon Rim."

I swallowed again. "Yes, sir."

"There's a rumor she's joined a gang. Is that true?"

I snorted. *Pink Girl?* "Riley?" No. Way. "I don't believe that. Not for a second."

"But you said you don't know her."

Oh, boy. Open mouth, insert foot. "I don't. Not really, I mean. But I know her type. She doesn't seem like the type of girl who'd join a gang. She's too smart for that." I hoped I was right. Riley? In a girl gang? With chains and tattoos and drug deals going down in alleys? I had an easier time picturing Jay Hawkins as the next Pope. "Seriously, Mr. Romero, someone's feeding you false information."

Mr. Romero pulled on his mustache. "My sources can be pretty reliable, Sam."

It was hard not to laugh. "I...I don't know what to say. I find it very hard to believe." Clearly Mr. Romero had watched too many teen movies.

"I've seen it happen, Mr. Tracy. I've seen it happen plenty of times to people you would never expect." He tented his fingers. "Well, this behavior is very sudden and very unlike Miss Berenger, and we are all very concerned. I'd like to stop it before it escalates."

"Uh-huh." At least I wasn't the only one who wanted Riley back to the way she was—back to not interfering with other people's lives. "Have you talked to her today?" My tone was hopeful, surprising me.

"She was in a car accident on Saturday, Mr. Tracy," he said, his lips pursing. "She won't be in school today."

It was like I'd been sucker punched. "What? Is she all right?"

"From what I understand, yes. She'll be okay. It could have been worse." I could tell that he was keeping something from me but, frankly, I was surprised that he'd told me anything about it at all. A million crazy thoughts ran through my head—was she driving? Was she drunk again? Or worse, was she with that tool Hawkins? I didn't know she had her license yet.

"Was she…with anyone?"

"I really shouldn't say any more," Mr. Romero said. "Anyway, anything that you can think of, anything you could share would be most helpful as we try to help Miss Berenger get back on track."

"Sure." My throat tightened. "Absolutely." There was so much more I should have told Mr. Romero but I couldn't push the words out of my mouth. "Um. Do you know when she'll be back in school?"

"Tomorrow, hopefully. Maybe Wednesday." He began to tap a pile of papers against his desk with his pencil. Message received: office visit over.

I reached for my backpack.

"And, Sam?" Mr. Romero said.

"Yeah?" I said, standing.

"If you hear anything, learn anything, will you let me know? I give you my word that anything you tell me will be kept in confidence."

I swallowed. "Yeah, definitely." I swung my backpack over my shoulder. The first bell of the morning rang, and I couldn't leave Mr. Romero's office fast enough. I needed to borrow Vernon's cell phone.

"Oh, and Sam?"

I stopped short at the door. "Yeah?"

Mr. Romero's expression softened. "Congratulations on getting nominated to the junior prom court."

"What?" I gasped. I felt all the blood drain from my face. First, Riley. Now, this? I was officially inside a full-blown nightmare. I had no intention of going to prom. Not now. Not ever.

"I learned about it in the teachers lounge this morning." Mr. Romero smiled wide, oblivious to my shock and horror. "The principal will be making the announcement during homeroom. Until then, keep it on the down-low."

One moment I was worried sick about Riley Berenger. The next, I wanted to strangle her. That was what this girl did to me.

I needed life to go back to the way life had been before I slid down that mountain after her. And I needed it now.

37

RILEY

I refused to wear the dorky neck collar, even when Mom insisted. I'd barely been injured in what could be described as a harmless fender bender on Saturday, maybe just a little twinge in my lower back, if you could even call that an injury. It was probably a leftover from my fall down the side of Mogollon Rim. But we both knew this was about much more than an ugly neck collar that rubbed my skin raw.

"I can't believe that you're making me stay home," I said to Mom as she flitted around my bedroom, lowering the window shade and picking up my discarded clothes as if I were a full-blown invalid. Then she tucked my laptop under her arm.

Wait. What. The?

At this very moment, I would be happier at school. In fact, in the last million moments, I would have been happier anywhere but at home.

"You're job today is to stay calm and quiet, Riley. Do you think you can handle that?" Mom's voice was measured and even, that perfect pitch. Not too loud or too soft. Suddenly I was one of her hospital patients. That tone grated on every last one of my nerves. She frowned at the neck collar lying beside me. "And you've got to wear that, too. It's not an accessory."

"If you say so." I didn't bother to hide my attitude as my fingers plucked the Velcro on the neck collar. It was as heavy as a bridle. Looked like one, too.

"I don't appreciate your tone."

"I didn't realize I had one." I shot her the stink-eye.

Mom sighed and then dropped to the end of my bed. She turned to face me, her fingers threading in front of her, as I tried to push through my headboard to the wall and then preferably to the outside of the house. "Riley. Talk to me." She spread her hands. "What is going on with you? I don't understand. Is this about a boy?"

I exhaled, rolling my eyes.

"Please don't be *that* girl, Riley. The one that does foolish things because she thinks she's in love with a boy. I beg you."

My voice shook. "This has nothing to do with a boy. Jeez, Mom. And even if it did, why can't I be as normal as everyone else?"

"This isn't just about the accident. You've been acting so different lately." She narrowed her eyes at me. "I raised you to be smarter than that." Then there was the tiniest of cracks in her voice. "And I just don't want you to make the same... choices...I did."

Oh, no. Here we go. This was when Mom usually reminded me that she'd gotten pregnant at sixteen. Apparently Ryan and I had a half sister somewhere out there, one she'd given up for adoption. She didn't like to talk about it with Ryan and me, because it hurt too much. I knew that I should feel more compassion for Mom, even guilty for feeling so resentful, but Mom had been doing everything in her power to make sure I was perfect enough for the both of us in everything that I did for as long as I could remember. It was exhausting. "All I did was borrow the car, and you're totally freaking out."

"You didn't ask! That's not borrowing, Riley. That's stealing. And you know you're not allowed to drive a car without a licensed driver. What were you thinking?"

"You never got mad when Ryan did it, when he only had his permit."

"I expected that behavior from Ryan. But from you? Never in a thousand lifetimes." Her voice grew louder. Her Doctor Voice was succumbing to Hysterical Mom voice. "You're lucky you weren't killed—or didn't kill someone."

I sighed, my nostrils flaring. This was the first time Mom had really screamed at me. Was it wrong that I wasn't too upset about it? Was it wrong that I even kind of liked it? "But the guy in front of me didn't even have any damage." Okay, I'll admit to it. Shame on me for following too closely and not braking in time at an intersection, but I'd been anxious to get out of the house. I was only going out for a chocolate mocha. I couldn't stay inside with Ryan lurking about, ready to jump all over me for not being his moldable younger sister who did everything he asked.

"That's not the point, Riley. Your behavior was irresponsible. It was careless and you're lucky it was only a minor accident."

"We've been over this, Mom." A hundred times already. I'd had to listen to Mom and Dad talk about it, over and over and over again, as they waited with me in the Emergency Room after the accident. They'd talked above me as if I weren't seated between them, either, as they both voiced their displeasure at my behavior, how they'd never expected me to get in trouble. What *did* they expect of me, anyway? Wasn't I allowed to be a teenager? Wasn't I allowed to do anything wrong? Ever?

"Well, then I think you'll understand why your father and I have decided that you won't be getting a car when you get your license—"

I almost leaped across the bed. "But you promised!" My hands squeezed clumps of the bedspread beneath me till my knuckles ached.

"Not until you can prove that you are a responsible teenager, Riley. Not one minute before."

"But Ryan got into all sorts of trouble and he still got his car! How's that fair?"

"Your father and I expect different things from you, Riley." Her steady hospital voice had returned. "I am more than a little disappointed."

I fell back against the pillow, breathing through my clenched teeth. I needed air. I needed to get away from here. "Well, that makes two of us."

"You're acting like a spoiled brat."

Yeah. I totally was.

Mom rose. Her chin lifted. "You are not allowed to get on the computer today. You're not allowed to use your cell phone." She looked around my room and spotted my cell in the middle of my desk. She snagged it, along with my laptop, even the power cord. "And needless to say, you are not allowed to leave this house under any circumstance today. Is that clear?"

I didn't answer. I refused to answer.

"Is that clear?" Mom said again.

I didn't answer. Again. I only saw red.

"I'll see you after work. We'll talk more then," Mom said, walking to the door with my lifeline to the outside world tucked beneath her arm. "Catch up on your homework. Mr. Romero tells me you're behind in every class. Unless you'd like to spend your summer in school, I'd suggest you get re-acquainted with your books."

My insides raged. I leaped off the bed and then spun around my room in a panic. Everything I cared about was missing. No phone. No laptop. Only my schoolbooks sat in a lopsided stack on my desk. I didn't have the desire to read any of them. For the first time, I didn't want to sketch, either. My fingertips pulsed. They tapped against the bed, faster and faster. I was afraid of what I would do, could do, wanted to do.

Mom shut the door. A minute later, the phone rang inside our house. I tilted my head but only heard muffled voices through the walls. Then footsteps shuffled across the hallway and a knock sounded at the door.

Instead of waiting for me to say something, Mom burst inside my room, pointing the cordless at me. "For you," she said.

My eyes widened. I was shocked that she was letting me take a call, especially since I was basically being held captive. "Who?"

"School," she said. "You have two minutes." She tossed the phone on my bed and turned to leave the room.

I gulped. School? A teacher? The principal? Was I being expelled? "Hello?" I said, my voice almost catching.

"Riley?"

My eyes narrowed. "Yes?"

"It's Sam."

"Sam!" How'd he get past Mom? I'd never been so happy to hear from anyone in my life. "Oh, my god, it's good to hear your voice."

"I just talked to Mr. Romero. I heard you were in an accident. Are you okay?"

"I'm fine. My parents are totally overreacting. I barely nudged a guy in front of me."

"It was your fault?"

"So it would seem."

"When will you be back?" he said.

"Not soon enough." And that was the truth. I'd rather be anywhere than inside my bedroom.

"Well, I'm sorry that you got hurt," Sam said. "But I'm glad you're okay." The phone went silent. "I was worried."

My throat tightened, feeling his concern. Hearing his voice. In the background, I could hear lockers clanging shut. A bell rang. I'd rather be there, with Sam. I'd rather be anywhere but here.

"Well, I better go—"

"Wait!" I sat higher. "Don't go!" Then I cupped a hand over the phone. There was so much I wanted to tell him, least of all the fact that he was the only outside contact I would probably be allowed to have until I turned twenty-one. "Sam…" I said, wondering how to say it. So I just said it. "I really need your help."

"What can I do?"

"If I don't get out of here, I'm going to lose my mind. I'm afraid I'm going to do something stupid." I paused. "I need you, Sam."

He paused. Finally, he said, "Don't do anything else stupid, Riley. Okay? Your track record hasn't exactly been great lately."

"Would you want to run away with me? Today?" I blurted. "I'll go anywhere." My voice caught again. "Please?" I'd never sounded so desperate in my life. In fact, I sounded so desperate that I was certain Sam must have considered me certifiable.

Sam paused. "Look, Riley, I've got two killer exams today—"

I wiped my hand over my nose, all of my excitement about running away fading in an instant. "Forget it," I said, sniffing, as tears leaked out of my eyes. "It was stupid. I shouldn't have asked. Anyway, thanks for calling. And good luck on your exams. I mean it."

"When you get back, we'll talk, Riley." Another warning bell rang in the background.

"Okay." My eyes turned cloudy. "But you better get to class."

And then I hung up before Sam could say goodbye.

38
SAM

The week dragged. It was Friday and Riley hadn't returned to school yet.

Sitting beside Vernon in homeroom, I listened to Principal Graser's monotone voice through the overhead speakers as he rattled off the morning's announcements. His words made my head hurt, especially when he mentioned prom. Thanks to Riley and apparently Jay Hawkins, I'd been nominated for the junior prom court and had gotten enough votes on the school's website this week to make it to the final five. How was that even possible? I was friends with, like, six people in the entire school. It had to be someone's idea of a bad joke, probably Hawkins. I'd never wanted anything *less* in my entire life and I had a sick feeling that Hawkins knew that already. He was the kind of twisted guy who'd appreciate something like that.

"Everything okay, Mr. Prom King?" Peter leaned over from the seat beside mine.

"Shut up." I sighed, rubbing the bridge of my nose.

Peter's face darkened. "I'm serious, dude. You okay or not?"

"No." I sank lower into my seat. "I don't know." Riley's offer to run away had been weighing on my mind. As much as I hated to admit it, I missed seeing her at school, in the cafeteria, at her locker. I even missed spending time with her after school, just the two of us. I had thought about borrowing Vernon's phone again and calling her about a dozen more times. Jeez, why couldn't I zap that girl and her crazy out of my head?

Peter lowered his voice. "Does this have something to do with Fred?"

I turned to him. "Fred?" I shook my head. Truthfully, I hadn't thought about Fred in a whole week. "No. Why?"

"I thought I heard she broke up with Berenger?"

"Another stupid rumor. Don't believe it." Fred had told me that she and Ryan talked the day after Jay's party and straightened everything all out. "They're very much together, believe me."

"Oh." He leaned back, considering that. He didn't sound convinced. "Saw you talking to her outside the cafeteria the other day. I just wondered. Well, you know…"

"No," I said. "I just needed—" But I stopped myself. I wasn't about to tell him I'd needed the Berengers' home phone number after Mr. Romero had dropped the bomb on me about Riley's car accident. And Fred hadn't asked why when I'd asked her for it. It must have been the desperate look in my eyes. "Nothing. It's nothing. Forget it."

Peter gave me a shoulder shrug. "Okay, bro."

"Oh, god." Vernon exhaled. "Dudes. You gotta see this." Vernon was looking down at the cell phone between his legs, careful to keep it hidden behind the person in front of him, not like it mattered very much. The homeroom teacher's eyes stayed glued to a sheet tucked inside a folder, his pen scratching checkmarks against the paper.

Peter and I nudged closer for a better look at his phone. "What up?" Martin whispered.

"Berenger's sister?"

My voice rose. "Riley?"

"Uh-huh," Vernon said, still staring down at his phone. "Hawkins plastered her pictures all over his Facebook page again. A few new ones, this time." He made a choking sound. "Must have been from the party on Friday night. Now I know what everyone was buzzing about in the parking lot." He sucked air between his teeth.

"Give me that." I reached over and yanked the phone from Vernon's hand. My thumb scrolled through a handful of photos as my breathing fought to catch up to my heartbeat. Riley with her eyes half-shut. Riley with her shirt lifted above her stomach. Riley chugging a beer bottle, smoking a cigarette. She barely looked conscious in any of them. Hawkins had labeled them *Good Girl Gone Wild*, even mentioning that this was a new feature on his Facebook page. *Feature!* What a great friend…

My fists ached to punch something. All I knew was that if someone posted photos like that of my sister, Cecilia, on his Facebook page—or anywhere—he would seriously wish he hadn't after I got through with him. How Ryan didn't know what was happening between Hawkins and Riley bothered me. Why didn't he want to take Hawkins apart, starting with his smarmy smile and then working his way down, limb by rotten limb?

I tossed the phone back to Vernon and then popped up in my chair at exactly the moment that Principal Graser started talking about prom. "I gotta get out of here," I said to the guys, not bothering to look at them.

"Where to?" Martin said but I ignored him.

I grabbed my backpack, hitched it over my shoulder and

then stormed down the row straight for Mr. Holdren, who suddenly decided to look up from his folder.

Mr. Holdren didn't ask why I needed a pass to see Mr. Romero before first period, and for that I was relieved. I had no intention of seeing my guidance counselor. It was too late for guidance.

As I broke out of homeroom into the empty hallway, I heard my breath whooshing out through my mouth and nostrils. It muffled the noises around me—a locker slamming, the creak of a classroom door opening, somebody's sneakers squeaking across the linoleum floor behind me. Principal Graser's voice was still filling the overhead speakers with updates and reminders, but all of his words blended together.

I walked to the middle of the hallway and faced the row of homeroom classrooms. There were at least six classrooms in this hallway and I knew Hawkins was in one of them. I waited, stuffing my clenched fists in the front of my pockets. I had no idea what I was going to say to him or what I was going to do but I knew we were *going to have words,* as my dad liked to say when he was upset with me.

The bell rang, buzzing throughout the entire school, and people began to shuffle behind the closed homeroom doors. Almost at the same time, all the doors opened and students streamed out and filled the hallway with clatter.

My eyes scanned heads as my heart thumped against my chest.

Fred and Ryan walked out of one of the rooms to my right, holding hands. For once, I was halfway glad to see them together. I locked eyes with Fred and she beamed at me, clearly pleased that she and Ryan reconciled, but I looked away in the next beat before she could read me.

I turned left, scanning the bodies for the obvious red-and-black letterman jacket, my eyes mindful of the clock that hung high in the middle of the wall. I had five minutes before I would be late for calculus.

The air in the hallway grew thicker as people pushed open the front doors behind me to cut through the courtyard. Just as I was about to give up and bolt to class, I spotted his grin.

Jay sauntered out of the middle room directly in front of me, surrounded by three of his friends. Typical. They cackled louder than everyone else in the hallway. My knuckles tightened.

As Jay stepped into the stream of students heading to the west wing of the school, I took my hands out of my pockets and took one step into the center of the hallway, blocking his path. He'd have to go through me if he wanted to get down the hallway.

Jay's jaw dropped with surprise, his face turning a shade paler, but only for a moment. Then his glare lifted to mine.

His friends stood beside him like a fortress, forcing everyone to squeeze around them. The odds weren't in my favor. There were four of them, two more wearing those lame letterman jackets, but I didn't care.

"What's up, Just Sam?" Jay said with a forced laugh. He even added a little military two-finger salute, causing more laughter from his minions. "Here to thank me for getting you nominated to prom court?" When I didn't answer, he added, "Don't mention it," before shoulder-shrugging at his buddy.

My nostrils flared.

"You know, it was Riley Berenger's idea," he said. "She practically begged me to get the prom committee to nominate you." Then he grinned. "Of course, I can never refuse a hot girl." His eyebrows wiggled like there was more to the begging. Like Riley traded him something for the favor.

I wanted to puke. What had she done? *Why* would she waste a second of her life with him?

Speaking became difficult, especially when Jay looked at me like he held all the cards. Instead of saying anything, I wanted to punch the grin off his face and be done with it. But I forced myself to say through gritted teeth, "We need to talk about Riley." First Riley, then I'd tell him where he could stuff his prom nomination. He only wanted me nominated to improve his chances of winning. Jay never did anything unless it could benefit him in some way.

Jay shook his head like he didn't know who I was talking about. Then his eyes narrowed and his grin spread. He was enjoying watching my frustration. "Wait. You and Riley?" He wagged his finger between us. His voice got louder, making sure the whole hallway, the whole world heard him. "You're not jealous, are you?"

It was impossible not to roll my eyes at him. "This has nothing to do with me and Riley and you know it."

He chuckled. "You know what I think, Just Sam? I think you're full of shit. You like her, don't you?" He was enjoying this.

I decided to listen to him blather for exactly five more seconds.

"Hate to tell you this—" he spoke out of the corner of his mouth, looking from side to side as if the hallway wasn't filled with dozens of students "—she sure didn't act like your girlfriend Saturday night." He was enjoying himself a little too much for my liking.

"What exactly is your problem, Hawkins?" I said through gritted teeth.

He waved me off. "Just yanking your chain, Tracy. Chill out." Then he paused. "You better keep a leash on that one. She's one hot tamale." He growled while he rocked his hips.

"Now who's full of shit," I said. Jay's overly white teeth

snapped shut when I took another step closer, my fists balled, even as a few nervous laughs floated around us.

Students began to form a tighter circle around us.

The circle grew three deep, then four. But my eyes stayed laser-focused on Jay. I noticed that the corner of his mouth began to twitch the closer I got. "You gotta take down those photos of Riley from your Facebook page," I said. It wasn't a request.

"Why?"

"Because I said so."

Jay's chin pulled back as he feigned innocence. "Humph. I wasn't aware that you and I were Facebook friends." His shiny lips pouted like a child's.

"You're a prick, Hawkins," I said. "Those photos are wrong and you know it."

His innocent smile darkened. "And you need to mind your own business."

"Riley is my business," I said before I could think of something else to say. People around us began to whisper and that's when I noticed that the hallway had grown quieter despite the wall of people surrounding us. No one seemed interested in making it to their first period classes on time.

"And those photos are mine," Jay said.

"You're an asshole," I said, closing the space between us. I was seriously considering snapping his head off his neck.

"Did you ask her?" Jay's chin lifted, challenging me.

I scoffed. "Don't need to."

"Ask her what?" said a voice behind me.

I turned. Ryan Berenger stood beside me, his eyes focused on Jay. He was surrounded by Vernon, Martin and Peter. Fred stood on tiptoe behind Vernon for a better look, her face frozen into a glare aimed at Jay and his buddies.

Jay fake-laughed. "No big, Ryan. Just had some fun with your sis last weekend at the party."

Ryan took a step closer until he was practically chin-to-chin with Jay. "Yeah? What kind of fun?"

"You were there. Remember?" His grin returned as his gaze swept between Ryan and Fred. "I seem to recall you were—" he cleared his throat, his eyes darting between Fred and Ryan "—rather occupied."

Ryan started to close the gap but I grabbed his arm. This wasn't his fight. This was all mine.

"Just check out his Facebook page," I said without turning to Ryan, my eyes still cutting razor blades into Jay's. "That should answer your question." It was hard for me to mask my irritation even with Ryan because, seriously, if I knew, how could he possibly not know what happened between Jay Hawkins and his own sister? He was at the party!

"Oh, I intend to," Ryan said. "And you don't think I'll be pressing the 'like' button on your Facebook posts anytime soon, Hawkins. I'd recommend you take them down."

"Ooooh," Jay said, puffing his chest. His fingers fluttered in front of his face like a fan. "The Lone Ranger and Tonto are suddenly making threats." His jackass friends snorted around him but there was a hint of fear in their faces, too. Jay was taking this further than they expected, that much was clear. "I am so scared," he added.

Unable to restrain myself a moment longer, I lunged for Jay, while voices chanted "Fight! Fight!" around us. I had grabbed the leather collar of his jacket with one hand and connected my other fist to his jaw when I felt hands pull back both my shoulders. A third pair of hands pulled on my backpack, still looped over my shoulders. I'd forgotten it still hung on my back.

Suddenly the hallway was a sea of blurry hands and arms

in front of my face, a hundred voices, hot sticky chaos. Hot skin. I was pulled backward and forward. I wanted to break free from all the hands and pounce right onto Jay Hawkins, but the hands and arms wouldn't let me. Someone launched a punch to my stomach and I felt bone against my right fist. Girls shrieked.

Out of nowhere, a security officer appeared in the middle of everything, one of the stockiest ones at the high school. "Break it up!" he yelled, his voice drowning out everyone else's, except no one broke apart, least of all me. I still had a grip on Jay's stupid wool jacket and my arm had just pulled back for another punch when two hands grabbed my fist and pulled back.

"Tracy started it," Jay yelled, pointing at me, retreating into the fold of his friends as the crowd reluctantly separated. Blood dribbled down the corner of Jay's mouth.

"He deserved it," I said, but not loud enough for anyone to hear.

I turned to see whose hands still pulled on my right shoulder. It was Ryan. "This wouldn't have happened if you kept a closer eye on your sister." I glared at him.

"What are you talking about?" Ryan's hands dropped from my shoulder. His blue eyes, carbon copies of Riley's, blazed like dry ice. "I know exactly what's going on with my sister. I live with her. Remember?"

"You know nothing," I said, waving away Martin's and Peter's hands. The security officer was barking information into a walkie-talkie attached to his shoulder. More bodies brushed by me as the distance between Jay and me increased. The air grew lighter.

Then I saw an opening among the bodies and backpacks.

Before anyone could stop me, I pushed through the glass door with my palm and sprinted toward the courtyard like my shoes had caught fire.

39

RILEY

I knew that Mom was right and I should study but I didn't want to. No—scratch that. I wouldn't study and give Mom the satisfaction that she had any control over what I would do or not do anymore. I'd rather that she and Dad see a few C's on my report card for a change, maybe even a D, because that's where I was headed. Thing was, I had never fallen behind before in anything in my entire life. I was usually two chapters ahead of everyone else, carefully planning my assignments and research papers before they were due, highlighting important parts of a textbook in yellows and pinks, even doing homework on Friday nights when Drew wasn't available for sleepovers.

Drew. I couldn't text her. Couldn't call. I didn't know if she wanted to speak to me again.

Another day at home and I was going to lose my mind. I felt fine, even if Mom didn't think so. And it had been four days already of solitary confinement—five, if you counted today.

I crept over and placed my ear against the door. I wasn't

sure whether Mom was still in the house. I knew that Dad and Ryan had left almost an hour ago.

The floors hummed. Connie, our housekeeper, was running the vacuum somewhere on the first floor. No doubt Mom had already advised her about my captivity.

I pressed my ear harder against the door. The humming seemed to be going in the opposite direction. With any luck, Connie would be occupied on the first floor for an hour or so and I could sneak into Mom's bedroom and hunt for my phone. She'd probably hidden it on the top shelf in her closet, where she hid the Christmas presents every year. I needed my cell phone. Just for a little while....

Outside, another hum started. A familiar hum.

I ran to my bedroom window and threw open the shade My hands reached for the glass as I squinted against the sunlight.

Sam Tracy was parking his motorcycle alongside the curb, his long legs still straddling the seat, in between the two pickup trucks and a trailer from a landscape company. Sam removed his helmet, dragging his hands through his hair, and then his dark eyes scanned our house, taking in the lawn guys first and then working their way up the front of our house. Almost as if he could sense someone staring back at him, checking him out. Which I totally was. The sight of him seated on his bike melted me.

I stared back, too stunned to wave. Sam Tracy was here? At my house? In the middle of the morning?

But how had he found me? How did he know? And could he see me through the window? I tapped on the glass.

It only took a moment before Sam's gaze locked onto mine.

My jaw quivered. I was too surprised to say anything, not like I could. The window was shut and there was all the noise....

Seeing me, Sam lifted his hand, waving, but almost like he was embarrassed. Or uneasy. He stayed on his bike, his hands dropping to his sides, as if he expected me to come outside.

I waved back, grinning like an idiot. "I'll be right down!" I said. I spread my fingers. "Give me five minutes." I pressed my hand against the warm glass, hoping that he understood.

To my delight, he nodded.

I felt an anxious smile build across my face. Then I turned and darted like a crazy person around my room. Busting outside was going to take a miracle. My hand reached for my hair. I'd barely combed it in days. I raised my hand over my breath and exhaled. Morning breath. Ugh.

In five minutes, I'd splashed ice-cold water across my face, brushed my teeth, ran a comb through my hair, slipped on a pair of jeans and a clean T-shirt, grabbed the five ten-dollar bills that I had rolled in my top desk drawer for emergencies and slipped on my pink Converse. Just in case, I grabbed a sweatshirt and tied it around my waist. I glanced quickly in the mirror over my bedroom dresser, realizing that I'd never gotten ready so quickly in my entire life.

I didn't know where Sam and I were going, but my shoulders lifted with the possibility that we were going *somewhere*.

I threw open my bedroom door, ran across the floor to the stairwell, flew down the stairs two at a time and then threw open the front door, ignoring Connie's perplexed expression as she stopped pushing the vacuum and stared at me.

"I'll be back!" I told her without more than a quick glance over my shoulder. "Don't worry," I added.

"But..." she yelled over the vacuum.

Before she could finish her thought, I was crossing the front porch and running down the path to the street, leaping over a leaf blower like it was a track hurdle, heat rushing up my neck.

Sam was still seated on his motorcycle, the helmet cradled in his arm.

"You came," I said. My smile returned. "I…I can't believe you're here."

He nodded.

"But it's Friday. A school day."

"So?" Sam said, surprising me.

"How did you find me?" I had to yell over the lawn mower.

He pointed to our front door. Welcome to the Berengers' was engraved on a piece of wood in the shape of a four-leaf clover next to our house.

"Oh. Yeah. I forgot about that." I glanced back at the house. I had exactly one minute before Connie ran out of the house, probably waving a vacuum attachment at Sam. Or maybe she was already on the phone to Mom. "Can you start this thing up? Like, as soon as possible?" I said.

"What's the hurry?" He handed me the helmet.

"I'll explain later. Just go. I don't care where. Please." I jammed the helmet over my head. Then I slipped my leg over the seat and wrapped my hands around his waist and squeezed him *hello*.

Sam twisted the throttle and then turned the bike.

I hugged him tighter.

In an instant we were cruising toward Pecos Road. I leaned forward, balancing my chin on Sam's shoulder, and smiled.

The day was turning out a lot better than I'd expected. I was seriously going to get in more trouble than ever before, and I didn't care one little bit. I guess that officially made me a crazy teenager.

Who cared? Thanks to Sam, I was finally free.

40

SAM

Riding with Riley on my motorcycle was better than spending the rest of the day in Principal Graser's office or, worse, trying to explain my fight with Hawkins in front of Mr. Romero. I was in deep. And maybe a part of me wanted this.

Now I was riding toward Pecos Road with Riley behind me, her thighs straddling mine, sending electrical shocks all the way up my back, her arms wrapped around my waist and the wind slapping against my face like a warning. If it was a warning, I didn't heed it. I pulled back on the accelerator.

Halfway down a mostly deserted Pecos Road, I drove off into the soft gravel, if only to wait for my insane actions to catch up to my brain. The Rez stretched south as far as we could see, acres of brown ground sprinkled between farms. Staring across the desert, my heart raced. I let the bike idle and turned to Riley. Her big blue eyes blinked at me through the helmet and I swallowed, hard. Her hands fell to the tops of her thighs and the electricity in my body slowed, allowing me a steady breath.

"Why are we stopping?" she said.

I cleared my throat. "We don't know where we're going."

"I know!" Her grin stretched wider.

My head tilted.

"Anywhere but here," she said.

"Anywhere's a big place."

"How about California?"

"California?" My eyes widened. I was hardly expecting that. "That's a six-hour ride."

"So drive faster."

When she smiled at me like that it was practically impossible to say no. I turned away, just for a moment, to get a grip on what I should say next. "Why California?" I said finally. It was a totally crazy stupid idea, and yet I liked the sound of it.

"I want to see the ocean," she said. "Haven't seen water in forever. And we've got the whole day in front of us."

The ocean? I inhaled, as if I could already smell the moist air. It'd definitely be a great ride. "Are you sure you can handle sitting all day on this bike?"

She smiled, patting the sides of her seat. "Positive."

"What about your parents? Shouldn't you call them?" It was the only sensible thing I'd said in hours. Days, even.

"They took away my cell." Her hands lifted in surrender. "Besides, we'll be back tonight. Right?"

"That would be the plan. But it'll be a long day," I warned.

"That works for me."

"Are you sure you'll make it?"

"Totally."

I pulled back the throttle, considering the idea a second longer. Then I said, "When we get there, we've really got to talk."

She sat straighter. "About what?"

"Stuff," I said, sighing. "Stuff you're not gonna like."

"I know. I figured this was coming. But could you save

it till we get there?" She cringed. "I don't want anything to ruin this ride."

I considered this plea. "Okay. Later, then."

Then I pressed down on the pedal and the bike growled louder. It even reared back, like a horse anxious to gallop, and Riley wrapped her arms around me again, resetting that electrical current in my veins.

We rode down Pecos Road until we reached the freeway. Then we drove south until we hit I-8 before we turned west, deep into the desert and straight for the ocean, although it'd be hours before we'd see anything but cactus and tumbleweeds. Whether Riley and I were racing away from our problems or toward more, I wasn't certain, but at least we'd see blue-green water stretching to infinity once we got there. That alone was worth it.

Life would have to wait.

41

RILEY

The sun beat down upon our backs but I was content to watch the world fly by with my chin resting in the slope of Sam's shoulder.

An hour into the ride, Sam leaned back into my arms rather than riding as if someone had duct-taped a ruler to his back. I enjoyed the feel of his back pressed against my chest and my arms wrapped around him. We melted into each other so perfectly. I could ride forever with Sam, just like this. I liked the comfortable familiarity that had grown between us. It was as though we could read each other's minds. I knew he was angry with me (what else was new?) but at least this ride gave me a reprieve. An afternoon at the beach had to soften him.

The wind roared against our ears, preventing conversation but, one time, when we passed a stretch of cotton fields around Wellton, I pinched his stomach just because I was bored. That's when I realized Sam's stomach was rock-hard and there was barely any skin to pinch. He jumped up in his seat, startled, and glanced at me over his shoulder. In the next instant we laughed. "So Sam Tracy is ticklish," I said, unsure if he could hear me through the plastic helmet and the wind. Sam just nodded and returned his attention to the long stretch of road in front of us, and I returned my chin to his shoulder. For some reason, you never think that big guys like Sam, who rarely cracked a smile, would be ticklish. It seemed like an innocent, little-kid thing. And I kind of liked knowing this tidbit about him. I wondered if anyone else knew. I wondered if Fred had ever gotten this close to him.

When we reached Yuma, I couldn't feel my legs, never mind my butt. Everything below my belly button was tingling numbness, like the feeling you get when you cross your legs for too long.

Sam pulled into a gas station. The little arrow on the gauge was past *E*. Once he parked alongside a gas pump, he had to help me step off the bike, because my legs had forgotten how to bend at the knees.

"Still doing okay?" he said, holding my shoulders until it was clear I wouldn't topple forward.

"Never been better." I shook my legs one at a time.

"Good," he said, placing his hands on his hips, still looking down at me. "Hungry?"

"Starved." I glanced across the street at a McDonald's as I unhooked the helmet strap beneath my chin.

"Mickey D's. Here we come," Sam said, unlocking the pump.

I pulled a couple of bills out of my pocket for the gas.

Sam lifted his hand. "I got it."

"Then I'll get lunch."

Sam smiled. "Deal. But I should warn you, I eat a lot."

"Good. So do I. Wanna bet who can eat more?"

"I'm done playing for a while," Sam said, his smile turning serious.

"Okay," I said, unfazed, "but you're gonna lose."

"I never lose."

★ ★ ★

Between the two of us, we ate: three cheeseburgers, two large fries, an order of chicken nuggets (Sam), a vanilla shake (me) and a chocolate shake (Sam). And Sam ate all the pickles, too. It was just your regular, run-of-the-mill McDonald's, but somehow it was the best food I'd ever tasted.

We finished driving through Yuma and then reached the state line where the freeway got busier and crazier. Somehow Sam knew where to go and for that I was glad because I sure didn't, even though I'd been to San Diego with my parents lots of times during summer vacations.

When Sam turned off an exit, I sucked in another deep breath. The air got moister. It was like breathing through cotton. Now I could feel it, taste it.

Sam pointed straight ahead, anyway.

I squinted.

The ocean loomed in front of us, twinkling below the sun. After so much brown desert, it was blinding.

In the distance, water sparkled a deep blue and stretched outward as far as we could see. White caps frothed along the surface like whipped cream. As we rode closer, the ocean peeked at us between buildings and trees, teasing us even more. I squeezed Sam tighter, and he pressed his palm over my hand.

We'd made it! On a Friday when we should have been in school, probably bored to tears in chemistry class or waiting in a cafeteria line for a tasteless sandwich, we were actually at the beach! How cool was that? I smiled at the sky. The sun was no longer directly overhead and I wondered how much more daylight we'd have.

Sam turned into a parking lot that overlooked the first beach we could find. Besides a couple of vans and cars, the beach parking lot was mostly vacant. The three lifeguard posts that lined the beach were empty. A surfer bobbed in the distance, but no one was swimming. It was as if we had the entire Pacific Ocean to ourselves.

My body felt lighter with each discovery. I knew that riding on the back of a motorcycle to San Diego was all sorts of wrong, but I couldn't deny that everything felt better than all right. Everything felt possible. Perfect.

Sam parked the bike in the spot closest to the beach entrance. We hadn't brought bathing suits or blankets. The water had to be freezing, even for May. Yet there was no way I was getting this close to the water without dunking my feet. I wanted my toes to squeeze in wet sand, and maybe I'd even make a sand castle. As soon as Sam parked the bike, I ran toward the beach and kicked off my shoes. In the next beat, I stripped off my socks.

"What are you doing?" Sam said.

"What's it look like?" My feet sank into the sand. "Aaahhh," I sighed, reveling in the warm goodness.

His lips twisted as he glanced at the parking lot.

"Oh, come on, Sam. Live a little."

Then he bent over and untied his laces. His shoes were the big, brown clunky kind that you see on construction workers.

We headed toward the water with our shoes dangling from our fingertips, sinking deeper and deeper into the warm sand with each step.

We walked in silence, the waves drowning out all other sounds. I closed my eyes against the sun, against the mist from the water, inhaling the air. When I opened them, the water glistened like diamonds against the blue sky. It was like staring at a postcard.

Sam's eyes smiled down at me. He was doing that thing again where his eyes did the talking instead of his mouth. I'd swear he wanted to kiss me.

But then the smile in his eyes faded. "Riley, we might as well get this over with. We really have to talk."

I faced the ocean, mist bouncing off my cheeks, Sam in my periphery. "It can't wait just a little while longer?" Maybe I could have handled the Sam Speech at the McDonald's in Yuma but this…*this* was like we were standing in our own paradise. I didn't want anything to ruin the moment, but I already knew his answer by the tilt of his head.

That couldn't be good. It might even be worse than I thought. It was obvious that I had disappointed Sam Tracy. I knew that I had gone too far the past couple of weeks. He was still angry about Friday night; so was my brother. My parents were freaking out at me. Join the club.

But now, standing beside him with an ocean stretched in front of us, I'd take it all back. Disappointing Sam felt worse than anything, worse than I had ever imagined.

42

SAM

I'd never been the type to talk about my feelings and problems. I would rather stick cactus needles in my eyes. But somehow being away from Phoenix, away from school, away from Jay Hawkins and all of the other useless distractions, suddenly my jaw didn't clench so much. My shoulders loosened. I could breathe. I could be me.

And maybe I could let Riley see beyond what I was normally willing to show. I only hoped that I wouldn't come off too righteous.

Riley and I walked to the shore, just before the water reached us, and we sat in front of an endless stretch of shiny wet sand. The beach was empty and a soft ocean spray cooled my cheeks. I squinted into the sun. I was ready to get everything off my chest but unsure how to start....

"So talk." Riley prodded my shoulder with her finger.

I jumped a little when she spoke, despite the pounding waves. I gazed back over the horizon for courage.

Then she reached down for my hand and held it in both

of hers as she looked at me. Funny how her touch seemed so natural now. I liked it.

"Is this about Fred?"

"No," I said, turning to her. "Yes." I sighed. "I mean, no. Not really." How could I say that? My crazy stupid love for Fred was what started this whole downward spiral and the intersection of our lives.

"Yes? No?" She chuckled nervously and I could tell she suddenly felt uneasy about holding my hand. "So which one is it? Did you finally tell her how you felt? Did you finally ask her out? Is that what you're trying to tell me?"

"This has nothing to do with Fred. I mean, it does and it doesn't. But this is about Jay Hawkins—"

"Jay?" She sounded disappointed.

"Yeah. We kind of got into a fight at school."

"*Kind* of?" Horror filled her face. "What? When?"

"This morning." Now she sounded like she was defending this guy.

But then she scanned my face, like she was checking for bruises. She examined my hand, but I pulled it away from her fingers and thrust it into the sand. "Are you…are you hurt?"

"Are you kidding?" A few bruises on my knuckles, but they blended into my skin.

"What's that supposed to mean?"

My voice rose. "Jay Hawkins? Please. Don't insult me."

"Is he…okay?" She cringed.

"He *might* have a black eye." It did not pain me to share this detail. "Or something." Hopefully he'd have to get his jaw wired shut for the rest of the school year.

"Gah! Why? Why did you get into a fight with Jay? That's totally crazy! After he got you nominated to prom court?"

I leaned forward. "Seriously? You seriously don't know?" Then I leaned back, already exhausted from talking in circles, from trying to explain and gauging her reactions, which changed every second. Was she really that naive? "And I didn't want to be nominated, Riley. Why would you even ask him to do that? Without asking me first?"

"So Fred would have a good reason for going with you to prom. Obv." Riley said it like I was an idiot.

"Be real. Fred is going with Ryan."

"But what if you needed a date? A date for the biggest night of your life? She'd go with you in a heartbeat."

"You don't know Fred."

"You don't know women."

Well, Riley had me there. But, still. There was no way Fred was going anywhere without Ryan. Not now. Not ever. "Wait. Stop." I put up my palm and closed my eyes, dizzy from Riley's logic and the weird way her mind worked. As usual, she was getting me off topic. "This isn't about Fred."

"But you brought up prom—"

"This is about Jay Hawkins."

Riley sat back, extending her legs. "Okay, so what about him?"

"Haven't you seen what he's been saying about you on Facebook?"

Riley sat straighter, momentarily excited. Then her shoulders slumped. "Can't. My parents took away my laptop."

"Well, you should check his page."

"Why?"

"'Cause he's been making fun of you, Riley. Jay, your best new bud. And maybe in other places, too." I paused. "He's totally been playing you, Riley."

"Playing me? That's ridiculous! You've got to stop saying that."

"Do you even know what happened Friday night?"

She turned. "Yes. I mean, no. I mean…kind of." Her voice

got softer. "I don't remember everything." Her shoulders pulled together, and she looked embarrassed. "And I haven't been able to talk to anyone about it, thanks to my parents."

I exhaled, running my other hand through my hair. "Jeez, Riley." I shook my head. "Guys like Jay Hawkins…well, they're the last guys you ever want to be alone with. *Ever.*" I drew back a breath again. "Did he do anything…you know?" I tilted my head like the question should be obvious.

She shook her head, blushed and buried her chin against her shoulder. Even quieter than before, she said, "No. I would know, Sam. And Jay's not like that." She turned to the ocean and said, "And I'm pretty sure he's taking me to prom."

I pulled back. "Are you serious?" It was hard to control my disgust. And some of my jealousy. "Has he asked you?"

She sniffed and looked away. "Not yet. Not officially. But I'm sure he will."

My voice got louder. "Riley, he didn't care that you had to walk home in the middle of the night on an injured leg. And after all the pictures he's posting of you online, you still like this guy?" My voice rose well above the roar of the ocean. "You'd still go anywhere with him? Are you that desperate?"

She couldn't answer—wouldn't answer—but I watched her nostrils flare with anger.

I grabbed her arm, turning her toward me. I needed her to hear me, every word. "Don't be so sure he'll ask."

She pulled away. "What's it to you? Why do you even care?"

I reached for her hand but she pulled it away. "Maybe because I feel like I kind of got you into this. I shouldn't have told you about Fred. I shouldn't have told you anything." My voice was tight. "I feel responsible." *And I'm falling for you, hard.* But I couldn't tell her that. Those words wouldn't leave my lips, not now. Maybe not ever. I didn't feel like getting my heart pulverized again.

Riley's lip quivered.

Tears welled in the corners of her eyes. She dragged her hand beneath her nose.

This time, her tears didn't stop me from saying what needed to be said. "And I don't need your help with Fred, Riley. There's nothing you can do. There's nothing I want you to do." Her lips quivered. "Fred belongs with Ryan. She's made that clear."

Riley looked away, the wind tossing her hair in front of her face. "Yeah, well, if I'd known you were going to give up so easily, I wouldn't have gotten involved. My bad."

I leaned back on my hands and laughed. "Oh, now I'm the bad guy?"

She sniffed.

"You think you can throw out an apology and everything goes away?" I said. "You think life is that easy?" I laughed, but nothing was funny at the moment. Nothing.

Riley's clouded gaze morphed into a full-on glare and her mouth opened. Her chest moved faster, like she was starting to hyperventilate.

"Wait," I said, raising my palm. "I didn't mean—"

She rose, still glaring at me. I wanted to say something that would make her feel better but in that moment I was struck stone-cold silent by the blue of her eyes. Fiery and mesmerizing at the same time, they matched the ocean. They were pure Riley. "Save it, Sam. You don't want to know. You don't know a single thing about me. You think you do but, trust me, you don't." Then she began to march toward the parking lot, the sand shooting up like daggers behind her heels.

"Wait up," I said. As usual, my words didn't come out like I wanted them to. "I'm sorry."

"Shut up."

I pulled back on her arm. "*Wait*. Hear me out."

"Oh, I heard you. Loud and clear. You obviously think I'm a total loser, too."

"I never said that!" But then my voice softened. "I was only trying to warn you about Jay Hawkins."

She yanked her arm but I held her elbow. "I already told you I have a brother," she said through clenched teeth. "I definitely don't need another one."

"And maybe…just maybe, I didn't want to see you get hurt."

"Like I said—"

Blacks and reds flashed in my periphery. "Oh, no." I glanced over her shoulder.

"What?" Riley snapped. She turned and looked at the parking lot with me.

Three beefy guys with jet-black hair and lots of arm and neck tats began circling my motorcycle like it was prey. One guy wearing a red baseball cap on backward hopped on the seat and twisted the throttle.

My heart raced faster. My hand squeezed Riley's arm. "Wait here."

She nodded. Her face paled as gray as the sand.

Quickly, I slipped back into my socks and shoes and then I jogged back to the parking lot, even as sand filled the heels of my shoes.

"Hey!" I said when I took my first step onto the pavement. My voice filled the parking lot. "Back off, dude! That's my bike you're messing with!"

The guy on my motorcycle, the biggest of the three, bristled. But then his irritation sprouted into a grin. I was close enough to see a snake tattoo curling up his neck. "Yeah?" he yelled back, a thin muscle bulging beneath the tattoo. "And who's the shithead that's gonna make me?" His friends laughed.

I ignored them.

"You?" he said, making a hand signal and pressing it against his chest.

I stormed toward them, anyway. Adrenaline raged through my veins. "Get. Off. My. Ride!" I was making everything worse, just like I had with Jay Hawkins. And this time there were three of them, but I was too furious to be scared.

When I got close, Biker Guy leaped off the seat. He proceeded to kick it to the ground with the heel of his boot.

My teeth clenched as the handlebars crashed in slow motion against the pavement. "You really shouldn't have done that," I growled.

Biker Guy stalked toward me, chest puffed, his friends flanked on either side of him.

The tighter the space between us, the less clearly my mind worked. I was reacting on pure rage.

Biker Guy stood below my chin, his chest grazing mine, taunting me. His breath was stale. "What's your problem, man? We were only admiring your wheels." He grinned at me with teeth stained from too many cigarettes. I should have my head examined for standing so close but I couldn't help it. He had *kicked* my *bike*.

"Yeah?" I said, closing the sliver of distance between us. He wasn't going to stare me down. "Where I come from, people usually ask before helping themselves to other people's stuff."

"Ohhhh." Biker Guy exhaled, turning to his friends with fake admiration. He backed off a hair, but I could still make out the teardrop tattoos that dotted the side of his face. I should be way more scared than I was. "And where's that, bro? 'Cause you sure don't look like you're from around here."

It was hard not to roll my eyes. The idiot was behaving

like I was from another country, which, I guessed compared to him, I probably was. "Just get away from my bike, man. Cool?" I lifted my palms, remembering that Riley was behind me. "No harm done."

His friends chuckled again in a way that said plenty of harm had already been done. The one on his right was probably around my age, looked Asian, skinny, with tattoos sleeved on both arms. He reached a hand behind his waistband. At first I thought he was pulling up his pants but then I froze.

Riley...

While I'd been staring down Biker Guy, one of his loser friends had slipped away.

Next thing I knew, Riley was squirming beside me. A guy more heavily tattooed than Biker Guy had her by the arm.

"Fine *mamacita!*" Biker Guy clucked, flashing a silver stud in the middle of his tongue. "Is this yours, too, bro?" He grinned, wider than before. His friends trilled their approval, as all three circled Riley like vultures.

"I'm not anyone's," Riley said, her voice trembling. Somehow she was able to shake off his grip.

This only made them laugh harder.

"She's with me," I said, stepping closer to Riley. I draped my arm across her shoulder, not casually but so I could push her out of the way if necessary. "Leave her alone," I said. "She's just a girl."

Biker Guy chuckled. "Do I look blind to you? I have two eyes," he said, as his gaze continued to sweep over Riley.

Frozen beneath my arm, Riley whispered, "Can't we just get out of here?"

"No one's going anywhere," Biker Guy said. "This party's just getting started."

My eyes shifted around the parking lot, toward the entrance. Except for a couple of empty cars, we were still alone.

All my senses heightened.

Biker Guy grazed Riley's cheek with the back of his hand. "Soft as butta," he said, turning to his friends. They chuckled with appraising eyes.

Riley sucked back a breath.

"Hey. Hands *off*," I said.

Biker Guy puffed out his chest again. "Who's gonna make me?" He jabbed a finger at my chest. "You?" The whites of his eyes flashed wilder.

"Just back off."

"Tell you what," Biker Guy said, pulling on his chin. "You give me the keys to your ride, and I let you leave in one piece. *Comprendes?*"

"What?" Riley squeaked beside me. "How will we get home?"

I ignored Riley. "Tell you what," I said, matching Biker Guy's grin. "You step out of our way, and I'll let you keep your pretty teeth."

Biker Guy backed away a fraction, his arms outstretched, as they shared another chuckle. Then Biker Guy's hand reached for the back of his waistband and his toothy smile disappeared. He pointed a gun at us.

Time froze.

I was hardly a gun expert but I knew enough to recognize a 9 mm. Icy nickel-plated, the gun was aimed straight at my chest.

Riley shook harder.

I raised my palm. "Whoa. Come on now, let's talk this out."

"New plan," Biker Guy said, his gaze darting over his shoulder for any type of audience. Unfortunately for Riley and me, it was just the two of us, three crazy guys and at least one gun—probably more from the way their hands twitched around their waistbands. "*Mamacita* comes with us and you get to keep your piece-of-shit ride."

Riley pressed closer to my shoulder like she wanted to hide inside my jacket.

I licked my dry lips. "No deal," I said with as much conviction as I could.

But Tattooed Arms Guy reached for Riley, yanking her away from me, while Biker Guy kept his gun trained on me. "Back off, dude," he said, his voice turning sinister. "The time for trash talk is over."

Riley reached out for me. I reached back, and our fingertips brushed together.

I started breathing heavy, trying to think of something to say, something more to do. Everything was happening in fast-forward. "Hey, the bike's yours," I said, dangling the rabbit foot in front of me. "Just let her go." Slowly, I stepped toward them. Riley wriggled like a catfish caught in a net. "Take the keys."

Then the most wonderful sound filled the parking lot.

Sirens. A whole symphony of them.

And they were coming straight for us.

Without a word, Biker Guy and his sidekicks stuffed their knives and guns back in their waistbands, looking sideways, back and forth. Before I could blink, they were inside their car, the engine revved, the accelerator floored. Biker Guy peeled toward the entrance, smoke spewing from the back tires.

In the next heartbeat, I had Riley by the arm and pulled her toward my motorcycle. I wasn't breathing. I was just moving, fast and slow motion at the same time. I lifted the bike off the ground as if it were lighter than air. The helmet was still threaded over the handlebar. Riley got on right behind me, her leg slipping over the seat. Her arms reached for my waist.

"Oh, my god, Sam." Riley's trembling voice brushed against my ear. Her entire body shook against mine. "Let's get out of here."

My key found the ignition, my hand pulled back on the throttle and we were racing toward the entrance.

And the army of police cars and fire trucks? They sped straight down the street, their red-and-yellow lights peeking through the trees that separated the beach from the street, as if we were never there.

43

RILEY

I flung my arms around Sam's waist, clinging to him as tightly as ever. It was an effort to keep myself from getting hysterical between his shoulder blades. It was a weird thing to watch your life flash before your eyes.

We sped down streets called Mission, Loma, Oceanside and Harrison, all happy-sounding names that cruelly masked what could really happen if you took a wrong turn when no one was looking. We made lefts and rights and more U-turns. We rode in circles till my head spun.

Finally I tugged on Sam's jacket. I had to yell over the engine. "Where are we going?" My hair flew around my face, sticking to my lips.

Sam turned a fraction so I could hear him. "Just want to make sure we lost them. I didn't want them to follow us."

My stomach tightened at the thought of seeing any of those boys again. Boys? Criminals, more like it. "Should we find a police station?"

"Do you want to?"

I paused, considering it. It was probably the smart thing

to do. Tell the police all about them, describe their tattoos and baggy pants; explain what they'd done to us, the green car they'd driven with the wide wheels and shiny hubcaps. How they'd threatened to kill us. And yet reliving it—any of it—was the last thing I wanted to do.

"Let's just go home," I said finally, burying my head and feeling another surge of tears thicken my throat as we approached the freeway ramp. This day had turned into one big bad dream. I was seriously cursed.

Instead of the freeway, Sam turned into one of those huge gas stations, the kind with endless pumps and a convenience store in the middle. Classic rock blared from overhead speakers, and I was glad to see that almost every pump was taken. I didn't want to go anywhere without a lot of people. Customers darted in and out of the store with sodas, cigarettes and six-packs of beer. Sam found an empty parking spot near a corner. He shut off the ignition and spun around over the seat so that we were facing each other, straight on.

"Riley," he said. He grabbed my arms.

I could see the apology in his eyes, one that I didn't deserve. I lowered my head and covered my face in hands that wouldn't stop trembling. Then before I could answer I jumped off the bike and ran to the blue Dumpster next to the air pump that no one was using. I fell to my knees on the pavement and puked.

After my stomach was empty, I sat back on my knees, struggling to catch my breath. I wiped my mouth.

"Riley?" Sam said behind me. His voice cut through the silence. He placed a hand on my lower back.

I sat up, embarrassed, and turned to face him. Puking seemed to have become a habit for me.

One thousand watts of more worry filled his eyes, and I fought back another urge to cry again, or worse. He knelt and then reached for me. He took my face between his hands, caressing my cheeks with his thumbs until I had no choice but to look at him.

We sat there, staring at each other, letting our eyes talk, especially since our words—mine especially—seemed to always be all wrong.

I'm sorry, his eyes said, so simultaneously fierce and gentle, the kindest eyes I'd ever known.

I'm sorry, too, mine replied.

I wanted to kiss Sam Tracy, right then and there, more than anything in the world, but I didn't think I had the right. Plus I'd just puked. So I took a deep breath and kissed him with my eyes and I let myself believe that his eyes kissed me back.

Finally, he stood and extended a hand to me.

I swallowed, praying I wouldn't hurl again, and threaded my fingers through his.

Sam wrapped his strong arms around me. His embrace stilled my shaking. Then it was like my whole body split apart, bone by bone, muscle by muscle. The dam burst and more tears flowed.

"I am so sorry," he whispered in my ear, warm breath against my skin.

I fought against my sobs. He crushed me against his chest. Speaking was still difficult. "Not…your…fault," I croaked. *I'm the reason we're here, remember?*

Sam's chin pressed against the top of my head. "What do you want to do? Should we call the police? Call your parents? I'll do whatever you want."

I shook my head, feeling his chin pressed against my head. "No," I said, fighting to speak. "I'll be okay." I breathed in his jacket. It smelled all-Sam, campfire and desert, and only brought more tears. I leaned deeper into his opened jacket. "Are you okay?" I asked him.

"I am now."

I cried harder. Sam didn't say a word. He just held me.

How long we stood by that smelly blue Dumpster, I didn't know. All I knew was that holding Sam was the only thing I needed.

Gasoline pumps beeped and people buzzed around us. A few people probably stared at the two crazy kids hugging each other for dear life, but I didn't care.

Finally, my breathing slowed and my sobs quieted.

Sam pulled back, his hands gripping my shoulders. His eyes, still warm and full of worry, found mine. And, hello? Why hadn't I noticed his impossibly long eyelashes before? Then his thumb grazed my cheek, wiping off a stray tear.

His beautiful eyes crinkled at the corners. "Home?" He said it like he knew the answer.

I nodded. "Home." I hiccupped.

A relieved smile erased the crease between his eyes.

His arm never leaving my shoulder, we walked back to the motorcycle. I took my spot behind him as he turned the ignition, returning the engine to life. My hands fell to his hips, my thumbs brushing his belt loops. He twisted the throttle and the bike roared, ready to fly us home.

We coasted out of the gas station toward the freeway.

Home had never sounded so good. *Home* with Sam Tracy sounded perfect.

44

SAM

The instant we reached the freeway, the sky changed colors. It was as if someone had pulled the plug on the blue and spray-painted it with gigantic swaths of black and gray. Thunder rumbled around us and the temperature dropped enough to chill me through my jacket. I pulled back on the throttle and opened up the engine. The sooner we returned to the desert, the better.

But outrunning the storm was impossible. Like a shadow, it followed us across the state line all the way to Yuma. Just my luck, it rained only a handful of days each year in the desert, and today, of all days, Mother Nature decided to gift us with an early monsoon. There was nowhere to pull over—not a gas station, overpass, ravine. Nothing. Just miles and miles of cotton fields and brown desert and Riley and me.

Riley's body pressed against my back. I felt every part of her. I rested one hand over the both of hers clutched around my stomach. At first it was because they still trembled. Once the trembling stopped, I guess I forgot to stop holding them.

In my side-view mirror I smiled apologetically as her chin

burrowed into my shoulder. Her cheeks, still splotchy from tears, pulled back in a smile and she squeezed me tighter, sending another kind of shiver running through my body.

Rain fell, only a few drops at first, but as heavy as pennies. Ice-cold, it pelted our faces. I had to reduce my speed because of the visibility and hunch lower in the seat to shield us both from the rain.

I squinted into the distance, desperate for someplace to wait out the storm. No such luck.

Then headlights glared like bloodshot eyes behind us. The beams glinted against my rearview as rain pelted the glass. Riley's breath hitched in my ear before she turned for a better look. For miles, we'd owned the road. Now we had company.

I decided to pull up on the throttle and veer to the right, giving the vehicle plenty of room to pass.

Except the car didn't pass.

It stayed behind us, matching us mile for mile. I had to squint even harder as its headlights bounced off both rearview mirrors on the handlebars, the right one still scuffed and bent from Biker Guy kicking over my bike.

Biker Guy...

My gut tightened.

The car closed the distance between us and I pulled back a little on the throttle. The car drove faster, less than a car length behind me now. Ahead, lightning streaked in crazy zigzags through the sky. The rain fell harder, drenching our hair, our clothes. I shook off droplets and concentrated on the road.

"What's going on?" Riley yelled against the rain, tugging on my sleeve.

"I don't know," I yelled back, scanning the rearview mirrors, the lightning. The monsoon was dropping on us. I squinted at the car in my rearview mirror. It was dark with thick front tires. I tried to see the driver through the windshield, but the glare from the headlights blinded me.

My heart began to race as fast as the storm. Riley squeezed tighter, and I revved the engine. The bike had to go faster.

"Be careful!" Riley yelled.

I nodded. I was trying. I was trying my best. But something wasn't right. And something was all too familiar about the car behind us. Would Biker Guy and his friends seriously follow us across state lines? All the way to Arizona? Were they that insane?

The answer mocked me in my rearview. *Yes, they were.*

A gush of air blew through my teeth as if I'd been punched. My mind raced with anger and frustration. Why did it have to monsoon now, of all times?

So I gripped the handlebars tighter. We wouldn't be safe until we reached the Rez. Another fifty miles? Maybe a hundred? We had to keep moving. It was the only option.

I lowered my head, my hair dripping with rain, and floored it. I knew it was crazy, given the slick road, but I couldn't take a chance again with those guys and their itchy trigger fingers.

Then red lights began to screech and swirl behind me. They lit up the sky.

Say what?

The lights lit up the sedan behind me like a psycho Christmas tree. I blinked in disbelief. I slapped my hand against the handlebar and swore into the wind, spewing every curse word I knew and even a few in Navajo that Martin had taught me.

"Are you kidding me?" Riley screamed, too.

I didn't know whether to laugh or keep cursing.

A voice boomed over a bullhorn through the pounding rain. "Driver!" he yelled. "Pull over!"

It wasn't Biker Guy. Not even close. We had a DPS patrol officer on our tail, driving an unmarked car.

"Great," I murmured, slapping the handlebar again as my bike slowed. "*Now* I get pulled over."

45

RILEY

I sat in the back of the patrol car, trying to see through the windshield, but it was practically impossible. Scratched plastic at least an inch thick separated the backseat from the front, perfect for transporting criminals and fugitives. The officer had left the car running and the heat blasting, but my whole body shivered with fright and confusion. Why did we get pulled over? Why was the officer questioning Sam?

Rain fell in gray sheets with blowing red dirt mixed in. The world inside and out was a mess, and it had nothing to do with weather. I wanted to be outside. I wanted to be beside Sam.

The officer wore a black hat with a wide brim and a fluorescent orange rain poncho. Seemingly oblivious to the weather, he tilted his chin upward as he talked to Sam, cool and calm. The officer had to yell to be heard over the rain, and for some reason he kept pointing a long flashlight in Sam's face. Unfortunately I caught only muffled words through the windows, along with a few unmistakable "yes, sirs" and "no, sirs" as they faced each other with puffed-out chests. A total guy thing. I hoped Sam would simply answer his questions so we could get out of here and get home.

"But what does he want?" I reached for the door release, but the panel was smooth. No handle. *Nice.* I was officially a criminal.

The officer kept one hand on the sidearm at his hip. The other clutched his flashlight, clearly ready to use it as a club if necessary. I wanted to scream at him, *It won't be necessary! The guys you really want are back in San Diego!*

After a century or so, Sam and the officer walked to the car. The officer pulled back on the handle to the back door.

I sat straighter. *Finally!*

Sam slid into the backseat, dripping wet. He dragged his hands through his hair, leaving thick ridges from his fingers.

"What's going on?" I whispered as soon as the officer shut the door.

Sam's eyes were shiny black but the whites of his eyes were wide. They weren't frightened. This time they were on fire. "They're taking me to Durango. You, too. I think."

"What?" I choked out. "What is that?"

"Juvy lockup. Downtown."

"Phoenix?"

"Yeah," he said.

I studied the officer as he walked around the car. He spoke into a radio on his shoulder. "Why? We haven't done anything wrong. Maybe if I talk to him…"

"Please don't say anything, Riley." He might as well have added, *You've already said plenty for one lifetime.* Then he said, "Seems someone phoned in a report about two runaways. We fit a description." He frowned and his face darkened another shade.

"Who?"

"I have no idea. Maybe the school. Maybe your parents."

"But we're not runaways."

The officer opened the driver's door and I lowered my voice. "What about your parents?"

"I doubt it was them." His arched eyebrow asked me a question.

"My mom?" I sighed, remembering our last conversation. Sam nodded.

"Yeah, knowing her, it's possible."

Then Sam said, "And he gave me a ticket for driving without a motorcycle license." He rolled his eyes and then looked out the window at his bike. It was parked in the gravel off the side of the road. "My mom says bad things always happened in threes. In our case, we're well past three."

I reached for his wet, ice-cold hand as the officer lifted a microphone attached to a computer thingy beside the steering wheel. I rubbed his hand between mine. He looked down at our hands, his face exhausted.

"I am so sorry, Sam." If I apologized a thousand times, it wouldn't be enough.

"Yeah, me, too."

"No, really. This is my fault. Everything is my fault."

Static buzzed across the microphone and the patrol officer rattled off a number of codes into the speaker. "Yeah, dispatch," he said as he removed his hat, revealing a round, bald head. He slapped his hat against the ridge of the passenger seat and let the water drip on the floor mat. "We've got a possible 702 and need a 926 out on I-8 at highway marker 402. I'll be transporting two to Durango for parent pickup." His voice was deep and calm, the voice of someone who did this a lot.

"Ten-four, 301," a woman's voice answered through more static.

"What about my bike?" Sam said, but the patrol officer raised a palm at the plastic divider, stopping his question.

"Couldn't he just drive us home?" I whispered, and Sam stifled a chuckle but it was hardly lighthearted. More like frustrated.

More codes and strange numbers sputtered between the dispatcher and the police officer.

"Your first arrest?" Sam said through an exhale, as if he wanted to make light of what was happening to us.

I nodded, forcing a smile, hoping to calm him. "How about you?"

Sam turned back to the window and didn't answer. But then he sighed, shook his head at his motorcycle and leaned his face against his hand. He dragged his fingers through his hair and the sides stood up in spiky peaks. Then he said, "We should have stayed in Phoenix. But there's no ocean in the desert," he added, like he was trying to reconcile our decisions.

"The ocean is overrated," I said, squeezing his hand.

The officer returned the microphone to the cradle. Just as I was about to tell him what had happened in San Diego, he reached for his hat and opened the driver's door.

Sam and I stole a quick glance at each other, confused

He walked around to the rear door with heavy steps and opened it. Rain splattered into the backseat.

"You need to step outside the car," he said to Sam. It wasn't an option.

"What now?" Sam said, stepping out into the rain. "Is it something about my bike?"

My whole body began to shake again. Something didn't feel right.

"You, too, young lady," he said to me. "You'll be riding up front with me."

"Why?" I snapped.

"Just do it," the officer ordered.

I stepped into the rain as he opened the front door for me. Cold drops pelted my face, sticking to my eyelashes. Meanwhile, the officer stood razor-close to Sam, his hand back on his sidearm. I slid into the front seat, the upholstery still wet from the officer's hat, and stared out the window, nothing but questions racing through my mind.

"I need you to face the car," he ordered Sam as rain pelted them.

"Why?" Sam said, pulling his shoulders back.

"'Cause I said so," the officer said.

Exhaling, Sam reached his hands against the side of the car.

"Spread your legs," the officer said. Then he began to search Sam's pockets. He patted both legs, from his thighs to his ankles.

"You mind telling me what's this all about?" Sam said again, loud, so he could be heard over the rain.

"I'll explain in a second. Just want to make sure you don't have anything that could hurt me."

"I don't," Sam snarled but the officer ignored him.

"You're a pretty big kid. This is more for my safety than yours," he added.

"Well, glad to be of service," Sam said, again with the sarcasm, but this time the corner of the officer's mouth twitched in a tiny smile that disappeared in an instant.

Sam's eyes locked with mine. They filled with anger and frustration as the rain pelted against his face.

I lifted my hand to the glass. *Don't do anything crazy*, I mind-melded with him as my body shuddered all over again. Was there no end to this nightmare? Just when I'd thought everything would be okay, something else mucked it all up. Why couldn't everyone leave Sam and me alone?

When the officer pulled out a set of handcuffs, I garbled back a scream. That had to be a mistake! Did you get hand-cuffed for driving in the rain?

"You have the right to remain silent," the officer began. "Anything you say can and will be used against you…"

Suddenly it felt like I was having a heart attack.

Thiscannotbehappening.Thiscannotbehappening.Thiscannotbe-happening.

The officer finished the little spiel about Sam's rights, except that nothing was right.

"Seems you fit another description," the officer said finally.

"Really?" Sam said, not bothering to hide his sarcasm. "And what the hell did I do now?"

"Armed robbery in Casa Grande earlier today."

"What?"

The officer slammed the door and I couldn't hear the rest.

He finally let Sam back into the car. With the handcuffs, Sam couldn't even drag his hands through his hair and nei-ther could I. I wanted to pound my fist against the plastic separating us.

We sat in stunned silence all the way to Phoenix. Sam rocked in his seat the whole way as if his chest was going to explode.

The day had just grown a million times worse.

46

SAM

The whole drive into Phoenix, all I could think about were the people who'd be disappointed in me, regardless of what I'd actually done or not done.

My parents: They would certainly kill me. My Dad? I was finally living up to his expectations.

My grandmother: She wouldn't say anything, but she wouldn't need to. Her disappointment would engrave itself in her face. I was the one who was supposed to go places in the family. The one who was supposed to do big things for our tribe. Going to juvenile lockup wasn't on the list.

Mr. Romero: Clearly I wouldn't be invited to next year's leadership conference, all fees paid. And it wasn't as much about the dumb conference as it was about him. He'd been the one person at Lone Butte who believed in me from my freshman year. He'd pushed me to take classes that I didn't think I could handle. He saw me as more than someone who could kick ass on a football team or a wrestling team or whatever. But now I'd have the cloud of this arrest over my head, even though I'd done nothing wrong—well, maybe except for ditching and driving without a motorcycle license.

Trevor: My bike would be impounded. It'd probably cost me a lifetime of bussing tables before I could get it back. I promised Trevor I'd take care of the bike and look what had happened. One cracked rearview and scuff marks all along the frame, and I'd only owned it a couple of weeks.

Riley: Because of my temper, she'd almost gotten killed. *Killed!* The word burned in my throat.

Myself: I could probably kiss any thought of an academic scholarship goodbye. I was pretty sure colleges frowned upon applicants with criminal records.

But here's who I hadn't added to my list: Mr. and Mrs. Berenger. They weren't part of my guilt-ridden equation. So how was it that they had arrived at Durango before Riley and me? Did white people have access to a secret police hotline that the rest of us didn't have?

I never caught the officer's name, and his badge was covered beneath his poncho. He parked the squad car at the front of the building and then led us through two thick doors and a glass-enclosed counter called Processing, his hand wrapped around my elbow tight as duct tape. And, seriously. How far could I get with my hands cuffed behind my back?

My shoulders ached from the pull and my clothes clung to my skin. The moment we were out of the squad car and Riley was beside me again, she reached up and ran cool fingers through my hair, lifting it from my forehead. Despite the chaos happening around us, my whole body shivered from that single touch. The officer glared at Riley, but she ignored him. I liked that. And what did he think she would do? Slip me a shiv that she'd whittled from a pencil in the police car on the way to this dump?

As we walked through the colorless hallways at Durango,

boys in orange jumpsuits filed toward us in a single line, some no older than ten or eleven. They were led by an officer at the front and the rear like teachers used to do in grade school. A few of the boys snickered when we passed. Riley pressed closer the deeper we walked down the hallway.

I glared at the inmates who snickered and the grins of at least two of the boys promptly disappeared. I towered over them. Truth was, I was scared, but I'd never let them see that. Never. I could never let anyone see I was scared. I just wasn't wired that way.

Jeez, the sooner my dad could get here and bail me out, the happier I would be. I didn't want to stick around long enough to be issued an orange jumpsuit and paraded about in single-file lines.

The officer led us into a windowless room with a gray metal desk and four chairs. Mr. and Mrs. Berenger jumped out of two of the chairs as if they'd just been electrocuted.

"Riley!" Mrs. Berenger yelped. I recognized her from the hospital after Fred's father's heart attack. Without her blue scrubs and stethoscope, she just looked like a mom—a mom who'd been doing a lot of crying. Splotchy dots covered her pale cheeks. She ran to Riley and enveloped her in a tight hug.

Riley's whole body stiffened. She stood in her mother's arms, speechless, as if she were as startled to see them as I was.

Mr. Berenger stood watching his wife and daughter, scratching the side of his head, as if he didn't know what to say. Silent, he put his arms around both of them, but kept one eye on me.

I heard a *click* and looked over my shoulder.

Officer What's-His-Name removed my handcuffs. Without a word, he moved to stand outside the opened door.

Instantly I rubbed my wrists, grateful to have the use of my hands again.

Mrs. Berenger released Riley, her eyes narrowing, her head shaking. "Riley?" she said again, this time in a hiss. "What happened? Where have you been? Your father and I have been worried sick. Are you kids all right?"

"You hopped on a motorcycle? And just drove off?" Mr. Berenger said, looking from me to Riley for an explanation.

It felt like I'd just swallowed a glass of sand. "Um…" I said.

"This is my fault," Riley said, taking a step back so she stood beside me again.

I stood straighter.

But then she started talking like she was in a race. "IaskedSamtoditch—"

"Ditch?" Mrs. Berenger interrupted, as if she'd never heard the word before. "Since when do you ditch?"

"Mom. Lemme finish," Riley said. "We just wanted to go for a ride. And we just decided to ride to…" Her face crumpled. "San Diego."

"San Diego?" Mrs. Berenger's voice turned to a roar. She looked from me to Riley. "But I told you not to leave the house. You disobeyed me."

Well, duh.

Riley drew back a breath.

"You should have called us," Mrs. Berenger said.

"You took away my cell phone!" Riley said.

"Do not lay blame on me, young lady." Mrs. Berenger jabbed her finger in the air. Then in a softer voice, she added, "Why, Riley? Why are you acting this way? This is not like you. I don't understand where this is coming from…."

Again Mr. and Mrs. Berenger's eyes darted at me and I just stood there, my tongue stuck to the roof of my mouth. They wanted—no, needed—someone to blame. And for now it was me. Standing there, wet and silent, I was the best candidate.

"This has nothing to do with Sam," Riley said, talking

full-speed again. "In fact, if it hadn't been for Sam…" Riley let her voice trail off. She looked at me for confirmation on what to say, how much to reveal.

Truthfully, I didn't know anymore. All of the lying had become too much.

Riley touched my forearm, and the only thing I could do was shrug my shoulders.

Then the officer was behind me again, his breath too close to my neck, like needles in my skin. "He needs to come with me," he said.

"Where?" Riley asked.

"Riley!" Mrs. Berenger said.

"What?" She spun around, glaring at her mother. "We've got to help him. This is all my fault."

"So you've stated," Mr. Berenger said, looking unconvinced.

My stomach tightened from the invisible gut punch.

"Dad!" Riley screeched as Officer What's-His-Name grabbed my arm again, tugging me toward the door. "Do something. Help him!" she pleaded, raising all ten of her bitten fingernails.

Mr. Berenger licked his lips but said nothing.

"Sam!" Riley said. She began to do that hyperventilating thing she did when she didn't get her way.

"Let's go, son," the officer said. "We've got some paperwork to do while we wait for your folks."

Good. They'd been called. Hopefully that meant I wouldn't be staying the night. Right?

Riley ran to the door. Her eyes begged me to do something, say something, but what? Anything I'd say or do would only make everything worse. All I could muster was a tired shrug.

When the officer and I turned a corner, Riley was still calling out my name, now through her tears. Her sobs echoed around me as we made our way down the hallway.

47

RILEY

I spent the rest of the weekend in a total emotional coma. I didn't eat, didn't speak and barely moved a muscle.

I was still on the No Phone and No Internet Privileges Till Further Notice Punishment Plan. My mother only begrudgingly returned my laptop when I explained that I needed to write an essay on *Lord of the Flies* for AP English, which she allowed as long as I did my homework in the kitchen with the screen facing her so she could check it whenever she walked by—which she did only about ten thousand times.

Whenever I asked, "What do you think happened to Sam?" my dad would shake his head, his gaze never quite meeting mine. He didn't like Sam; that much was obvious. But he had no right. He didn't even know him. He didn't know—couldn't know—all the things Sam had done for me. And all that he meant to me.

"Have you forgotten Sam Tracy saved my life?" I said over my laptop.

Dad didn't answer. He returned to rustling the newspaper

and snapping the sports page in my direction. Mom emptied the dishwasher in silence.

I sighed, loudly, and returned to my English essay, despite not having finished the book yet.

Ryan was as distant as my parents, acting like I'd suddenly developed leprosy. When I thought about all the times I'd covered for him, supported him when he screwed up, it only fueled my anger, bubbling inside me like a volcano.

But Ryan was my only link to life outside the walls of our house. "Could you ask Fred to call Sam?" I begged him when my parents weren't eavesdropping. "Would Fred know if he made it back home?" Like Dad, Ryan only grunted noncommittal answers.

By Sunday, I was too sick of everything to care. I needed to see Sam. In all the chaos of the past few weeks, I had come to realize that he had been the only constant. He saw me and that crazy ninja alternate-personality who lived inside of me and didn't run away—well, not totally. He saw me at my worst and found a reason to still be my friend.

The thing was, I got him, too. He couldn't fool me with his brooding, stoic personality. He was a total pushover when no one was looking. I liked that—no, scratch that. I *loved* that about him. I just hoped I hadn't ruined everything that was beginning to become clear between us.

I hoped I still had a chance.

Unable to concentrate on my essay, I sketched instead, pushing down on my pencil until my fingers ached.

Monday morning, Mom wouldn't let me ride to school with Ryan. She insisted that Dad drop me off on his way to work, which he did. If only he could have dropped me off behind the school or in another country completely.

The second I turned away from Dad's car, two hundred

pairs of eyes watched me walk from the curb down the side-walk. It was even more intense than the Monday following the rescue on the Mogollon Rim. At least that morning I'd felt a little special. Today I felt like I was carrying the bubonic plague.

I threaded my messenger bag across my chest and pretended everybody was invisible, which worked for about .00001 seconds. For the first time, I actually heard the spray from the courtyard fountain. None of the students seated around it uttered a word. It was a little creepy.

I was halfway to the double glass doors when someone said, "Hey, Wild Girl! Where've you been? Over here!"

Jay Hawkins.

"Long time, no see," he added but there was something else in his tone, a familiarity that I didn't care for. His eyes never spoke to me with quiet kindness like Sam's did. Jay's eyes were cold and empty. Why hadn't I noticed that before?

My stomach did a somersault as a few snickers and giggles spread throughout the courtyard. I could hear the muffled voices drumming through my body.

I swallowed hard, lifted my chin and leveled Jay with a steady gaze.

Jay was wearing a white bandage across his nose but acted like it was invisible. Both cheeks, I noted with some satisfaction, were purple, just below the eyes. He was flanked by two other juniors from the wrestling team. I recognized them from yearbook pictures but didn't know their names.

I nodded at them, even forced the tiniest of smiles to show him that nothing that he could say or do would bother me. And kept walking.

"Did you hear the news about your boyfriend?" Jay called out, a happy-bearer-of-bad-news tone in his voice.

Boyfriend?

I froze on the sidewalk and glanced back at him over my shoulder.

Beneath his bandages, a toothy grin spread across his face as I waited for him to speak. "Just Sam got suspended till Thursday. Got lucky," he said. Then, in a voice that made the hairs prickle on the back of my neck, he added, "He won't be so lucky next time."

Good, I thought with relief. That meant Sam was home. Didn't it? I needed to find Fred. She would know.

But then I remembered how awful I'd been to her, how I'd lied and interfered with her and Ryan. She probably didn't want anything to do with me, and I couldn't blame her.

I barely wanted anything to do with me, either.

I swallowed again and nodded at Jay as if I could not have cared less what he had to say. Then I locked eyes with Drew, who was watching the exchange from outside the front door. *I'm sorry*, I mouthed to her.

Drew gave me the hint of an apologetic smile and a little wave and then turned around for the cafeteria. I supposed that would have to do for now.

First thing I needed to do was find Fred. I darted straight for the library.

It was too early for the library to be busy. Even the librarian was missing. I walked to the gray cubicles beneath the *Ww-Xx* bookshelf sign. Fred was inside one, her back to me, a strand of her shiny black hair wrapped around her finger as she huddled over a book.

"Fred." I exhaled an urgent breath behind her. There wasn't much time till the first bell.

"Riley?" She stood one second after turning. Before I could utter another word, her arms wrapped around me in a hug that I didn't deserve. "Jeez," she said, pulling back to look at me, shaking her head. "I am so glad you're okay."

"I'm fine," I said.

"If you're looking for Ryan, he won't be back till noon."

I shook my head. "No, I'm not looking for him. I was looking for you." My tongue dragged over my lips. Then the words rushed out like a waterfall. "FredI'msosorryIdidn't-meantointerfere—"

Fred reached out a hand. "Whoa. Slow down, Riley."

I drew in a breath. Then I started again. "I didn't mean to get between you and Ryan. It was stupid stupid stupid. I am so sorry. This is all my fault." I paused for another breath, surprised to find that my eyes had welled with relieved tears. I blinked at her.

Fred's mouth opened a fraction. Clearly she hadn't been expecting this. She was acting as if she wasn't even aware of my meddling, and that made me feel worse. She deserved my apology more than anyone else. Then she chuckled, "It's okay, Riley. It's okay. Everything's gonna be okay." She hugged me again, stroking the back of my head until my breathing calmed.

"What do you know about Sam? Is he okay?" I sniffed back my tears. "I suppose you heard everything from Ryan."

Her head tilted. "Not everything. Just bits and pieces."

"What can you tell me? Did you see Sam over the weekend?"

She shook her head and my body felt like it could crumple. "Not since his fight at school with Jay Hawkins."

I pressed my hands against my stomach. "Oh, god," I said. "I hope he's not still at…"

"Durango?" Fred finished for me. "No. My brother spoke to him yesterday. Sam's home."

I reached out for the edge of the cubicle. "Oh, thank god," I said, my knees turning wobbly. "I've been so worried about him."

Fred reached out her hand, finding my forearm. "Didn't Ryan tell you?"

"Ryan doesn't tell me anything."

Her eyes narrowed, as if she didn't believe me. "Your dad...?" she said it like a question.

"What about him?" My dad and I were barely speaking to each other.

"Your dad went back to Durango. He talked to the judge. It was all a big stupid misunderstanding or something."

"Dad? *My* dad?"

Fred nodded.

Dad had dropped Mom and me off at home, and then he'd said he had to go back to the office. I would have bet every dollar in my college fund that he'd never go back downtown to check on Sam Tracy, not after the way he'd glared at Sam like he was some kind of seasoned criminal. "But...I..." I stammered "There was something about an armed robbery. They said he did something he didn't."

Fred's eyes softened. She returned her hands to my shoulders to steady me. "I know. At the same time that robbery happened in Casa Grande, your Dad was able to show that you and Sam were pumping gas in Yuma, a million miles away— well, maybe not a million, but you know what I mean. The gas station had cameras. Your dad got the tape and showed it to the judge. Case closed. Your dad totally rocks."

"Yeah, rocks." My vision turned fuzzy. *My dad did that?*

"Even the ticket got changed to a warning."

I leaned against the cubicle wall for more support. And to think I'd ignored Dad all weekend. Even this morning on the drive to school, when he'd tried to make small talk about my art class, I hadn't answered him. I officially felt lower than dirt.

"But what about his scholarships?" Sam had mentioned

that he'd been contacted by a couple of college recruiters already for interviews.

"Shouldn't make a bit of difference," Fred said.

"But he was suspended…." That couldn't be good.

Fred paused and said, "Riley, are you sure you're not sick or something? Your face just went pale."

I shook my head, like I was trying to keep myself in one piece. "Yes. No. I don't know."

"You really care about Sam, don't you?"

I nodded.

Fred squeezed my arm. "He's lucky to have you as a friend."

I choke-laughed. "Yeah, well, I'm not sure he feels the friendship at the moment. Anytime he's around me, there's police intervention or a rescue operation. I'm officially cursed."

Fred chuckled. "With Sam, you just got to be patient. It'll be okay. You'll see."

"No, it won't!" I almost shouted. "Sam got suspended because of me." *He almost got killed and he was thrown in jail—all because of me.*

Fred lowered her voice. "No, Riley. That wasn't because of you. That was because…well, because that's just Sam. It's who he is. He's always carried the world on his shoulders. You've just got to understand him."

"I know," I said. *And I've been so terrible to him, making him be someone he isn't,* I wanted to add, but I couldn't. I think Fred already knew, and that made me feel even worse. Fred was the kind of person whose respect you wanted, and now I wasn't certain I would ever have it.

The bell rang above us. There was so much more I wanted to ask her, so many more apologies to make, but I was having trouble finding the words. Sam, Dad, my parents, the suspension. My head was spinning. I should have been the one who got suspended, not Sam.

"Riley," Fred whispered. Her face lowered, the tip of her nose inches from mine. "Tell me. You're not still hanging out with Jay Hawkins, are you?"

Tears clouded my eyes. I shook my head.

"Good," Fred said. "People like Jay Hawkins can only lead to trouble. I hate to say it but he's just not a nice person. You need to trust your brother on this."

I couldn't think about Jay. He could never compare to Sam. And Sam wouldn't be back in school till Thursday.

Thursday was a lifetime away. I wasn't sure I'd survive without seeing him till then. I wondered if he felt the same way.

48

SAM

After my parents left for work, I stuffed a half-dozen cheese sandwiches, apples and water bottles inside my backpack. I didn't even take the time to spread mayonnaise on the bread. I had to leave the house before my head exploded.

So I did what I always did when I wanted to be alone, really alone, not-seeing-another-human-being-for-miles alone. I started walking toward the Estrella Mountains, an imperfect line of jagged teeth in the distance. The Estrellas were my drug of choice and I needed an overdose.

As expected, the car ride back home with my parents from Durango had been as quiet as a funeral—after Dad yelled the disappointment and frustration off his chest, that is. I was never certain if Dad's frustration was directed at me or himself. Until recently, I hadn't given him cause to be frustrated with me. I was never certain if he was frustrated because he couldn't figure me out or frustrated that he finally had. Anyway, I had expected the lecture. In a weird way, I had wanted it. "What are you doing with that girl, anyway? She's been nothing but trouble," he had said. "Aren't there enough girls for you on the Rez?" The one-sided yelling match had lasted half the car ride. I deserved his wrath. Dad was right. Mom didn't say a word—she didn't need to. She wore her disappointment on her face. But I knew that with her it would eventually disappear. With Dad, all bets were off.

I couldn't have stayed at the house one more minute, watching Grandmother weave another dream basket while her eyes lectured me. *We believed in you, Samuel Joseph,* her eyes seemed to say. *You let us down. You let the whole tribe down.*

All right, already! I get it! I wanted to scream at them, even Grandmother. *I screwed up! Give me a break!* I wanted to scream at the whole stupid mixed-up world.

As bad as it was, my criminal record with Phoenix's finest would have been a lot worse had it not been for Mr. Berenger. That weighed heaviest on my mind. Seriously, my jaw had hit the ground when Ryan's dad strode back into the lock-up room. Initially I had thought that maybe Riley had returned with him and my stomach had twisted like it always did whenever she was around, but Mr. Berenger had returned alone. He marched into the room with a no-nonsense, let's-get-this-over-with lawyer face. He was the last person I'd expected to see, one of the last people I'd wanted to see, too. And yet he was probably the one I needed the most. Just my craptastic luck.

I knew that I should have been more grateful to him for springing me from that hellhole, but a part of me resented it, too. The Berengers were always fixing things, floating in at the last minute like white knights and snagging hero status. Like father, like son.

My parents hadn't liked accepting Mr. Berenger's help, either, but what could they do? Mom's brother, my uncle Silas, was a lawyer, but he lived all the way out in New Mexico. We'd needed a lawyer now.

If it hadn't been for Mr. Berenger, I might still be in Durango with my own personal extra-large orange jumpsuit, walking in straight lines up and down colorless hallways, with all my dreams of college scholarships reduced to just that—unrealized dreams. Just the thought made me sick to my stomach. I'd worked so hard in school my whole life. Everything would have been for nothing because of one wrong decision. One wrong girl.

So I'd figured that, since I had a little forced time off from school thanks to my suspension from Principal Graser, I might as well go somewhere where the breathing was easy, where I could get my head screwed back on straight. I'd left a note for Mom and Dad, said I'd be back in a day or two when my food ran out. They wouldn't mind too much, as long as I stayed on the Rez.

I heard Martin before I saw him. I'd been walking toward the Estrellas for twenty minutes. The air was crisp and the sky was postcard-picture blue when a truck engine chugged behind me.

I bit back a smile. As much as I had wanted to be alone, I wasn't exactly sad to see Martin, either.

He drove alongside me, slowing the truck to a crawl. "Figured I might find you here," he said through the open passenger window.

"You should be in school, Martin. What are you doing out here?" I didn't stop.

"Same thing as you." The old truck kept pace with me, so close that I could see more spots where the paint had peeled off.

"And what's that, exactly?"

He ignored me. And then he did what I'd taught him to do to keep the upper hand whenever he didn't want to answer a question: answer a question with a question. "And give up the opportunity to go camping with my bestest bro?" He flashed a toothy smile.

"You've just come from my house, haven't you?" It wasn't a question.

"Yup," he said, a toothpick twirling between his teeth.

"My grandmother say anything?"

"Does she ever?"

"You're gonna get in trouble, you know, being here when you should be in school."

Martin waved his hand at me. "Won't be the first, won't be the last." He paused. "Hey, are you gonna hop in or what? I'm pissing away gas here."

"What's wrong with walking?"

"Why walk when you can ride?"

I inhaled another gulp of the morning air and squinted at the horizon. With the sun behind my shoulders, the mountain range glowed a deep red. I finally stopped, letting my backpack drop to the ground. "Anyone ever tell you you're a real pain in the ass?"

The truck's bald tires squeaked to a stop. "Yeah?" he said, draping one arm over the steering wheel. "Well, I'm the pain in the ass who's got a tent and two sleeping bags in his truck. What've you got?" His eyes peered at me above his sunglasses.

I shook my head and opened the door. Martin was the only person I knew who kept sleeping bags in his truck on a regular basis, mostly because he usually left his trailer whenever his mom and dad started fighting. Their fights were epic, totally knock-down, drag-out. When he was really young, before he could drive, he used to walk the two miles to our house and stay with us, sometimes in the middle of the night, showing up at our door shaking and crying. Dad had comforted Martin way more than he ever did me. Sometimes I thought my dad would rather have had Martin as his son than me. "I *get*

Martin," Dad had joked once when we were around four-teen years old and having a barbecue. Martin had wanted to horse around in the front yard, and I'd wanted to read *The Call of the Wild*. "You?" Dad had said. "You're not as easy." It was around that time that Dad and I forgot how to talk to each other so, in true Tracy fashion, we'd simply stopped talking altogether. It seemed easier that way. For both of us.

"Nothing as good as what you got," I said to Martin, nod-ding at his sleeping bags in the back.

A smug smile curled his lips. "I knew you'd see it my way."

"You should go to law school, you know that?"

Martin turned away, mostly to hide the blush in his cheeks. "Naaawww," he drawled. "School's your job. I'm just eye candy for the ladies." Then he said, "Where to?"

"Somewhere where we'll only hear coyotes."

Martin chuckled. "Are you saying I can't talk to you?"

"I'm warning you, Martin. I won't be much company."

He smirked. "Seriously, dude. Are you ever?"

"Shut up and drive," I said and then turned to the open window, letting the morning air wash over my face. We drove the rest of the way in silence.

Martin parked the truck at the bottom of the mountain where the dirt road ended and left the keys in the ignition. We hiked up to a ridge of smooth boulders that dotted the mountain. It was a high enough climb that we needed some water by the time we reached the first flat rock.

"This looks good," Martin said, a little out of breath.

"You tired already?" I chided him.

"I didn't see you breaking your hump carrying the tent."

"I don't know why you brought that thing, Martin. Sleep-ing bags are good enough."

"You'll be thanking me in the morning when you're freez-ing your face off."

I stood on the ridge and looked down at the Rez. Trailers and cotton fields dotted one half. A sea of brown desert as far as I could see dotted the other half. No one around for miles. I inhaled. "Perfect."

"Good," Martin said, letting the gear land on the rock with a *thump.* And a *clank.* Like a can *clank.*

My eyes narrowed. "What else did you bring?"

"Just some refreshments for later." His eyebrows wiggled like caterpillars. "You'll thank me, bro."

"Doubt it," I muttered. I wanted to clear my brain, not muddle it even more.

It took Martin about five minutes to set up the tent, mostly because he'd had years of practice. I had to admit that sitting inside the tent would probably be a relief when the sun started to blaze around noon.

I rolled out the sleeping bags and dug a hole for a fire. We'd need it come sunset. I walked higher up the mountain and found some dried saguaro stalks and a couple of mesquite trees. With my knife, I cut off a few of the thinner, deader branches. By the time I was done, we had enough, with some to spare.

Then Martin sat across from me on one of the rolled-out sleeping bags. They smelled the same as always, a fragrant mix of motor oil and campfire. I offered him one of the sandwiches. We ate in silence for a couple of minutes. I avoided Martin's steady gaze and the questions that I knew lingered on his lips.

Finally he said, "So what's up with you?"

I stopped in midchew. "What are you, my mother?"

"Seriously, Sam. Talk to me. Your dad said you haven't been yourself lately."

I laughed. "And how would he know?"

"Hey, cut the old man some slack."

I took a swig from a water bottle, stalling. "I just wanted to get away for a while. That's all." I wiped my mouth with the back of my sleeve. "You know the feeling."

"Yeah," he chuckled. "I know the feeling. But I also know you like a brother. There's something else going on."

"Well, I was almost kicked out of school and I came this close—" I indicated an inch with my fingers "—to getting thrown into juvy." I didn't hide my pent-up sarcasm. "My parents think I'm a lower life form. Life's just peachy."

His eyes narrowed. "Yeah," he said, unconvinced. "I know all about that shit. It's all over the Rez." His head tilted toward me. "Your dad pretty mad?"

"Yeah. I think. Of course he'll never really talk to me. You know how it is."

Martin chuckled. "No, not really. You know my dad. When he's angry, he just throws a punch."

"Yeah. That sucks. Sorry, Martin." I got a sour taste in my mouth.

"Nothing to be sorry for. It's just the way it is." Then he paused. "You know, I always wished your dad had been my dad."

I smiled tiredly at him. "Well, if it's any consolation, I think the feeling is mutual."

"He's a great guy—"

I raised my palm. "Save it, Martin."

"Like I said, bro, you got to cut your old man some slack. He means well."

I laughed. "Does he? He doesn't know a single thing about me. Or care."

"That's not true."

"Trust me on this, Martin. He's never been interested in anything that I've been interested in. Hell, I'm not even sure he knows I'm alive sometimes."

Martin leaned back, studying me. Then he said, "You don't know, do you?"

"Know what?"

"You don't know that your dad can't read, do you?"

It was as if all the oxygen had been sucked from my lungs. "What are you talking about?"

Martin leveled his gaze at me. "Your dad can't read, Sam."

"What?" My voice got louder as Martin's grew softer. "How do you know?"

"One time when we were kids, maybe when we were seven or eight. I was staying the night at your place. You asked your dad to read one of your books to us." Martin paused. "I saw how he looked at that book and then looked at you. His face turned all red. His hands even trembled a little bit. Then he said he'd rather hear you read it. Which you were only too happy to do, being the nerd that you always were." He paused. "That's when I knew. I just knew."

I looked down at my water bottle without really seeing it. I turned it over in my hand. Could this be true? "Are you sure?"

"Takes one to know one, bro. I'm an expert at getting people to believe I'm something I'm not."

"But," I stammered, "I'm his son. I would know. He would tell me."

"Your dad?" Martin's lips pursed. "No way. Too proud."

My mouth opened and closed again. I was too stunned to speak.

"That's probably why he doesn't ask about school. Maybe even why he avoids you, Sam. He's embarrassed."

"How come you never told me, Martin?" I whispered.

"Not my place. Besides, I thought you already knew. I'm sorry, Sam. Really, I am."

My head was a little dizzy with the news. I lost my appetite for the sandwich. Across from me, Martin ate another sandwich and drained another water bottle. We didn't talk for the longest time, long enough for the sun to change position in the sky. Then he said, "But there's something else eating you. I know it."

I turned away. "Don't want to talk about it." Especially after learning that my dad couldn't read. It was hard for me to believe. Mom had to know. Why wouldn't she have told me? Did Cecilia know? Had I been too absorbed in myself to notice? I didn't know whether to feel guilty or angry.

"I know you don't." Martin paused again. "But you should." Then he grinned. "And who better to tell than me?"

I almost grinned back at him, mostly because he had one of those smiles that was a combination of innocence and pure crazy. I turned away, pretending to be interested in a dove cooing at us from the end of the rock. It flew into the sky and my eyes tracked it till it was just a gray spec. "Nothing to tell, Martin. Let it be."

But he wouldn't. "It's Berenger's sister. Riley? Isn't that the white chick's name?"

I nodded, tasting dryness, hating to hear Martin refer to Riley that way. *Jeez*, I was one messed-up fool. There I went again, defending her, even in my head.

"Are you mad because she's dating Hawkins?" he persisted.

I turned to him, feeling that all-too familiar surge of jealousy swell inside my chest. "She is not dating Hawkins." I tossed a pebble over the ridge.

"If you ask me—"

I lifted my palm, stopping him. "I didn't, in case you've forgotten."

Martin ignored me again. He leaned back on his hands, extending his legs and crossing them at his ankles. "If you ask me," he said again, slowly, like he was waiting for me to catch up, "you like her. A lot." He paused. "Maybe even more than you ever liked Fred."

I swallowed, hard. "You're insane."

"She's completely different from Fred, too. I think that's a good thing."

"They're not so different—well, in some ways." Wait. Why was I rationalizing this to Martin? It would only encourage him to continue.

"And the whole Fred thing. It really did a number on you. Peter, Vernon and me, we were real worried about you. You barely talked to us for months. It was like you were alive and dead at the same time. Riley's brand of crazy has been good for you." When I pretended to ignore him, he added, "You hearing me?"

I shook my head. "No," I said, but it was a lie. I had withdrawn after Fred told me she only wanted to be friends, that much was true. Watching her walk off into the sunset with Ryan Berenger was like a baseball bat to the kneecaps.

Martin grinned. "You're such a liar. You know exactly what I mean."

I leaned forward. "And hanging with Riley has made all my problems go away? Made me a better person?" More sarcasm. "That girl is a walking train wreck."

Martin barely flinched. "Nothing wrong with shaking up the status quo."

My chin pulled back. "Status quo? Big words."

Martin ignored me again, surprising me. Usually I was the one giving him advice. "You needed something besides school all the time. And pining away for Fred? You were really starting to become a huge bore, bro."

My breath hissed between my teeth. I couldn't help but glare at him but that only made his grin spread. "Thanks for the warning."

"Hanging with Riley has put a little of the life back in you. Admit it."

I rolled my eyes. "She's crazy."

"Besides," Martin said, still all casual-like, "it's obvious you like her."

"Who?"

"Riley."

"You're crazy, too."

"I might be crazy but I also know I'm right."

I waved him off and then lay down on my sleeping bag, half inside the tent. My feet fidgeted. The nervous tic climbed up the rest of my body. It was as if spiders crawled over my body. I couldn't sit still, I couldn't concentrate and I definitely couldn't lie down for the rest of the day inside Martin's tent. Annoyed, I got up. "I'm gonna go for a hike."

Martin leaned forward, pulling his knees to his chest. "Just listen to what I'm telling you for once."

"Do I have a choice?"

He smiled up at me. "Nope."

"That's what I'm afraid of."

Martin's smile faded. "Seriously, dude. There's something about Riley and you. I've watched you around her." He paused. "And I've seen the way she is around you. It's like you two are doing a mating dance and don't even realize it."

"Shut up."

He lifted his palms. "All I'm saying is…maybe you should give her more of a chance."

My eyes widened. "Who says she's interested?"

Martin laughed. "And I thought you were the smart one!"

Grabbing my water bottle next to the fire pit, I stormed away.

"Hey, I've seen the way she looks at you, too."

I stopped but didn't turn. "When?"

"Around. In the cafeteria."

I glanced at him over my shoulder. His expression had turned completely serious.

"And I see the way you look at her," he said. "Stop denying it."

"The girl drives me crazy. And not in a good way." I started walking again, higher up the mountain. "You don't know what you're talking about!" I yelled without looking at him.

"Like hell I don't," he yelled back, his voice bouncing all the way up the mountain, whether I wanted to hear it or not.

49

RILEY

During homeroom, I'd planned to beg Mr. Holdren for a pass to see Mr. Romero. It wasn't necessary.

"Seems he beat you to the punch, Miss Berenger," Mr. Holdren said, handing me a folded paper. It was a note from Mr. Romero, instructing me to see him before first period. I stuffed the note in the front pocket of my jeans, squared my shoulders and darted for the door, but not before at least two boys taunted "Wild Girl" underneath their breaths. Junior jocks and friends of Jay, I was fairly certain. Apparently even being Ryan Berenger's sister wasn't working to my advantage anymore. I scowled at them, anyway.

Except for a couple of security guards, the halls were empty, so I arrived outside Mr. Romero's office in a matter of seconds. I knocked on his door.

"Come in!" he said.

I opened the door and entered.

"Miss Berenger." By his tone, I knew that this wasn't a social visit, if there even was such a thing with guidance counselors. But, for once, I had something to tell him, too.

"Nice to see you back at school," he added, almost as an afterthought. "Feeling better?"

If feeling numb and confused was feeling better, the answer was *yes*. I nodded and sank into one of the chairs in front of his desk, waiting for my heartbeat to slow. I sat with my bag in my lap, even though there was an empty seat beside me. I had a feeling I was going to need something to cling to. "I'm glad you asked to see me, sir, because I needed to see you, too."

"Oh?" Mr. Romero removed his glasses.

"Yeah. I need to talk to you about Sam Tracy."

"I'm afraid I can't talk to you about other students, Miss Berenger. You know that."

"I'm hoping you'll make an exception, especially after you hear what I have to say. The fight with Jay Hawkins, for starters. Sam tried to warn me about Jay, but I didn't listen."

His eyes widened. "A fight is a fight, unfortunately." He leaned forward. His voice softened, as if he didn't like what he was about to say. "And by all accounts, Mr. Tracy started it."

"But Jay's been taunting him. Egging him on. I think he's jealous of Sam or something." I paused to swallow. "Sam was just...protecting me." I wondered if I should also tell him about the photos Jay had posted to Facebook, but I was still pretty embarrassed by them. It was even worse now that my parents had seen them.

Mr. Romero exhaled like he was considering this.

"He shouldn't have been suspended, Mr. Romero. Sam is one of the smartest guys in school. This could hurt his chances for scholarships."

"Yes, that's true. But there are consequences for our actions, Miss Berenger."

I hadn't expected him to discuss Sam's future so cavalierly.

"Yes, I know. That's why I think you should punish me and not Sam."

His fingers tented. "Tell me why." He waited for my answer but by the tilt of his head, I could tell he'd already made up his mind. And I was about to blow that right open.

So I proceeded to tell Mr. Romero everything—and I mean, *everything*. I told him about how it all began with Sam's rescue on the Mogollon Rim. My cheeks flushed when I told him about how we'd shared our deepest, darkest secrets. I told him about all the trouble I had been getting into since I started hanging out with Jay Hawkins, both intentional and unintentional. I was probably breaking every unwritten Student Code in the History of Student Snitch Codes when it came to Jay Hawkins, but I didn't care. I even told him about San Diego and how I'd roped Sam into ditching school. When I shared almost getting mugged by a bunch of gang members at the beach, he didn't blink for a full ten minutes. By the time I'd finished, the bell to second period had rung and Mr. Romero hadn't uttered a single word.

Watching him watch me, I wondered whether I'd hung myself with my own rope or if I'd actually done something good. Either way, I was feeling the weight of my lies and bad decisions lifting from my shoulders. "Sam's been the best friend I've ever had," I told him.

And I had repaid him by messing up his life.

50

SAM

Our food and water ran out the next day on our impromptu camping trip, not a huge surprise, but that was okay. Martin turned out to be good company.

We talked about old times as we watched sparks and ash float from our campfire into a blue-black sky. We talked about some of our earlier camping trips, like the time Dad took us to Woods Canyon to fish, or all the times we went to the county fair and got sick on too many fried Snickers bars after riding roller coasters. We even talked about some of the old legends our dads used to tell us around the campfire when we were kids. They were the kind of mystical stories about coyotes and bears and shooting stars that we could never forget, that we were never supposed to forget. And that we were supposed to pass down to our own children some day.

The subject of Riley Berenger did not surface again. But that was Martin: once he got something off his chest, he moved on. So by the time we drove down the bumpy dirt road that led to my house, I was feeling like I could face the world again. I even thought about what I wanted to say to Dad.

My state of bliss came to an abrupt end the moment we reached my front yard. When I saw it, clear as day, I didn't know whether to whoop with joy or scream into the sky.

"Is that what I think it is?" Martin said in a semistunned tone, after the truck lurched to a stop.

I was half out of my seat before Martin cut the ignition. I ran straight for my motorcycle. It was propped up by the kickstand, its silver handlebars gleaming in the afternoon light. It had been washed—no, more than that. It had been scrubbed clean. The key was in the ignition, the rabbit's foot still dangling from the ring. My palm pressed against the engine. It was cold.

The bike was supposed to be locked up in a city impound lot somewhere on the south side of Phoenix. We'd driven by it the night we got back from Durango. Dad had pointed it out. The impound lot was surrounded by barbed wire and fencing that reached halfway into the sky. No doubt a dozen rabid pit bulls patrolled the inside, too.

"What the...?" I touched the handlebars—also cold, still scratched, but sparkling clean.

"Um. Dude. How'd this get here?" Martin asked.

My voice sounded as numb as I felt. "I have no idea." I stood there, staring at it, shaking my head. It was supposed to cost two hundred to spring it out of impound. I figured it would take me at least two busy weekends at the restaurant to earn the money to get it back.

"Your dad?"

My head shook faster. "No way."

"Trevor Oday?"

I dragged my hand over my chin. "I really don't know. Doubt it." No one I knew could part with that kind of green and I'd taken enough from Trevor as it was.

The front screen squeaked open and Grandmother walked

out the door, leaning against her cane. She walk-limped faster than usual.

"Who drove this here, Grandmother?"

She waited to answer till she was standing right in front of me. "The white boy with the yellow hair. Brought it here yesterday." She pointed to my bike with her cane. "An older man followed in another car. His father, I think."

"What white boy?"

Grandmother shook her graying head as if she was trying to shake out the words.

I put my hand on her bony shoulder, steadying her. I leaned lower. "Did they give you their names?"

"Berenger," she said. "He said his name was Berenger."

"Holy. Sh…" Martin hissed beside me.

"Ryan?" I said, my voice flat. *Riley.* I bet she'd talked her brother into this, too. That made me angrier. Didn't she think I was capable of getting back my own bike?

Grandmother nodded once.

My hand dropped from her shoulder. I looked at the bike, then at Martin, then at Grandmother and then at the bike again. Finally my head fell back, my eyes squeezed shut and I cursed to myself. I didn't need Ryan Berenger's help. I didn't need Riley's help. I didn't need their charity. I didn't want it. I'd rather have worked for the rest of my life as a busboy to get my bike back.

"Du-u-uddde," Martin said in a long exhale. He clapped his hand against my back. "You owe that guy. Big-time."

I glared back at him.

"What?" He took a step back, confused. "What'd I say?"

I shook my head. I wasn't about to explain it to him. Again. Didn't he get it?

Martin's eyes narrowed as he studied me warily. For once, his mouth clamped shut.

I toed the dirt, deeper and deeper. Then I kicked the ground as hard as I could. Pebbles and dirt flew across the yard.

No words could express the burn inside me.

I stormed into the house, feeling more frustrated than before I left.

51

RILEY

Ever since I learned that Dad had helped Sam in Durango, things had been better between us. It wasn't like my dad never did nice things for people. It was the fact that he'd known how much this would mean to me.

Things improved—between all of us. I wouldn't say it was great; it had never been great. But I would say that things had the potential to get better, and I supposed that was sometimes all you could ask for with your family.

The time between Monday and Thursday rolled by as slow as the world's slowest freight train on the world's slowest train tracks. Why was it that, when you needed your days to speed ahead, time always laughed in your face? I counted down the hours, even the minutes, till the moment when Sam would finally return to school. I memorized at least a dozen things to say to him, with "I'm sorry" on the top of my list followed by "Please, please, please forgive me."

When Thursday arrived, I asked Dad to drive me to school a little earlier than usual so that I could wait for Sam at the edge of the courtyard by the curb. When Mr. Oday's van pulled up, I would be waiting.

I sat on the curb, my bag beside me and my knees pulled up to my chest, rocking in place. From the corner—the farthest point from the school buses—I watched as car after car pulled into the school parking lot and then dropped off one load of students after another, mostly freshman and sophomores and those who didn't have their own cars.

Finally, the Oday van arrived. It chugged into the parking lot, a thin veil of gray-blue smoke trailing behind it. Like some kind of welcome committee, I stood as soon as it rounded the drop-off point in front of the courtyard, biting back the anxious smile toying with my lips.

Fred got out first. Two boys followed, one really tall and skinny—Vernon Parker, I think his name was. The other was Peter Begay, a junior like Sam.

I gave a tiny wave to Fred and she waved back. But then she slid the van door closed and I felt my smile fade. I could hear the door slam from where I stood.

No Sam.

As if reading my mind, Fred yelled out, "He's right behind us, Riley. He rode his bike."

I bounced in place. I wanted to hug her. "Thanks, Fred!"

Fred nodded knowingly.

My smile returned just as Sam Tracy coasted his motorcycle into the parking lot toward the bike rack where students were supposed to park motorcycles and bicycles. He was wearing sunglasses, and his hair must have been pulled back into a ponytail because it wasn't flying past his shoulders. And he wasn't wearing his helmet.

I jogged toward the bike rack, my messenger bag bumping against my thigh, as Sam coasted his motorcycle into a corner spot.

When I reached him, I was out of breath. "Hey!" I said, unable to hide my nervousness as Sam shut off the engine. I let my gaze trail across his face. It felt as if I hadn't seen him in centuries.

"Hey," he said with noticeably less enthusiasm. He sat on his seat and seemed to take an extra moment before he lifted his leg over his bike.

I swallowed. "You're back." Brilliant observation.

"Yeeeeppp." The word popped between his lips.

"I'm glad," I stammered. "You being back, and all." And it had only been three days, twelve hours and fifteen minutes, but who was counting? "I've missed you."

"Thanks," Sam said, hitching his backpack higher on his shoulder. Once again, way less enthusiasm in his voice than I'd expected. But what should I expect? The last time I'd seen Sam, the poor guy had been handcuffed and soaking wet. At least he'd gotten his bike back.

The sun was at Sam's back, framing him. I lifted a hand over my forehead, squinting against the glare.

Sam exhaled.

Then I said, "Sam, I am so sorry. About everything. I shouldn't have interfered—"

"No, you shouldn't have. On that we can agree. And we've already been over this. Forget it."

I swallowed. "I know. But I'm sorry. I just had to say that again."

"Okay, apology accepted." Sam's nostrils flared. "Just…just leave me alone. And stop interfering in my life. Okay, Riley?"

It was as if I'd been punched in the stomach. We'd been through so much together. And he was talking to me like he didn't know me. "If you'd just let me explain—"

Sam raised a hand, stopping me. "I've let you explain too much as it is."

"No, you haven't."

His gaze dropped to the ground as he prepared to ignore me.

"You know, I can't believe I've been sitting here all morning waiting for you."

"Nobody asked you to."

My temples began to pound. "Jerk," I spat. "All I wanted to do was see you and tell you again how sorry I was. I felt terrible about everything that happened."

"And I said, 'apology accepted.' What more do you want from me?" His palms spread open.

"Thanks for making me feel like shit."

"Oh, so this is all about you again, is it?" He grabbed my arm. "You Berengers…" He paused. "You know how to turn everything around. You got nerve. I'll give you that."

Fire exploded in my chest at his words. I backed away from him. "I was totally wrong about you." I paused. "You're an idiot."

"Can't disagree with you on that!" A maniacal grin spread across his face.

"Who *are* you?" I said.

"The same guy I've always been, only more honest."

"I hate you," I said.

"Thank you," he said, but now his grin had faded.

I reached inside my bag and pulled out the dream basket that his grandmother had made for me the day I'd cut his hair. The day we'd played chess. The day, in retrospect, when I'd fallen for him. The day I'd let myself wish that someday Sam Tracy would love me as much as he loved Fred Oday. "Here." I thrust it in front of him. "This is for you. I don't want it anymore."

Sam's chin pulled back. He stared down at the basket and then he looked at me, saying nothing. With a shrug of his shoulders, he reached out for the basket, both of us watching as it got swallowed up by his hand.

I spun around and stormed toward the courtyard so that Sam wouldn't read the hurt in my eyes.

52

SAM

I almost didn't recognize Riley when I drove into the school parking lot. Pink Girl was back in full force. Her face looked pretty again instead of shellacked with the scary makeup she'd started wearing while she was hanging with Jay Hawkins and the rest of his loser friends. The closer she got, the more I could see the freckles that sprinkled across her nose. Her eyes were no longer darkened with too much eye shadow or whatever it was called. Good thing I was wearing sunglasses, or she might have thought I was staring, which I kind of was.

But then before I knew it, her cheeks were growing splotchy and her eyes were turning shiny. I knew that I was upsetting her. My words had spewed out before I could stop them. I should have just told her that I needed to be alone for a while, that I had a lot on my mind and stuff to sort out. That I wasn't ready to talk to her or anyone for that matter.

My first day back at school was off to a lousy start. A shadow stretched in front of me. *First, Riley. Now, Mr. Romero?*

"Sam?" Mr. Romero said, his footsteps stopping right in front of me. "Nice to have you back."

I wasn't sure if *nice* was the word I'd use so I just said, "Thanks."

"Got a minute?"

Like *no* was an option. "Okay."

"Walk with me."

I followed Mr. Romero toward the football field, away from the courtyard and the parking lot. Away from nosy ears. We crossed a stretch of recently mowed grass.

"I see you got your bike back."

"Yeah."

"I understand Ryan Berenger got it back for you."

"How do you know that?"

"I gave him the pass to leave school."

"Was Riley involved in this, too?"

"Getting your bike out of impound? Riley may have known about it. I don't know. You'll have to ask her but this was all Ryan's idea."

It was hard to hide my frustration. A low exclamation seeped between my teeth before I could hold it in. "I really wish you hadn't done that, Mr. Romero."

He stopped walking and then looked across the football field. "And why's that?"

From his tone, it was as if he already knew the answer. He didn't respond.

"Now I have to pay him back," I said.

"Of course you do. But thanks to him, you'll owe him a lot less cash. Those impound lots charge you for every day your property sits unclaimed."

I swallowed. "I didn't know that."

"Could have cost a small fortune."

It already has, I wanted to say. "Yeah. I need to thank him," I said, although my tone hardly sounded thankful.

Mr. Romero turned to face me. "You know, Sam, there's

no harm in letting someone do a good thing for you, especially when they want to."

My insides twisted. How could I answer that? How could I explain to Mr. Romero that the Berengers—Ryan, especially—were the last people on earth I wanted anything from? If Mr. Romero noticed how uncomfortable he was making me, he didn't show it.

"Kind of like what you tried to do for Riley Berenger," he said, his head tilting. "You helped her. You wanted to do a good thing. That's what people do, Sam. It's called being a human being. In her way, she's just been trying to thank you, although I gather that hasn't been going so well."

My breathing quickened a little. "Riley? That was different."

"Not really."

I looked away in frustration before looking at him head on. "It's just that Ryan and me. Well, we have a history." Slight understatement. I wasn't about to tell my guidance counselor all the sordid details involving me and my formerly wild crush on Fred.

"You're more alike than you know, you and Ryan," Mr. Romero said, placing a firm hand on my shoulder.

I wanted to shrug off his hand but it pressed down on me like a barbell. "We are nothing alike."

Mr. Romero chuckled a little. "Really? Okay, let's see." He lifted the thick fingers of his other hand in front of my face and got ready to count off. "You're both extremely bright, stubborn as mules, hot-headed and always ready to defend your girlfriends." He paused. "Oh. And you have families that care about you. How am I doing so far?"

I forced a bored expression. "Seriously, Mr. Romero, I'd prefer it if you just didn't say his name around me."

"Which one? Ryan or Berenger?"

"Both."

"Well, that might be tough. Because Riley Berenger spilled the beans to me on Monday about your recent escapades. She's the reason I'm working with Principal Graser to get your incident with Mr. Hawkins erased from your permanent record."

My jaw dropped. "What?"

"You heard me."

My mouth opened to speak but no words emerged.

"You know, Sam—" Mr. Romero's hand dropped from my shoulder and angled at his hips "—you'd feel a lot happier if you could drop that sizeable chip from your shoulder."

"I don't have one." I *didn't* have a chip. I just had too many people messing with my life.

"You could have fooled me."

"What did Riley tell you?" I asked, changing topics. I hope she hadn't made a bad situation even worse which, it had been my experience, was completely possible.

"Among other things, she told me you were the best friend she's ever had."

My eyes narrowed. "Riley has plenty of friends."

"Apparently none like you."

"Okay, you've totally lost me."

"You heard me," he said, backing away, his palms in the air, before he turned for the front doors.

I remembered that I was still holding my grandmother's dream basket. For some reason, I lifted the round woven lid. Inside I found a folded piece of white paper. Carefully, I unfolded it, holding the single white page so that it wouldn't flap in the breeze. With a black pencil, Riley had sketched a girl and a boy on a motorcycle, the girl holding on tight, her chin resting on the boy's shoulder. I had to say, she had talent. The girl wore a helmet, but the boy's black hair was long, longer than mine now, and it stretched backward in the wind. Their profiles looked straight ahead. They were smiling dreamy cheesy smiles and I liked it. Somehow she was able to capture that moment, the one where words weren't necessary but yet being together said everything. Below the sketch, in pink ink it said:

Riley loves Sam

53

RILEY

On Saturday, I spent most of the day on the window seat in my bedroom overlooking the street, watching the day pass by. Cars, delivery trucks, people walking yellow Labs. Mrs. Exeter across the street, planting pink-and-purple petunias in the window boxes next to her front door. She even looked up and waved. I didn't think she saw me beneath her pizza-box-sized straw hat.

The biggest excitement of the entire day was when a black limousine pulled up in front of our house just as the sun dipped below the mountains, turning the sky the color of a bruise. That was when someone knocked on my door.

"Riley?"

"Go away." I gathered my knees to my chest and stared at the shiny limo. A palm tree reflected in the hood of the car. The setting sun glinted off the windows.

Ryan opened my bedroom door.

I sat straighter. "Knock much? Jeez." Ryan was dressed in a black tuxedo. If I hadn't already known he was going to prom, I would have pegged him for best man at a wedding.

A cobalt-blue handkerchief thingy was stuffed like a triangle in his front pocket. I assumed that meant that Fred would be wearing blue, which would be a perfect color for her. Even though he was my brother, I had to admit he looked pretty handsome, although I'd never tell him that. I'd rather that he think that I was still pissed at him, even though he kept giving me reasons to love him even more.

He ignored my frown. "Are you ever going to talk to me again?"

I turned back toward the window. "Don't feel like talking."

"That's what you said yesterday. And the day before."

I shrugged. I really didn't have the energy to talk to anyone. I still had a lot on my mind—school, Sam, the possibility of changing schools. I was seriously thinking about asking my parents if I could transfer to the Catholic school up the street. New school, new friends (in theory), a new start. I just wanted to be left alone to feel sorry for myself, as if holing up in my bedroom all weekend didn't make that painfully obvious. Although Mom had left a plate of homemade brownies dusted with powdered sugar outside my door, baiting me outside my bedroom. Must admit, I wasn't too offended by the offering.

Ryan walked closer, unbuttoned his jacket and then sat opposite me in the window seat as I pretended to be intrigued by Mrs. Exeter's flowers, which looked pretty gorgeous, actually. I thought about sketching them....

Ryan tugged on his collar. "Look, Riley, I'm sorry for being such a crappy brother."

I rubbed my arms and looked from Ryan to the window. My tongue thickened and I had a feeling I was going to cry. I absolutely did not want to cry, not in front of Ryan. It's just that everything was making me sob today—Taylor

Swift songs, television commercials, an elderly couple walk-ing down the street this morning, hand in hand.

"I'm sorry for not being there," he said, "especially after all the times you had my back. I'm sorry I didn't warn you sooner about Jay. I'm just…sorry, Riley. I wish you didn't hate me so much."

Tears built behind my eyes but I blinked them back. I forced an eye roll. "I don't hate you." *I could never hate you, you idiot*, I wanted to say. *But you do drive me crazy on a regular basis.*

"Then what's the problem?"

"This isn't about you." For once.

"I get that."

"No, I don't think you do." I paused. "Don't I get to flip out every now and again? Why am I always expected to be perfect?"

He blinked back at me. "Because you are. You always have been."

"Stop it."

"Well, it's true."

"How come you get to mess up and I don't? It's like you have a Get Out of Jail Free card with Mom and Dad, and I… Well, I just don't. I get the silent treatment and the removal of all my electronics." At least I got my cell phone back, not that I'd been using it very much. The only one who'd texted me was Drew, and even her texts had been few and far be-tween. At least she'd started talking to me again.

"You're too smart to make the same lame mistakes that I did, Riley. That's why. You're better than that."

My voice rose. "Maybe I'm not. Maybe I don't want to be. Maybe I don't know who I am yet. Is that so bad?"

Ryan's voice only got softer, totally surprising me. "It's not bad, Riley. You're not bad. Not at all. In fact, as far as little sisters go, you're pretty…awesome."

"That's debatable." I shook my head, wiping my nose with the back of my hand. "I didn't mean to drag down Sam with me. I hadn't planned on that."

"I think he feels pretty awful about everything that happened, too."

"He shouldn't feel bad. None of it was his fault."

"I don't think that's how he sees it," Ryan said.

"Who told you that?" I sniffed.

"Fred."

"Well, for once Fred is wrong. I tried to apologize to him on Thursday and he pretty much told me to get over myself."

Now it was Ryan's turn to chuckle. He even sighed a little bit, like he was relieved, like he was happy that we were actually having a fairly civil conversation. "You got to cut the guy some slack, Ri. He'd just gotten back to school after being suspended."

My voice rose again. "You think I don't know that?"

Ryan leaned back, his palms up. "Hey, don't bite my head off. I'm just sayin'. Sometimes a guy just needs his space. We don't react at the speed of sound like you do, okay?" He sighed, loudly. "So now what?"

"What do you mean?"

"Are you going to spend the rest of your life in your room? Are you going to talk to Mom and Dad again?"

My chin dropped to my knees. "Yeah. I've just been feeling kind of embarrassed about everything." I looked across the room at my laptop.

"Hawkins took the pictures down from his Facebook page. I think he's officially scared of Sam, despite the phony tough-guy act. Thanks to Sam, he's been knocked off his mighty perch. That's a good thing for everybody, especially him."

"Good. But it wasn't just the pictures. It was that I thought

Jay was someone he's not. How could I have been such a poor judge of character?"

"You wouldn't be the first to make that mistake, Riley. Don't beat yourself up over that."

"Yeah, but it was also how I let him treat me." I squeezed my legs tighter, remembering the party. "How could I have been so desperate? It was stupid."

Ryan's jaw clenched.

"It was also how I tried to manipulate Sam. You. Fred. It was…everything. I'm a fool."

"No, you're not."

"Am, too."

Ryan sighed. Then he rose to button his jacket and looked down at the limousine. "Just don't take forever to sulk, okay? I miss you, Riley. We all do."

The lump in my throat grew to the size of a peach pit. I looked away but couldn't stop the tears trickling down my cheeks. "Your limo awaits," I croaked. "Go have a good time at your prom." I wiped my nose. "Tell Fred I said hi."

And then Ryan did something that he hadn't done in years. He leaned over and wrapped his arms around me, drawing me close to his chest, sloppy tears and runny nose and all. I was afraid I'd stain his pretty blue handkerchief with my tears but he didn't seem to care.

I didn't know how long he held me or how long he kept the limousine waiting but I did know that it was long enough that I finally felt like everything could be okay—not perfect, just okay. And I could live with that.

54

SAM

I rode north on my motorcycle, the sun setting over my left shoulder. The freeway was buzzing with Saturday-night traffic but it was easy to weave in and out of the lanes.

Martin had offered his truck but I couldn't take the chance of stalling in the middle of the Rez before I reached the freeway, which, with Martin's wheels, remained a certainty. I was already late and a little petrified, but I knew my bike wouldn't fail me, despite a few new nicks and scrapes. So I took a deep breath and stepped on the accelerator.

By the time I reached the door, the sky was purple-black with a faint strip of wispy orange in the horizon. I dragged my fingers through my hair a couple of times, straightened my tie, rang the bell and prayed that I wouldn't start sweating. Despite the crisp air, heat rose up my neck, threatening to choke off my air supply.

The door opened and he smiled.

"Hi, Mr. Berenger," I said. My voice echoed in the entryway.

"Hey, Sam. Good to see you again." I hoped that was true.

We shook hands. Mr. Berenger had been friendly on the phone when I'd called earlier. I'd thanked him for helping me out at Durango, and that seemed to please him. Then I'd told him I really wanted to take his daughter to the junior prom—and I wasn't certain he'd be pleased by that request given that Riley and I seemed to attract disaster whenever we were together. To my surprise, he'd said, "If you can pry our daughter from her bedroom, you'd make her mother and me the happiest parents on the face of the earth," which I thought was a little over-the-top. But I did appreciate his enthusiasm, not to mention the fact that he didn't hang up on me.

Mr. Berenger opened the door wider and then pointed to a set of wooden stairs that curved up to the second floor. "Her bedroom is the second room on the left. Godspeed," he said, grinning at me. From the tilt of his head, I was guessing he gave me about a fifty-fifty chance.

My shoulders pulled back. What did I have to lose? Well, tons, if I was being honest, like my pride and my heart. But if there was one thing I learned from Riley Berenger, it was that sometimes you had to take a chance. "I'll do my best."

He clapped my back. "I know you will." But then he gripped my shoulder. "And, Sam?"

"Yeah?"

"Nice suit."

My smile finally matched his. Little did he know that it was the best I could do. The suit belonged to my dad, along with the blue-and-green striped tie. Dad had said I could borrow it the day after Riley and I got into our big fight at school—the night Dad and I stayed up till three o'clock in the morning, talking. I'd decided to take Mr. Romero's advice and start to chip away at the boulders on my shoulder. Dad and I had talked about many things for the very first time. First I apologized for giving him and Mom more reasons to worry. Then I'd told him I knew that he couldn't read. I'd told him that I wanted to help him learn. Instead of storming away like I'd figured he would, Dad had nodded and said, "I think I'd like that, son. I've put it off long enough." We both got teary-eyed from all the talking and sharing and the late hour, but it had felt good. Calm had returned to our house again, like a cloud had lifted. Maybe things could be better between Dad and me.

Good thing Dad's suit fit. With dinner, gas and the prom tickets, I hadn't had any money left for a tuxedo rental. My savings account was officially tapped dry, three times over. Mom had stuffed an extra twenty in my wallet when she didn't think I was looking.

Mr. Berenger released my shoulder. The dance technically started thirty minutes ago, so I was already late, but, when she was helping me with my tie, my sister, Cecilia, had told me that showing up on time to prom was not cool. Without another word, I ran up the wooden stairs, taking two at a time, trying to reach Riley's bedroom before I lost my nerve. The last time I'd taken a chance on a girl, I'd been shot down like a wild turkey during hunting season. I had planned a little speech on the ride over but, for the life of me, I couldn't remember a single word as I raced up the steps. I was sure it was lame.

I stood in front of a dark wooden door, second from the left, exactly as Mr. Berenger had instructed. Then I listened outside the door for movement but heard nothing, not a radio, cell phone or computer hum. For an instant, I thought about bailing. But in the next instant, my hand raised and rapped on the door, loud. I didn't mean for it to be so loud, but everything seemed to echo inside the Berengers' house, even my own breathing.

"Go away," Riley answered. Her voice sounded tired, de-feated.

I knocked again. This time, louder.

"What?" she snapped.

I reached for the knob, cold and polished. I turned and pushed the door open.

Riley was sitting up against the headboard on her bed. She clutched a white pillow to her chest that was half as big as she was. Her jaw dropped the moment I entered.

"Hey," I said, weirdly casual, as if I popped into Riley's bedroom all the time. I was expecting to see lots of frilly girly things and pink, but the walls were painted sky-blue. Art-work was taped haphazardly all over the walls—Riley's art-work. Wasn't expecting that. But Riley Berenger had turned out to be nothing like I'd expected, either.

Riley blinked at me. "Hey…?" she said finally, numblike, as if she'd just woken up from a coma. In the silent seconds that froze between us, she watched my gaze travel around her room and her cheeks flushed, especially when I took Grand-mother's dream basket from behind my back and walked to a desk in the room, placing it on the corner along with a pink rose. If Riley looked inside the basket, she'd find a new slip of paper wrapped around hers. "This belongs to you," I said, motioning to the basket and the flower. "Oh, yeah. Mind if I come in?"

"Um. S-sure," she stammered. Then she rose to her knees on her bed, letting go of the pillow and at least a half-dozen wadded up tissues. A notebook on the edge of her bed flopped to the floor. The pages fluttered open to another one of her sketches. "I mean, what are you doing here?" Her eyes swept over me. "And why are you dressed like—" she pointed at me "—that?"

My hands found the front pockets beneath my jacket. I

hated to admit it but they were shaking a little. This was new territory for me. I wasn't used to feeling so vulnerable—at least not on purpose. "It's junior prom tonight. Remember? And you only told me a million times that you wanted to go." *Though not with me.*

"Um. Yeah." She stammered again. "But. Well…"

"Is someone else taking you?" I couldn't even mention Jay's name but it was on my tongue, along with the usual bitter aftertaste that accompanied anything having to do with his existence.

"Of course not."

"As I recall, you're the reason I was nominated for prom king."

"And you're here because you need a date?" Her expression fell.

I took a step closer. I wanted to make sure she saw the naked honesty in my eyes. "No, I need you."

"So this is a pity date?" Her arms moved to her hips.

I took another step. "I want to take you to prom. If you'll have me."

Riley climbed off her bed. She was barefoot. Gray sweats hung on her and a pink T-shirt dipped low on her right shoulder. Her hair looked like it hadn't been combed all weekend, which was probably true, given what Mr. Berenger had told me of her self-imposed exile. Instead of pulled back or swept behind her ears, blond hairs stuck straight out around her head like she'd just stuck her finger in an electrical socket. I wanted to run my hands through her hair. I wanted to know if it was as silky as her skin. For once and for all, I wanted…

"So you want to take me to the prom because…?" She stood inches from me, her arms wrapped around her chest. Her tone hesitant.

I took another deep breath, digging deep for more nerve. "Didn't you hear anything I just said?"

"Every word. But your eyes tell me there's more."

"You're right. There's a lot more." I swallowed. "First, I want to apologize for how I acted on Thursday."

She raised her hand, palm toward me.

For some reason I grabbed it and her teeth snapped shut. I squeezed, just a little, when I felt her fingers shake. I looked down at her hand. Her fingernails were still jagged. A tiny lump rose up my throat, seeing them so short. "I was an asshole. I'm sorry." Again, she tried to speak but I stopped her. "Let me finish, Riley."

"Sorry," she whispered.

"What I've been trying to tell you for the longest time—" I paused "—is that I've really started to like you. A lot. I've liked all the time we've been spending together, even the crazy times."

Riley was speechless. I wasn't sure I'd ever seen her speechless.

"It's not always easy for me to say the words, but that's how I feel," I said. Her mouth opened again, a tiny O. She hadn't been expecting any of this. "And I would really, really like it if you went to the prom with me." There. I said it. I said it all.

Riley finally blinked. "You like me?"

"More than *like*."

"So…you love me back?" Her eyes got wider.

I chuckled. An uncontrollable smile spread across my face. "Yeah. I do. I love you, too, Riley." This time, it wasn't so hard to say the words. "Sorry it took me so long to say it."

"Wow…" she said, looking down at our hands, my fingers threaded with hers.

"Wow," I said, too, because it was as though the Grand Canyon had been lifted off my shoulders.

Then her face turned up to mine. "You could be prom king tonight, you know." I could see the wheels beginning to recharge inside her head.

"I don't care about being prom king. I'd just like to go with you." I stared at her lips. They were soft pink like her shirt. "I'm really not the prom-king type, in case you haven't noticed."

"Not true."

"Totally true." She looked toward her closet. "But I don't have a prom dress," she whispered.

"Well, I didn't exactly bring a limousine, either. Or a tux. So I guess that makes us even."

"But—"

I pulled her closer. I wanted to feel her body pressed against mine, more than anything. "Riley. Seriously. I don't care what you wear. Go like that! You look great." It was taking all my strength not to completely bear-hug her. "Please. Please just go with me tonight."

Her cheeks flushed and I took another chance and pulled her closer. It would be just my luck if her dad was eavesdropping right outside the door, especially with a crazy big Native in his only daughter's bedroom. I'd already won back a little of his trust; I didn't want to lose it again.

"Please?" I said again. This was me, begging. And I didn't care. I was wearing my heart on my sleeve before this girl and I didn't care. This was me taking the biggest chance of my life tonight.

Her eyes moved to my lips and lingered there for a few seconds and I felt the heat rise up inside me again. Then a tiny smile curved at the corners of her lips and my breathing stopped.

"You're doing it again," she said.

"I'm doing what again?" I said, confused.

"You're kissing me with your eyes."

"I am?" Light filled my face, my chest, my whole body. All because of this perfectly imperfect girl whose hand I held in mine. "Well, then you've probably noticed that I've been doing it for a while now."

"I hoped that you were."

"How about if we try it for real?"

She thought about it for a moment. Then another moment passed and it was all I could do to remain still. Finally, she nodded.

I leaned over, drew back a breath, closed my eyes and slowly pressed my lips against hers. They were nothing like that time on the Mogollon Rim.

They were better.

I drew her closer, feeling the entire length of her body melt against mine. I was afraid to pull back and lose this moment. I was afraid to open my eyes. But breathing became necessary. Dammit.

Riley looked up at me, her palms flat against my chest.

My forehead stayed pressed against hers, eager for more. Hot skin against hot skin. *Did you feel what I felt? Did the world just spin around ten times at lightning speed as it did for me?*

She grabbed hold of my lapel. "Sam?"

"Yeah?" I pulled her tighter but braced for the worst, her body still molded against every inch of mine. I braced to hear that I was the worst kisser, the worst dresser, the worst person, the worst everything. But Riley Berenger surprised me again.

"You're perfect," she said, and I lowered my head for another kiss.

Just that second, Riley's dad knocked on the door. "Kids?" he said.

We snapped apart like a rubber band. Heat, zapped. The

moment, lost. Quickly I adjusted my tie and remembered to breathe.

"Yeah, Dad?" Riley's voice squeaked. She looked back at me with scared eyes. Was her dad going to bust down the door?

"Your brother just called."

"Yeah. So?"

"Guess what?" Excitement bubbled in his voice.

Riley's eyes were still locked on mine. We were still trying to catch our breaths as we waited for her dad to burst into the room. "What?" Another squeak.

But he didn't barge in. "Thought you might be interested in knowing that Sam just won prom king."

Riley's eyes grew as big as moons and I was pretty sure mine did, too.

We both gasped at the same time. "You have got to be kidding me!" I shouted. This was completely unbelievable. Completely impossible. Me? Lone Butte High Junior Prom King? "Is this a joke?"

"No joke, Sam. Very real," Mr. Berenger said, still from behind the closed door.

It was as though someone kicked me in the chest. I had to bend over and clutch my knees. It felt like I could be having a panic attack.

"Sam?" Riley whispered, her hand found its way to the small of my back. "Are you okay?"

I was half hunched over, still unable to stand. She led me to the edge of her bed.

"Yes. No," I finally whispered back. "I have no idea."

Seated on the edge of the bed, we listened as Mr. Berenger cleared his throat and then walked away down the stairs. "You still want to go to prom?" Riley asked me, still whispering.

"Do you?" I said, still dazed from the news.

She didn't answer right away. I could see more wheels turning inside her brain and picking up speed, like a train getting ready to leave the station. That wasn't good.

Then I said quite possibly the most difficult thing in my entire life. "If you want to go to the prom, I'd be honored to take you. Just say the word."

Riley bit the bottom of her lip, watching me. More wheels turning.

My heartbeat ratcheted up again in full panic attack mode. Another century of silence passed between us.

Instead of rushing to her closet to pick out a dress, which I kind of expected, Riley surprised me with six words. "I want to kiss you again."

My world started spinning again.

Slowly, she wrapped her arm across my chest and the next thing I knew we were horizontal on Riley's soft bed—well, I was horizontal. Riley straddled me. Mind blown! I was euphoric. My adrenaline was racing.

She leaned over, her hair falling alongside her cheeks, her eyes locked on my stunned ones. She placed her hands on either side of my head and smiled at me. I think I smiled back. I think I was breathing.

Then she leaned down and pressed her lips against mine. A heartbeat later, I reached up for her with both arms and crushed her into my chest.

Yeah, we kissed. A lot.

Again.

And again.

We had to make up for lost time.

In those moments, I realized that there would be about as much chance of Riley Berenger breaking my heart as I would hers.

We never made it to the prom. We clung to each other

and kissed some more and in between we played chess when Mr. Berenger's footsteps became suspiciously more frequent outside the door, especially as it got later. Who could blame him? But we never left Riley's bedroom (and her parents never questioned it), which was totally fine with me. Riley won both chess games, by the way. I mean, *chess?* I was too busy memorizing the flush in her cheeks.

And prom king? Jay Hawkins took second place and he could have the crown with my compliments. I didn't need it. I had something way better. I had Riley Berenger's heart and that crazy girl owned every bit of mine.

The proof was tucked inside Grandmother's dream basket.

★ ★ ★ ★ ★

ACKNOWLEDGMENTS

Someone very wise once told me that publishing your second book can be tougher than publishing your first. For the record, this is true.

Once again, I'd like to thank my literary agent, Holly Root. I'd hate to think where I'd be without her steady guidance and superadorable Facebook baby pics that always make me smile when I need it most.

At HarlequinTEEN, I am forever grateful to Tashya Wilson, Annie Stone, Lisa Wray, Kathy Lodge and about 1000 other behind-the-scene people who acquire, edit, market, promote and generally just love the heck out of TEEN books.

To all of my Native friends and beta-readers who've graciously and tirelessly read multiple drafts of *Hooked* and *Played* and answered my endless questions about Native life. You've taught me so much, more than you know. If there are any errors in my stories, they belong to me.

To the wonderful and generous people of the Gila River Indian Community. Thank you for letting me explore your beautiful reservation and not minding when "that crazy girl driving the white pickup" crisscrossed your community, simply trying to get a feel and sense of the land after the first seed of this series popped into my head with Fred Oday waving a golf club at me on the side of Pecos Road.

To anyone who has read *Hooked* and *Played*, particularly Native teens across the country who've sent me emails and left notes on my social media. Thank you for taking the time to tell me your stories and sharing your personal experiences. It's your letters that make writing books worthwhile and, frankly, why I'll continue to write for kids.

To Arizonans and other readers familiar with the American Southwest, where my books usually take place. Many of the places mentioned in my stories originated in my wild imagination but most are based on real, live honest-to-goodness places. For example, Lone Butte High School? Wild Horse Restaurant? These come from my brain. Pecos Road? Very real.

To parents, teachers and librarians. Thank you for teaching your kids the lifelong joy of reading.

To book bloggers across the globe. Thank you for your tireless passion and support of young adult literature.

To the small but growing global YA Revolution crew, affectionately known as The Crew. Thank you for helping to spread the word about books with diverse characters and consequently demanding more diversity in children's literature. Your involvement makes a difference.

To my family.

To my mom and dad. I miss you!

And especially to my husband, Craig. This one's for you. Finally.

DISCUSSION QUESTIONS

1. Riley and Sam seem to live in two different worlds, but they have more in common than they think. In what ways are they alike? What do you see in the story that shows they are more in tune than they first realize?

2. In what ways are Sam and Riley different from each other, and how might that help them to build a strong relationship? What obstacles do they have to overcome?

3. Why does Riley decide to help Sam win Fred's heart? Where does she go astray in her evaluation of Fred and Ryan's relationship? What could Sam have done at the start to stop her plans, and why do you think he didn't? What communication gaps do they need to overcome and what aspects of their characters exacerbate the problem?

4. How does Riley feel about popularity at the beginning of the story, and what is she willing to do to gain it? How does her view change and why?

5. Social media plays a large part in many teens' lives today. What does the author of *Played* show about social media through Riley's experience? Did Jay Hawkins have the right to post pictures from his party online?

6. At the beginning of the story, Riley lets her friend Drew talk her into a BOTOX-like injection. How much pressure does society put on teens, particularly teen girls, to look beautiful? What can teen girls do to push back? What should girls do?

7. How does the author make setting important to her story? In what ways does the setting complement the story, and in what ways does it affect the action?

Discover one of Harlequin TEEN's most
authentic contemporary voices,

Katie McGarry

Available wherever books are sold!

Praise for Katie McGarry

"A riveting and emotional ride!"

–*New York Times* bestselling author Simone Elkeles
on *Pushing the Limits*

**"Everything–setting, characters, romance–about
this novel works and works well."**

–*Kirkus Reviews* (starred review) on *Dare You To*

www.HarlequinTEEN.com

HTPTLTR6R

HTPGAHYTR

HTITR2